"Classy series . . . a compelling story of political int[...] trayal, and growing romance. Strong ch[...] title stand out from other more [...]

—*Library Journal*

"*The Eldritch Conspiracy* is fast-pac[...] [...] action and a lot of familial drama. Continues the thrill ride that Celia's life has become."

—*Fresh Fiction*

"Bodyguard by profession, vampire by accident, and siren by heritage, Celia leads a life of excitement and turmoil. This series just keeps getting better, maintaining a delicate balance between urban fantasy and paranormal romance. The emotional components are just as strong as the action sequences, set against an increasingly interesting world."

—*Publishers Weekly* on *Demon Song*

"Thrilling urban fantasy . . . endlessly entertaining."

—*All Things Urban Fantasy* on *Demon Song*

"The author has created a paranormal fantasy world that leaves the reader wanting more. Interesting characters, wonderful world-building, and a mythology that gets more interesting with every character they throw into the mix. Fast-paced, with twists and turns and excitement galore, *Siren Song* does not disappoint."

—*TeensReadToo* (5 stars, Gold Award)

"The action-filled narrative of this engrossing novel never lags, and the authors skillfully keep the various plot threads all going simultaneously, scoring extra points for a style of smooth readability. *Siren Song* will please urban fantasy fans. [An] exciting, highly satisfying series."

—*Bitten by Books*

CAT ADAMS

ALL YOUR WISHES

A TOM DOHERTY ASSOCIATES BOOK  NEW YORK

ALL YOUR WISHES

Copyright © 2016 by C. T. Adams

A Tor Book
Published by Tom Doherty Associates
175 Fifth Avenue
New York, NY 10010
www.tor-forge.com

Tor® is a registered trademark of Macmillan Publishing Group, LLC.

The Library of Congress Cataloging-in-Publication Data is available upon request.

ISBN 978-0-7653-7571-1 (trade paperback)
ISBN 978-1-4668-4786-6 (e-book)

Our books may be purchased in bulk for promotional, educational, or business use. Please contact your local bookseller or the Macmillan Corporate and Premium Sales Department at 1-800-221-7945, extension 5442, or by e-mail at MacmillanSpecialMarkets@macmillan.com.

First Edition: October 2016

Printed in the United States of America

0 9 8 7 6 5 4 3 2 1

This book is dedicated to my mother, a strong, generous woman with the kind of kindness and determination worth emulating. I love you, Mom. You're the best.

ACKNOWLEDGMENTS

As always, there are a million people I should thank for the help I have received in this book. First, my son, James, for everything. Cathy Clamp, my frequent coauthor, who may not have participated in the writing of this particular book but is always a great sounding board, and a better friend. Melissa Singer, the esteemed editor at Tor, who makes every book *so* much better; my agent, Lucienne Diver, and the folks at the Knight Agency; all the people at Tor who walk my books from start to finish and produce a product we can all be proud of; Charles, for his gun and police knowledge (and willingness to use it!); Shawn and the beta readers, who let me know when I've run off the rails.

Thanks to you all.

ALL
YOUR
WISHES

AUTHOR'S NOTE

I made it up.

I have created the culture and significance of the djinn in the world of Celia Graves from scratch. The terms *genie* and *jinn* and *ifrit* are used, but that is not to say that they bear any resemblance to any other beings in any religions or books of fiction or nonfiction currently existing. I do not mean any offense to any member of any religion.

Also, while I tried to be as accurate as I could, I made a couple of changes to the bridge on the causeway to Treasure Island. It is a drawbridge, and I tried to be pretty accurate. But there is a concrete barrier between the traffic lanes and the sidewalk that didn't "work" with the action I had planned. So I took it out. You'll note that the authorities decide to put one in after our heroine's little adventure.

1

I **took the** third exit off Oceanview and drove toward my new office. Despite the fact that I'd had a huge fight with Bruno last night—well, actually in the wee hours this morning—I was in a pretty good mood. I'd given everyone on staff the morning off today because of the great job they'd done last night; my new desk and safe were being delivered today, and, with any luck, I'd actually be able to unpack and get my personal office organized.

Dawna and I were finally in the process of moving Graves Personal Protection into our spiffy new digs.

We'd managed to purchase a decommissioned, Mission-style church complex from my friend, Emma Landingham, who had spent a fortune renovating and upgrading the property. She'd have kept it, but her new husband got transferred to Seattle. Her loss was Dawna's and my gain. The place was absolutely gorgeous, with Old World charm and all of the modern amenities and security. Best of all, thanks to the on-site cemetery, it was, and always would be, holy ground. Bad ghosts, demons, and vampires couldn't cross onto it.

But my absolute favorite thing about the office was that it existed.

My previous office had been close to downtown, in a three-story Victorian. It had a big porch and a little balcony that opened right into my office. I'd loved it, and probably would still be there if it hadn't been destroyed by a bomb meant for me.

That little fiasco had been all over the local news, so no one would rent to me. For months we'd been working without an office—and I'd had to put up with having boxes of stuff filling my home, and Minnie living with me.

Now I could get my house back to normal. *Woot!* No more tripping over boxes. No more looking for things here, only to find out they were packed somewhere else. No more litter box in the bathroom. Just the thought of being able to walk easily from room to room made me giddy with pleasure.

I would always have a soft spot in my heart for my dear, departed Victorian, but this office, while a completely different style, was still wonderful. The main structure was a big old stone building with beautiful architectural details and a pair of bell towers. I was a little surprised the church had decided to part with it. Then again, it wasn't old enough or important enough to qualify for the historical society's mission trail, and the church itself was small and outdated by modern standards.

Too, the grounds had to have been expensive to keep up. Em had been forced to sink a lot of money into landscaping the courtyard area alone. What had been barren dirt and mown-down weeds was now an aesthetically pleasing area planted in xeriscaping, with wildflowers and native trees. There was a fountain, too, and if I listened hard, up in my office, I could hear the water burbling in it. It was very soothing.

In all, the complex took up more than an acre, including the walled compound with a parking area on the east side and the small cemetery, which held the remains of the first missionaries who had been stationed there, on the west.

There was a rectory attached to the main church by a covered walkway that also passed the graveyard. We had a couple of spare bedrooms in there for when we needed a safe place to stash a protectee, or an employee needed a place to crash. One of the rooms had been Kevin's before Emma moved out, and he was still using it, with my permission. It seemed more than a fair trade since he was letting a former client use his place in the desert while she acclimated to being one of the monthly furry.

The third building was a small, detached storage shed for the mower and lawn equipment. Since the parking lot was bigger than we really needed, I'd chosen the north end as the location for the casting circle.

Approaching the entry, I hit the button on the automatic gate opener clipped to my sun visor. The gate looked like wrought iron, but was made of heavy-duty, spelled silversteel; it rolled smoothly out of the way. There was barely enough time for my rear bumper to clear the perimeter before the gate began moving back into place. And that perimeter! The magic of it hit my senses like a ripsaw, making me gasp. I keep telling myself I'll get used to it—but so far, no such luck. I've been able to sense the magical perimeters around buildings for a while now. Most are no big deal. The better ones are a little uncomfortable. But this one hurts. Still, it's only for a minute, and the security it provides is worth the bother and expense.

I was surprised to see a car parked in the lot—a silver-gray Mustang convertible, it belonged to our newest employee, Tim Sawyer.

Tim had been hired just last week to replace Dawna's cousin, a mage who had been injured in the line of duty. I already liked him. He's twenty-two years old and biracial, with skin the color of heavily creamed coffee and curly, light-brown hair cropped close to his head. He has a sunny disposition and the kind of grin that lights up a room. He jokes around but knows when to settle down to work. I'd been a bit worried about him, but in the past two days I'd given him two serious challenges. Both times he'd risen to the occasion. As a result we now had no sound problems in the office *and* a portable spell-casting circle. Fifty percent of that would belong to Graves Personal Protection, and unless I was off on my estimates, it would be bringing us in a very nice chunk of change.

After slathering on sunscreen, I climbed out of the car. It was only a pair of steps from my reserved spot to the door, but even in that short distance I could feel the heat of the sun trying to burn me to a crackly crunch.

I'm an abomination, a human who has been partially turned by a master vampire. It's caused me a slew of biological changes, including problems with solid food and a severe allergy to sunlight. I've been like this for quite a while now, so I've worked out some coping mechanisms, but it's not something I'm happy about. Still, it's not all bad. Vampire speed, strength, and healing can be damned handy in my line of work—particularly since I find myself protecting clients from the monsters often as not.

I punched in the security code and the door latch clicked, the light on the electronic lock flashing bright green. Stepping from bright sunlight into the shadows of the side entrance was like stepping into a cave. The temperature inside was easily ten degrees cooler, and it took a few seconds for my eyes to adjust to the relative gloom. There was also that sense of calm and peace that so many holy places have, as if years and years of prayers and ceremonies have seeped into the structure itself. I wondered if after we'd been here a while, that feeling would wear off. I hoped not.

"Hey, boss. What're you doing here?" Tim's voice came to me from the main area.

"I'm supposed to meet the guys delivering my desk and my safe."

"Ah."

"You?"

"I wanted to finish getting my desk together so I can get the patent paperwork done and have the attorney go over it." He was grinning, his face alight with pride and excitement. I didn't blame him a bit.

"Well, I'll leave you to it. I'm headed upstairs."

He nodded and went back to work.

I strolled down what had once been the main aisle of the church, looking around with proprietary pride, checking out how much of the move had been accomplished. I was pretty pleased with the result. Oh, it was still chaos, but it was organized chaos. The conference table was in the altar area, just below the big screen that could serve as both a television and computerized video display. Separate work areas had been set up on the main floor.

It was all very high tech, and the geeky part of me was overjoyed. Never again would I have to make do with makeshift, thrown-together tech. I was glad my staff hadn't wanted cubicles. Not only did an open floor plan mean less expense (yay!), cubicles would have ruined the aesthetic. Instead, the four employee desks sat two by two in the main area.

Bubba's was the desk closest to the dais. I could tell because his desktop was already organized and decorated with a perfect model of a yacht, a photo of him with his wife, Mona, and their daughter, and a baseball autographed by Mr. Cubbie himself, Ernie Banks. A box of files in a banker's box sat atop the black two-drawer cabinet beside his desk.

Kevin Landingham had taken the desk directly across the aisle from Bubba. Because of his PTSD he has a service dog, Paulie, a golden lab. Her doggie bed and a chew toy were tucked discreetly into the corner formed by his desk and credenza. Kevin's our tech guy, and despite the PTSD, a complete badass, a former member of a quasi-military organization. He keeps more secrets than a mob boss's priest. He is also one of the monthly furry.

Tim's station was in the next row, and it was as messy as the other guys' were neat. The clutter included papers, books, spell components, a stuffed bat, and God (and Tim) alone knew what other unidentifiable stuff. But I didn't give him crap about it. First, we were just moving in. Second, I had a sneaking suspicion that he was one of those folks who would be able to find what he wanted in an instant despite the mess, even if no one else could.

The fourth desk was empty. Someone had set it up with all the right stuff—stapler, two-hole punch, the works. But it was, and would remain, barren, until and unless we hired another person.

Since she was my partner, Dawna had an office. On the main floor, it had one glass wall that looked out on the main area. Glancing in, I could see that she was well on the way to having her stuff unpacked and organized. Lucky her.

I kept walking, heading toward the lobby and the stairs that led up to my office in the former choir loft. Emma had used it as her spare bedroom. I'd chosen it as my workspace because I liked the idea of being able to look down and see everything that was going on. I also liked having a bit of privacy. And I absolutely loved the stained-glass windows.

When my old office had been blown to bits, one of the things that grieved me most was the loss of the big stained-glass window that had adorned the stairs leading up to the third floor. Now I had a similar window in my actual office. Mornings like today's, when the sun shone through the colored glass, were like standing in the midst of a rainbow.

Looking up, I could see over the half-wall that someone had gone to the trouble of assembling most of my office for me. Sweet.

Oh, there were still boxes everywhere, but it was starting to look really good. It sounded good, too. When we'd first moved in there had been a terrible echo problem. Tim's very first project had been to come up with a spell that could contain the problem but still leave us able to hear each other. It had been a real challenge, but our new mage had done a fine job with it. Now someone just had to refresh the spell, along with the perimeter, once a week.

I'd barely made it to the top of the stairs when the phone rang. Tim answered it on the first ring. A second later, the intercom buzzed. It took me a minute to find my phone in one of the boxes on the floor. But eventually I was able to answer.

"Yes?"

"There's a guy named Justin on the line. He says his people are at the front gate with your new safe. Shall I let him in?"

"Please." I hung up and turned around, trying to figure out how to arrange the boxes and chairs so that they wouldn't be in the way while the safe was installed. The other day, Justin had taken one look at the narrow stairway, with its worn wooden treads, and decided there was no way in hell they were bringing a safe up that way. So he'd charged me to hire four mages to levitate it up from the first floor and maneuver it over the half-wall.

I bent down to shift a bunch of boxes to one side and Minnie the Mouser leapt out at me. I let out one of those "eepy" screams that are so embarrassing, leaping backwards and tripping on something behind me as she bolted between my feet, a little orange and white blur of fur headed for the staircase.

I sat down abruptly in the nearest chair, my heart racing, my breath coming in short little gasps, feeling like an idiot as adrenaline poured through my body from having been startled.

Thus I was right by the phone when it rang again. I picked it up without thinking, from habit. "Graves Personal Protection." My voice on the line sounded almost normal, not at all like my pulse was pounding.

"Celie, it's me. Are you okay?" "Me" was Bruno DeLuca, mage extraordinaire and love of my life—at least at the moment. Whether that was going to continue was becoming increasingly dicey if last night's argument was any indication. I shoved that thought firmly back down and answered.

"Fine. The cat was apparently playing in the boxes and we startled each other."

He laughed, but only for a second, and it wasn't the hearty guffaw it normally would've been. Something was up.

"What's wrong?"

"I just hung up with Matty. Mom's worse. I'm headed to Jersey on the next flight out."

Oh *hell*. Bruno's mom, Isabella Rose DeLuca, was a force of nature and one of the most powerful magic-wielders on the planet. But not so long ago, a group of rogue mages had tried to use the node near a supermax prison known as the Needle for dark purposes, and she'd been one of the four mages to step up and stop them. During the battle, more magic than any human body could handle had coursed through her. The instantly visible signs were that her hair turned snow white and she went blind. But the power had done other, and worse, invisible damage. She was dying a slow, agonizing death that I wouldn't wish on anyone.

While I would never say it where Bruno or Matty could hear, I was pretty sure that part of why she'd been so badly hurt was because she'd chosen to take most of the magic into herself rather than allowing it to harm her sons—Bruno and his brother Matteo, also a magic-wielder. She was their mother. She'd protect them. She just would. It did make me worry a little about John Creede, the fourth participant in that working. Him she wouldn't have gone out of her way to protect.

"I'm so sorry." I meant it. Isabella and I have had our issues in the past, but I respect the hell out of her, and that last adventure had brought us to something of a truce. I might not be the woman she would've chosen for Bruno, but at least she didn't hate me anymore. "Do you want me to come with?"

"No. Not yet anyway. The doctors think it's going to be a while still. But she's asking for me. I notified the university. They've got people covering my classes."

"Do you want me to take care of the house?"

"Please."

"Is there *anything* else I can do?" I felt helpless, frustrated, and sad. I could tell just from the sound of his voice that he was hurting so badly. But while I could guard people's bodies from the monsters, I couldn't protect the man I loved from this kind of pain. Nobody could, and it sucked.

"You're doing it. I love you, Celie. And I'm sorry about last night."

Last night, after an impromptu celebration here at the office for having slain a big bad monster, Bruno and I had gone home together. I would've loved to have continued celebrating. Instead, we'd had a fight: Maybe not a break-off-the-engagement and end-of-the-relationship fight, but a big one. It had been about the kind of issues you can't compromise on. It looked as if his dreams for the future and mine weren't the same—weren't even close.

But just the thought of breaking up with him made my throat tight enough that I had a hard time speaking normally.

"Me too," I croaked.

"We'll talk when I get back."

"Take care of yourself?"

"Always do," he answered. "You'll be careful?"

He worries about me. I know that. I understand. He loves me. And seriously, some of the cases I've had the past couple of years would scare the hell out of anybody. Unfortunately, understanding our problems doesn't solve them. Still, I tried to reassure him. "Dawna and I agreed. No cases this week. We need time to settle into the new office."

"Right. Look, I've gotta go. Love you."

"Love you." My voice sounded almost as rough as his. Not that either of us was on the verge of crying or anything.

I hung up the phone and spent a few seconds blinking: First to clear my blurred vision, then in shock. While I'd been distracted by the phone call, the delivery guys had set to work. In midair, directly above my head, a safe that I knew from the specs weighed nearly eight hundred pounds was bobbing gently along. The X drawn in chalk imbued with magic on its base was seeking a similar X on the floor of my office where the boards had been reinforced in preparation for it.

I didn't move. Sitting right where I was, I was out of the way. Besides, I didn't want to distract anyone or do anything that might screw with their concentration and cause them to drop the safe on me. That would be bad—probably very, very bad.

As I watched, the safe settled onto the floor, gentle as a feather. Impressive.

As soon as it was in place, I walked over to inspect it. When I got within three feet of it, I could feel the spell work buzzing against my skin. Excellent! Since this was the same model I'd had in my old office, I knew exactly how to set the biometrics and magical settings, and I knew that my weapons and other important gear would be safe against pretty much all comers. Good. I'd been a little nervous, keeping them at the house.

Not terribly nervous—the estate was pretty secure. But I'd had bad experiences in the past. Once, the bad guys had murdered the pool boy and cut off his hand so they could use it to get onto the premises.

And people wonder why I'm so obsessive about security.

I made my way downstairs to sign the receipt for the safe and thank the installation team. I knew they'd relay my thanks to Justin, too. Yes, I paid him well, but over the years, what with him coming by the office to renew the spell work every week, he'd become a buddy. More than once he'd gone above and beyond to help me out, and I always tried to make sure he knew I appreciated it.

The mages passed Dawna on their way out the door.

"Hey, you're here early." I greeted her with a grin that won me an answering smile. Dawna Han Long is one of my best buds in the world, despite the fact that she is flat-out gorgeous. Tiny and of Vietnamese descent, she has long black hair, perfect features, and the kind of effortless style that makes cheap clothes look expensive and expensive clothes look dynamite. Today she was wearing a gray sports bra with neon green piping, matching sweatpants, and neon green sneakers. Her hair had been pulled into a ponytail—with a matching green tie—and though she wore no makeup, she still looked stunning. It's enough to make you sick.

"I remembered they were going to deliver your safe first, then the desk. So I figured I'd come down and wait for the second delivery so that you could move the weapons out of your house. I know you've been fretting about them."

She wasn't wrong. I have a *lot* of weapons. Most are valuable. Some are irreplaceable. And it had been a damned nuisance having to run back and forth to get things. I could have put things in the general vault on the ground floor, but I just wasn't comfortable doing that. I trusted my people not to steal. That wasn't an issue. Unfortunately, not all of our clients were completely trustworthy, and the vault wasn't always locked during the workday.

There's a reason why "lead us not into temptation" comes *before* "deliver us from evil" in the Lord's prayer.

"Thanks, Dawna."

"No problema." Her smile grew into a grin that flashed a hint of dimples. "And don't forget to drop your clothes off at the cleaners. You don't want the blood of an über-bat like the one you dealt with last night damaging the spells on one of your best jackets." Her grin faded a little around the edges as she spoke, but she stayed rock solid. Ten points for her. Last night's vampire had been the sire of Lillith, a vampire that had tried to make Dawna her Renfield. He'd come after me because I'd killed Lillith and freed Dawna.

Dawna was still in therapy to deal with the aftereffects of what Lillith had done to her, even though that had happened years ago, and I'd worried about yesterday's events being triggering for her. But she seemed okay and, as usual, was on top of the details.

"Hit the cleaners on the way in, but thanks for the reminder. And if you're serious about your offer, I'll head back to the house and pack everything up."

"I am. Go."

I went.

2

Heading back to the office a couple of hours later, I was very careful to obey all traffic laws and stay well within the speed limit. My relationships with the various members of law enforcement varied from very good to incredibly bad, and I was currently transporting enough weaponry and magical geegaws to take over a developing nation, or arm a Texas nuclear family. All of it was legally acquired and perfectly justifiable given my line of work. But if I got pulled over with it I would still be in deep caca.

Not that speeding was an option at the moment. It wasn't. I was stuck in traffic. It wasn't bumper-to-bumper. But one of the narrower sections of Oceanview had been blocked for a while by a wreck and things were still pretty backed up.

I couldn't believe it was already one o'clock. The day was racing by. I took a sip of the warm beef juice I'd fixed myself for lunch and felt some of the tension ease out of my body: Tension that came right back when an asshole in a blue Mercedes cut me off.

I considered giving him a one-fingered salute, but decided

to take the high road instead. Who knew, he might be a future client—assuming his driving didn't get him killed.

The phone rang and my nifty new view screen flashed Dawna's picture. Pressing a button on the steering wheel, I accepted the call.

"Hey, Dawna, what's up?"

"Where are you?"

"In the car, stuck in traffic. Why?"

"We have a client on the way."

I fought not to sigh. Dawna and I had agreed: No clients this first week so that we could get unpacked and set up properly. We'd already broken that rule once. And now someone else had shown up. *Ugh.*

"I thought—" I began.

"Yeah, I know. But we kind of blew that out of the water last night."

True enough. And that had been my fault. "All right, who is it and what do they want?"

"His name is Rahim Patel. He's flying out from Indiana in his private jet. I've just started researching him, but what I've found so far is impressive. He's a full professor at the University of Notre Dame, in their Metaphysics department. He specializes in magical beings, particularly the djinn. He's written the go-to book on the subject. He's a fully certified pilot, qualified to fly pretty much anything up to and including big commercial planes, *and* he owns his own jet—one of those brand-new Sparrowhawks. Oh, and he's apparently got more money than Bill Gates."

I let out a long, low whistle. The Sparrowhawk was the

newest, flashiest thing in personal aviation. There was a long waiting list to get one. A four-seater jet, it had all the best spells for protection and fuel economy and all the creature comforts, plus leather interior and real wood trim. There was an on-board bathroom and a small interior compartment for luggage. The Sparrowhawk was a little bigger than the average corporate jet and had a top speed approaching five hundred miles per hour. I'd heard all about it because a rock band for which we'd done a protection detail had been lusting after one—but had decided it was just too pricey.

"Good to know he can pay the bill," I said with a laugh.

"No kidding. Anyway, he called ahead. Says he's desperate. He sounded pretty panicked, swears it is imperative he see you *immediately*. His wife is a seer and she says you're his only hope. I told him we were closed for the week and he literally begged me to make an exception. Lives are at stake, apparently."

Well, hell. That wasn't good.

"Did he give you any details?"

Her voice grew icy. "No."

Not good. Dawna's my partner, not a lackey, and clients should be able to tell her anything they'd tell me.

"What does Dottie say?"

Dottie was our receptionist, an elderly woman with fluffy white hair and a penchant for brightly colored tracksuits. She was also a highly skilled and well-trained clairvoyant. My great-aunt Lopaka, queen of the sirens, said that Dottie was my "prophet." Dottie took the responsibility very seriously and kept close tabs on what the future had in store for me.

"I wasn't able to reach her. Fred said she was on her way to the office, though."

"Okay, I should be there in an hour." I'd even packed a couple of changes of clothes that I'd intended to keep in the office in case of emergency, so I could change into something more client-appropriate than my current sweats and ratty Bayview tee.

"Good. See you then."

I leaned back in my seat, stretching a little, to think things out.

Clients lie, and they hide things. They just do. Sometimes, like the night the vampire tried to turn me, it's a setup. More often, they just try to put themselves in the best possible light. I get that. But I need to know the down and dirty if I'm going to protect them. By the time I arrived at the office Dawna would have dug up everything there was to find on Mr. Patel. In the meantime, I pondered what little we knew.

He was an expert on the djinn. And he was in trouble.

I felt my stomach roil a little, the beef juice I'd been drinking for lunch sitting uneasily. I really, really hoped that our extremely urgent problem didn't have anything at all to do with the djinn. That would be so bad. Seriously. There are three types of djinn. All of them are dangerous, alien beings that are unimaginably powerful both magically and physically. They can, with a thought, alter reality in serious ways. The jinn are the most benign—mainly because they never willingly come to this dimension. They stay home and leave humans alone. Genies are bad. Exiled to the human world, they have to earn their way home by proving themselves worthy through doing good works: sort of a preternatural probation. The trick is, humans aren't supposed to know. If we find out, it doesn't count. So, nobody much runs into the genies either.

Then there are ifrits.

Ifrits are bad news: really, really bad news. Fortunately they are so rare that the last known encounter with an ifrit was centuries ago—well before the founding fathers brought forth this great nation.

So, maybe it wasn't a djinn problem. I mean, just because Patel wrote about them and was a world-renowned expert on them didn't mean that he couldn't have a much more ordinary problem.

I told myself this. Unfortunately, I didn't believe it. That little niggling voice in the back of my mind was pretty sure we'd be dealing with the djinn and that I should "just say no."

I should listen to my instincts more often.

3

I **saw Rahim** Patel before he saw me. Weapons stowed and outfit changed, I was coming down the stairs from my office and spotted him standing in front of the reception desk.

First impression: he was pretty. He was not handsome, at least not to my mind. His features were too soft for that. Slender, he stood five foot six or so. His eyes were lovely, wide and dark, with just a hint of laugh lines at the corners. His lips were full, with a cupid's bow, very kissable, but not very manly. While he wasn't a big man, he held himself with poise and confidence. His suit was high quality, well tailored, and immaculate. The white shirt he wore stood in stark contrast to the dark caramel color of his skin, and against his black suit it was so bright that it practically glowed.

His appearance was perfect—which seemed a little odd to me in light of the fact that Dawna claimed he'd been in such a panic. I've found that people who are that upset don't take time to polish their appearance. Then again, he might have stopped at a hotel to change so he would make a good impression.

"Good afternoon, Mr. Patel."

He turned to face me and extended his hand. "Ms. Graves, thank you so much for agreeing to see me. I know this isn't a convenient time for you, but the situation really is urgent."

He looked me up and down as I approached. I could tell from his expression that I didn't quite look the way he'd expected. Oh, I was still five ten and leggy, but I hadn't had a lot of publicity since the debut of my new, very trendy, very short hairstyle. And my eyes were no longer gray; they were blue, thanks to a brush with the same heavy-duty magic that was killing Bruno's mother.

As we shook hands, I caught a glimpse of what looked like it might be a curse mark on his wrist, peeking out from beneath the cuff of his shirt. Interesting.

"Would you like something to drink?" I really hoped he wouldn't. The kitchen was at the far end of the building—next to what had once been the altar area. It hadn't occurred to me until just that moment how inconvenient that was going to be for Dottie, who had to use a walker to get around. Crap. Then, out of the corner of my eye, I saw she'd already taken measures. A small table had been set up in her corner, with a coffeemaker and bowls of sugar and packaged creamer.

"Thank you. Your receptionist offered me something, but I said no."

I glanced at said receptionist, trying to get her nonverbal take on our client. Aside from the fact that she's a powerful clairvoyant, she's smart and observant. She doesn't miss a thing, and she is cheerfully capable of using her age and seeming disability to gently bully people into revealing more than they intended . . . and doing things they hadn't wanted to do.

In short, she's an absolute gem in the front office. I honestly don't know what we'd do without her. Dottie doesn't put in quite as many hours now that she's married to Fred, but she gets the work done. In exchange, she gets a salary that is just barely below the amount that would screw up her benefits—and the opportunity to spend time with her beloved Minnie the Mouser, though the cat was nowhere to be seen at that moment.

"Let's head up to my office." I gestured to the staircase, letting him take the lead. I don't like having people behind me, particularly in an enclosed space. It makes me twitchy. Gwen, my long-term therapist, says I have trust issues. Talk about your understatement of the millennium.

"Dottie, will you please buzz Dawna and ask her to join us?"

"Of course."

Walking into my office was like stepping into a rainbow filled with boxes. The sun wasn't yet shining directly through the stained glass, but it was bright enough outside that the colors shone like jewels just the same. Patel stopped and stared.

"Wow." He smiled as he turned his attention to carefully removing Minnie from her seat on the visitor's chair facing the desk. He brushed the seat with his hand to clear away any stray cat hairs, then sat. Minnie, offended at finding herself on the floor, gave him a baleful, green-eyed glare.

"It is pretty impressive," I agreed. "It almost makes up for the temperature difference." Actually, it more than made up for it to me. I could get another fan or a room-cooling unit easily enough, and the play of light was beautiful and unique.

I moved a stack of boxes from atop the desk to the floor so that I could see my guest, then settled in. Dawna arrived and took the chair next to the client, shifting it close enough to my desk that she could set her iPad on it and take notes. "So, Mr. Patel, what is it you need from our firm?" she asked.

"I am about to undertake a very dangerous quest. My wife tells me that I need you," he stared directly at me when he spoke, to make his point absolutely clear, "to ensure that I survive long enough to complete it."

I blinked. I hadn't heard someone seriously refer to something as a "quest" in a while—if ever. But he meant it. His expression was terribly serious, and there was a hint of sadness in those beautiful brown eyes. "Your wife?"

"Abha is a level six clairvoyant. She was *most* insistent."

Dawna and I traded a knowing glance. You ignore the advice of a seer at your own peril. That explained why Patel was here, in spite of his visible misgivings.

He reached into the pocket of his jacket and pulled out a device approximately the size of a cell phone. I recognized it immediately. It was the latest piece of technology to take the market by storm. Ridiculously expensive, it combined magic and electronics and was the darling of law enforcement agencies, criminal defense firms, and more. It used a spell disk to create a holographic recorder and projector and could produce accurate, three-dimensional scenes that seemed so real you could practically touch them. The little machine even incorporated smell. The movie industry was desperately scrambling to find a way to incorporate the technology into the theater experience, although, honestly, I wasn't sure having slasher flicks seem that real was a particularly great idea. And really, who'd want to live through the explosions in action movies? I've been in real explosions: there's nothing fun about it.

Still, I'd bought one when Isaac Levy first got them in stock. I wasn't sure what use I would make of it, but I'd splurged on one just the same. I mean, seriously, it's a tech toy. How could I resist?

"May I?"

"Sure, go for it," I answered.

He set the device on my desk, pressed the button, and "poof," just like that, I was on the holodeck of the old science-fiction show I'd watched as a kid. Well, not really. But I might as well have been. My office disappeared and while I knew Dawna and Rahim Patel were there, I couldn't actually see them unless I concentrated really hard. Instead, I was sitting in a well-lit room full of shelf after shelf of . . . djinn jars.

Shit, shit, shit! I cursed inwardly. *I knew it. I just knew it.*

Stationed at regular intervals on the shelves, the ancient jars were absolutely gorgeous. They varied in size, each one a completely unique and beautiful cloisonné creation, tiny jewels set with shining gold or silver wire to form unmistakable patterns on each individual jar. A large jewel sealed each vessel—precious rubies, diamonds, and sapphires, at least the size of my fist, being used as stoppers to keep über-powerful creatures trapped inside. The jewels were sealed in place with black wax delicately inscribed in runes, and while I knew I was looking at a projection, I would swear I could feel the power of their magic pounding at me hard enough to give me a blinding headache.

The air in the room had that stale, canned quality that you get when a place is biosealed and the air is filtered and recycled repeatedly. The ambient light was gentle, but bright enough to see clearly, and, since I couldn't see any source, I assumed it was magically generated.

I looked carefully around the room, my stomach knotting in dread as I counted more and more jars. Then I saw what had brought Patel to my door.

One jar was not where it was supposed to be. Two feet tall, patterned in smoky gray, dull red, and bright orange with brass, it lay on its side on the white tile floor, its seal broken, the stopper gem missing. I shuddered at the realization of just how big a problem that might be.

"His name is Hasan." Rahim Patel pronounced the name in a tone fraught with . . . well, it sounds melodramatic, but "doom" was the word that sprang to mind.

I didn't answer or react, mainly because the name meant absolutely nothing to me.

"Hasan is one of the most ancient and powerful of the beings which my family guards. There are tales—" he stopped speaking and I heard him swallow hard before he resumed. "It is my duty to protect the world from the creatures contained

in those urns. I have failed. Because the urn itself is still secure, there is . . . hope. I may be able to recapture him—to
fix this. But I must live long enough to do so. If I die, my replacement will be my ten-year-old son. He is a good boy, but
he has not learned all that he needs to serve as Guardian
even of the jars contained in the vault. My family will help
him, but he has nowhere near the knowledge and skill required to contain this disaster. I must recapture Hasan before the unthinkable happens."

"Why do you think you can recapture him?" Dawna's tone
was businesslike. If the thought of dealing with the djinn
spooked her, you certainly couldn't tell.

"I have the jar. They tried to steal it, but they were unable
to get past the perimeter. They tried to destroy it—there is
evidence of that farther along in the video. They were unable to do so. The worst they were able to manage was to
free him. They took the jewel, which means that they have
a bond with him, but they will not be able to control him.
Not," he added quickly, "that anyone has ever truly controlled a djinn. A djinn must grant the human's wishes, but
they always twist the granting to do the most possible harm
to the person manipulating them—and that is the best
of them, a genie. An ifrit of Hasan's power . . ." Again, he
stopped talking. I stared through the projection and saw
Patel shudder.

"Why would Hasan kill you?" I asked.

"Three reasons: First, because I am the Guardian; I am
the only one with the knowledge and power to trap him, to

seal him away again and render him helpless to do harm. He hates being imprisoned. Second, he hates me personally for being from the line of the man who originally ensnared him. He is an eternal being. His hatred is eternal as well."

"And the third reason?" I asked.

"Power. Ifrits lose power during the term of their imprisonment. The stones which serve as a stopper on the jar drain them until, eventually, they are . . . neutered, for lack of a better term. If freed before that happens, they try to replenish their magic by draining it from other sources. Places, things . . . *people*. Given the opportunity, Hasan will gladly drain me dry."

I'd seen a mage drained once before. An ancient artifact, the Isis Collar, fell into the wrong hands and was used against a friend of mine. If Bruno hadn't stepped in, John Creede, one of the most powerful mages in the world, would have lost his magical abilities permanently, and might even have died.

As I focused on the jar it came into sharper focus. It was a lovely thing. Glossy black at the bottom of the round, lower portion of the jar. Red and orange flames had been worked into the brass in a pattern of flames that actually seemed to flicker upward to an indentation, before bowing out and up to a long, narrow neck that was colored with the grays of smoke.

Still, beautiful as it was, I wouldn't have wanted to touch it. Not for a million bucks. It just reeked of bad mojo.

I tore my eyes away from the jar long enough to meet Patel's gaze. "I don't see any way that we can protect you from a being like that." I didn't like admitting it, but it was the truth. I knew my limits. This was beyond them. It was a damned shame, but he was screwed.

He gave me a sad smile. "I know. Nor do I expect you to. There are certain . . . measures . . . things that have been done that protect members of my family—for the most part—from the ifrit we guard."

"But—"

He interrupted me. "I will have to lower those protections to recapture Hasan. It is the only way. I ask that, if for any reason I am unable to, you safely transport the jar with him in it to my wife and son. They will return him to the vault."

"So—"

Again he interrupted. He was either very stressed, very arrogant, or both. I stifled my irritation before he could notice. "I would have you guard me from the people who tried to steal the jar, who released the ifrit. My protections are against actions by the spirit itself. But he can, and will, manipulate humans against me—and them I have no shield against. A small group of intelligent, magically powerful people managed to get through the vault's defenses and to that specific jar. They knew exactly which jar they wanted—none of the others were touched. Whoever those people are, they will be your opponents."

"Well, then," Dawna said reasonably, "the first logical question is, who are we up against? We need to concentrate on finding out who tried to steal the jar." Her fingers moved swiftly across the surface of the little computer.

"No. That is not your problem. My family is taking care of it. I don't want you interfering or wasting time looking into it."

Wrong answer, bucko, I thought, but kept my mouth shut.

Dawna simply gave him a sweet smile and said, "Actually, it *is* our problem. We can't manage the logistics of this without knowing who we're up against and what they are capable of." She continued, "Obviously, they are very powerful and well connected. I assume the existence of your vault is not common knowledge, let alone its location and the specifications of your protections. And yet your enemies managed to find it, got in, and very nearly managed to remove one of the jars. From the look of it, they even knew which jar contained the particular djinn they wanted."

He glared at her. She pretended not to notice.

"It sounds to me as if someone is feeding them inside information," I said.

This time I got the glare.

"And then there is the problem of what they're going to be doing with him," Dawna continued. "It's not as if anyone can actually *control* an ifrit. He'll be wreaking havoc."

She was right, of course. It wasn't like we could expect Hasan to sit around twiddling his incorporeal thumbs while we moved against him.

"My people are taking steps that will keep Hasan occupied."

"And if there is a traitor in your camp, the people who liberated him will be taking countermeasures." Dawna responded.

It was interesting watching the ever-so-polite battle of wills. Dawna is so much more diplomatic than I am that it isn't even funny. That meant that in situations like this, she got to do the bulk of the talking.

I sat silently, listening and thinking. We should turn down the job. I knew we should. It was such bad news. But I remembered case studies I'd read back in college, reports of what an ifrit had done.

Hasan needed to be captured. If he wasn't . . . well, that didn't bear thinking too closely about.

"Is there anyone in your organization who might have a grudge against you? Someone with a personal axe to grind?" I asked when there was a pause in the conversation.

Rahim Patel looked at me with his mouth slightly open. I could almost see the gears grinding as his personal feelings warred with what was obviously a very logical and necessary question.

"I trust all of the members of my family implicitly," he said, but his tone, and the flicker of doubt I saw pass through his eyes, told me otherwise. On the other hand, it looked like pushing him would get me absolutely nowhere.

"What about outside the family? Anybody else have access to the vault or know what you keep there?"

"No." His eyes had narrowed, darkening until they were nearly black. I could see he was clenching his jaw. He was getting pissed.

"So you want me to keep you alive long enough to capture Hasan, and if you die in the process, I'm to transport the hopefully filled jar back to your wife and son. Is that it?"

"Exactly," he said, and pressed the button that shut off the recorder. My office was once again an office.

That it was more of a relief than it should have been told me just how afraid I was. The job sounded simple. But simple is not the same as easy. I met Patel's gaze across the desk. Beneath the calm veneer I could sense a level of fear and desperation. But I didn't think it was for himself: for his son, perhaps, and the rest of us.

I traded looks with Dawna. Since my siren heritage gives me a limited ability to speak mind-to-mind, I sometimes talk to her that way when there are things I don't want the client to overhear, but we've known each other for so long that I often don't even need to.

If we took this case, and that was still a big if, we'd work it on our own terms. If the client didn't like that, he could damned well fire us.

I was afraid. I did not want to do this. But if I didn't, and Patel failed, I would never forgive myself. Every death, every injury would be on my conscience.

"When would we start?"

"Now would be good. Abha insisted I retain you before I even begin working the tracking spells." His voice grew annoyed, and his face showed apparent frustration. "I do not know why."

That was a seer for you. Tell you what they wanted you to do, then clam up tight about anything else. If you pressed, they'd give you a lecture about "changing the possible futures." That was *so* annoying. I loved Dottie and Emma, and Vicki Cooper had been my best friend up until her death.

But there were times when I'd wanted to throttle each of them for doing to me what Abha had apparently done to her husband.

"When we finish our negotiations, you're welcome to use our casting circle. It's brand new, so there's no chance of any residual magic fouling your work." Not that I'd let Tim get away with using the circle without cleansing it after—or that he'd even try. He wasn't stupid, or, as far as I could tell, lazy. If he had been, we wouldn't have hired him.

"Thank you. I wish to get moving on this as soon as I possibly can."

"Fine by me," I agreed, then continued. "Now, is this a short-term job, or long-term? If it's long-term, we normally work with at least a three-person team."

He shook his head, jaw set like granite, lips compressed into a thin line. "It should not take long. I would not even have involved you if my wife had not insisted." He was obviously unhappy. "It took time to get here—time I did not believe I had to spare."

"But you did it."

"Yes." He didn't say, "Duh," but the look he gave me implied it.

"Which may mean there's more to the situation than you originally thought," Dawna added. "So we should probably consider a long-term plan, just in case."

"No team. Just you," he said flatly, pointing to me.

I sighed, but kept my voice free of the irritation that was starting to build within me. "There are physical limitations involved. A person needs to sleep, eat, go to the bathroom. It's very hard to protect somebody when you're taking care of your own bodily functions. I can go without sleep for a while, same with food and other things. But eventually your body's demands can't be ignored, and that will ruin your effectiveness."

"I can stretch my power to protect myself and one other from the magic of the ifrit. Only one."

"One person will be guarding you each shift. You won't need to protect the two who are not on duty." I kept my tone calm, reasonable. I didn't want to. I absolutely hate it when amateurs try to tell me how to do my job. It could get them killed. It's even more likely to get *me* killed. And while Bruno had accused me of having a death wish when we were arguing, I really don't.

"Not acceptable."

I came *this close* to telling Patel to take a hike. I'd actually opened my mouth to say the words, when the intercom buzzed. "Excuse me, this must be important. Dottie wouldn't interrupt otherwise."

"Of course."

I picked up the line. "What?" I sounded more annoyed than I intended.

Dottie's voice had the far-away quality it gets when she's in the middle of a vision. A powerful clairvoyant, she's guided me through seriously dangerous waters and I'm still here to tell the tale. Because I listen—most of the time.

"You need to do this. It's important."

Well, crap. "Dottie . . ." I started to argue, though I knew it was pointless.

"Your future depends on it as much as his." She hung up.

Shit.

4

When we'd finished the paperwork and gotten a retainer, I escorted Patel to his car, where he retrieved a worn leather medical bag that was stowed next to a duffel. The medical bag, I guessed, held his magical gear, while the duffel was probably clothes. Then I showed him to the circle.

He examined it closely, walking over every inch, nodding with satisfaction when he was done. And well he should. It was a very nice circle.

The very day we'd closed on the property I'd had specialists come and install the circle under Bruno's direct supervision. It took up the north half of the parking lot, and while we could probably park on top of it, nobody ever did. It wasn't silver—too expensive and not suited to being out in the elements. But I'd invested in good-quality silversteel, which was practically indestructible, wouldn't tarnish, and wasn't valuable enough for thieves to dig out of the concrete.

It had been interesting, watching the construction team set the connecting plates of silversteel into the concrete. Each plate was engraved with runes and sigils that enhanced the metal's ability to both amplify and contain magic. I'd actually felt the power snap into place when the last plate was set. I'd winced at the cost, but paid it willingly. In the long term, good equipment is a good investment.

I leaned against my SUV, in the shade, watching Patel work. First he stripped off his suit jacket and set it aside, then rolled up the sleeves of his dress shirt. Next, he used a whisk broom to sweep the metal and the concrete around it perfectly clean. He swept the debris into a dustpan and emptied it into a white plastic trash bag he'd brought with him.

That was when I learned just how meticulous, or anal, Rahim Patel actually was. Most people would've considered the clean sweep enough. Bruno, John, and Isaac were the only three people I knew who would have done what Patel did next.

He took a box of sea salt from the medical bag and sprinkled a trail of it all around the circle, being meticulously careful not to miss a spot. Then he swept up every last grain. The used salt went into the same white trash bag, which he then stowed in the trunk of his car.

Next he used a spray bottle to spray holy water over every inch of the circle—something even my three guys wouldn't have done.

When he was finally satisfied with the state of the circle, Patel took five votive-style candles from his bag. Using a compass to determine the precise location of each of the prime compass points, he placed a white candle at each spot. The fifth candle, which was the color of old blood and was visibly flecked with what looked like herbs, he set at the precise center of the circle.

Walking clockwise from due north, Patel began muttering a spell in a language I didn't recognize, the words rolling fluidly off his tongue. One by one, he lit the outer candles. Each time he did, I felt a surge of pure power wash across my othersense. When he went to his knees and lit the red candle, power roared to life, filling the circle with shimmering light that cast actual rainbows and was so bright it was physically painful to look at.

His preparations had been good enough, thorough enough, that not even a frisson of power bled out past the metal of the circle. The heat within it might have been as intense as a bonfire, but that heat was contained and controlled. As the power built to a crescendo, the air almost seemed to thicken, as if I were watching what was happening through a thick pane of old, wavy glass, or clear Jell-O.

That was an impressive amount of power. I'd seen one or two people who could do as much, but not easily, and Patel didn't even seem to be working up a sweat. Then he surprised me again.

I would've expected him to use something connected with Hasan as a focus, maybe wax from the seal that had held the stopper in his jar, or a scraping of paint from the jar itself. But he didn't. Instead, Patel drew a knife from his pocket, flicked it open, and drew the blade up the inside of his forearm, making a shallow incision about five inches long in his smooth brown skin. Blood welled rapidly to the surface, staining the knife, then dripping onto the ground with the same sizzling sound bacon makes in a hot frying pan.

Patel's voice rose to a crescendo as he called out Hasan's name, once, twice, and the final third time. The word rang out clear as a bell, seeming to spread in echoing waves out from the circle, the force of it felt as much as heard as it moved across the ethereal plain.

And that was when things went spectacularly wrong.

It was a trap. Someone, a powerful mage, judging by what happened next, had been waiting for Patel to do just what he'd done. The instant he created that opening to the ethereal, he was attacked. First, the circle flared, the power locking my client inside. A sulfurous fireball the size of my head appeared in midair, flying at Patel's head at the speed of a major-league fastball. He dived sideways and it missed, but the heat was intense enough to singe the back of his shirt, and the smell of burning hair and cotton filled the air.

Whoever was going after him didn't give him time to recover. The fireball was followed by a lightning bolt intense enough to blind. The detonation of thunder when it struck, a mere inch from Patel's rolling body, was loud enough to shake leaves off the nearby trees. Every hair on my body stood on end.

If I were a mage, crossing into that circle would have made my power react—badly enough that it would have likely incapacitated me. But I'm no mage.

When I was fifteen, a pair of boys got into a fight in the gymnasium over Cindy Malden, the head cheerleader. Not a big deal normally—but the boys were both talented mages, and things escalated from a fistfight to a full-out magical duel with the jump circle on the basketball court serving as an improvised, but fully working, casting circle. Ryan Thompson and Alan Brady went at it with everything they had, fire bolts, lightning, you name it. It was fascinating, brutal, bloody, and terrifying. Ryan hit Alan with a lightning bolt that had him down on the ground. He had drawn up more power, intent on finishing him off, actually *killing* him, when Ms. Lindell, the PE teacher, came tearing into the room, realized what was happening, and caught Bobby in a flying tackle that knocked him out of the circle, diffused the power, and saved the day. Bobby wound up with a broken collarbone, and one of Ms. Lindell's wrists was shattered. Alan was covered with bruises and minor burns.

Breaking the barrier had worked for Ms. Lindell; it should work for me. And really, there wasn't any choice—not if I wanted Rahim Patel to survive. He was flat overmatched.

As I sprinted over the edge of the circle, the power stole my breath and gave me instant first-degree burns. I wondered if Ms. Lindell had been as scared at that moment as I was now. My crossing the barrier *should* have broken it, and I prayed that it had. Because if it hadn't, I was as trapped as my client.

5

Things looked very different from inside the circle. For one thing, I could see a rip in the fabric of reality that let me see Rahim's attackers. There were three of them. At a guess, based on relative size, it was two men and a woman, but it was hard to tell. They'd taken pains to conceal their appearance. Not just with illusion, but with the low-tech solution of wearing baggy clothing and hoodies. The hoods were drawn up over their heads, so that only their faces needed magical concealment. The largest figure, on the left, made a flinging motion with his right hand. A flash of searing white light flew toward the tear—directly at me.

I couldn't turn my head quite quickly enough for it not to affect my vision. Not that it mattered. I didn't need to see what he was throwing to know it would be deadly. Pulling on my inner bat gave me the ability to move with blurring speed, away from the blow. Using my sense of smell, I moved across the circle to where Rahim lay.

Grabbing blindly at him, I got hold of a leg that was stiff

as a board. Apparently one of the baddies had hit him with a full-body bind that he hadn't been able to shake. My vision was still blurry and I was blinking back tears as I dragged Rahim—by the ankle—to the edge of the circle, moving as fast as I could. It might have taken one or two seconds, but that was still enough time for them to send magical blows whizzing around me. One of the three was canny enough to aim ahead of me, and I barely managed to dodge the fireball he threw. It passed so close that I felt my skin blistering beneath my slacks and smelled a nauseating combination of burnt flesh and melting polyester. The fireball flowed like lava down the invisible magical barrier in front of me.

When it hit the metal of the circle, the fire grounded out, and I used that brief instant when the flames vanished to drag Rahim across the barrier, which parted around me like a curtain made of heat. The instant the last of his body crossed that barrier, his part of the spell collapsed, closing off the portal and effectively slamming the door in the enemies' faces.

"Strip off your pants," Dawna snapped at me. "You don't want them to stick to your burns."

I blinked, a little startled by the fact that she and the others were waiting for us. When had they arrived?

"Shit," Dawna swore. "She's in shock. Kevin—"

I shook my head, trying to clear my mind. Now that she'd said it, I felt the burns on my leg. I dropped Rahim's leg and tried to work the buckle on my belt with fingers that simply refused to function. Looking down, I saw why; they were a swollen mess of blisters—although when and how they'd been burned, I had no clue. Kevin acted without hesitation. Batting my useless hands gently aside, he deftly unfastened my belt. An instant later he had the button and zipper undone, and my pants were pooled on the ground at my feet. I stood in my underwear as Dawna knelt in front of me and broke a healing spell onto the ground at my feet.

Cool, soothing magic rolled upward, easing the agony of the second-degree burns that covered the lower half of my right leg and washed over my hands. The blisters receded, leaving my hands red and sore, but usable.

Tim, meanwhile, was using first-aid spells on Rahim, who was beginning to stir, his breathing ragged with pain.

The relief was enough to make my knees buckle. Kevin caught me and half-carried me to the fountain and sat me on the ledge. "Put your hands in the water. It will help."

I did and it felt wonderful. I sat there, basking in the cool, soothing feeling of water on my overheated skin, my mind drifting aimlessly. If this was shock, it really wasn't so bad.

"Celia. *Celia!*" Dawna's sharp voice brought me back to the present. I blinked a few times, bringing her face into focus. She looked worried, but more than that, she looked *angry*. Her face was flushed, her jaw was clenched, and the knuckles gripping the handle of the first-aid kit were white with tension. "Kevin, get her inside. Put her in one of the spare rooms and him in another. Chris is on his way."

She turned to Tim and snarled, "Make sure that circle is

shut down, cleansed, and sealed off. I don't want them sending us any nasty surprises."

"Yes, ma'am."

I woke up in one of the spare bedrooms. There wasn't a clock handy, but judging by the angle of the moonlight streaming through the window, it was probably around two in the morning. On the nightstand next to the bed was a tray of food: a little plastic tub of applesauce, a jar of turkey baby food, a nutrition shake, and a thermal mug. I sat up in bed and grabbed the mug first. When I twisted the top open, the smell of tomato soup hit my nose and my stomach growled in response.

As I was taking a big swig, I heard voices in the hall outside my door.

"They should both be all right now."

"Good. Thank you. Have the Company send us a bill." Dawna's voice was brisk, businesslike.

Chris answered with a sigh and a soft, "No. This one's on me. But this is the last time. You need to hire a medic of your own."

"You're right," she said, and I heard him take a sharp, surprised breath. "Do you know of anyone?"

"No. But you should go with a veteran—a combat medic. They'll have seen the kind of trauma she comes back with and will know what to do about it."

"I'll ask my cousin. Maybe she'll know of somebody. About what should I offer as salary?"

"You?"

It was her turn to sigh. "Yes, Chris. Me. I'm a partner. I get to make hiring decisions, and I'm making this one. We absolutely need a healer on staff. I can't keep relying on you. I know that. So, what do you recommend?"

There was a long pause. When he spoke again, it was with great care. "I'll make a couple of calls and get back to you. But Dawna," his voice faltered just a little, "you can always rely on me. Always."

He didn't wait for her to answer. I heard his footsteps moving away. After several long moments, during which I finished every bit of food on my tray, she opened the door. I pretended not to notice that her eyes were red from crying.

"I figured you'd be up by now," she said.

"You figured right." I managed a smile.

"Did you hear that?"

"'Fraid so. You want to talk about it?"

"Just the business part."

I could understand that. Right now, Dawna was as reluctant to talk about Chris as I was to talk about Bruno, and probably for the same reasons. I knew she and Chris loved each other desperately. But their relationship had some fundamental problems that they'd have to iron out if it was ever going to work.

"Fair enough," I said, and meant it. "You're both right. We need a medic. And while it'll be a stretch, it shouldn't break the budget. I trust you. Do what you need to do."

She gave a brisk nod, then, smoothing her skirt, sat down on the edge of the bed next to me. "I spoke with Dottie and

Emma. They both say you need to take this case, but I don't like it. I didn't like it before what happened in the circle. I like it even less now. Djinn are bad business . . . and I don't trust our client as far as I can spit."

"Why not?" Dawna has excellent instincts. If she was twigging onto something weird about the client, I wanted to know what it was.

"He reminds me of my uncle Hoang."

"Hoang?" I riffled through my many memories of Dawna's extended family but couldn't place the name.

"You haven't met him."

The tone of her voice told me that I probably wouldn't, either, which kind of surprised me. Dawna's family is very large and very close. They may drive her crazy occasionally—well, actually, more often than not—but I'd never heard of anyone she disliked before. And she obviously didn't like Hoang. Not even a little. In fact, her tone was almost as bad as mine gets when I have to talk about my mother.

"Hoang is one of those people who hide how ruthless they are by being charming and pleasant," she said. "And while Mr. Patel is far too stressed to be charming at the moment, he's almost *exactly* like my uncle."

I gave that the consideration it deserved. Finally, I said, "You may be right."

"But you're not going to walk away from this, are you?" She didn't bother to hide her unhappiness.

"I don't trust Rahim," I admitted. "But I do trust Dottie and Emma. They've never steered me wrong before."

"Fine," she conceded. "But do me a favor?"

"What?"

"Be careful. I'm no John Creede."

It was her not-so-oblique way of reminding me to be extra cautious.

John Creede was a friend of ours, and one of my former boyfriends. He'd taken over the reins of the company he'd run with his best friend after the other man was killed.

"You'd do fine if it came to that." And she would.

"Yeah, well, let's not find out."

6

Rahim needed to rest and recover, and he was as safe in one of our spare rooms as he could be pretty much anywhere on the planet. Meanwhile, I went to join my team in the main office. Everyone but Dottie was there, and they'd all been busy, researching the djinn and trying to track down the human angle. Yeah, the client didn't want us to. None of us cared. He could fire us if he wanted, but I didn't want to take the case blind. It was just too dangerous. Rahim would probably be annoyed. I could live with that. More to the point, he could *live* with that.

Tim, Bubba, Kevin, and Dawna had spread out papers over most of our conference table, which seats twelve. The video screen was on, and Gordon Waters, Warren Landingham's graduate assistant, was on video chat, his face hovering above the table.

Gordon was a small man with a big talent and even bigger brain. His bright blue eyes peered out at the world from beneath a shock of reddish-gold hair, and his abundance of freckles contributed to the impression that he was a kid, despite the fact that he was older than I was. Despite the hour, he was dressed in a blue-and-white-striped dress shirt, untucked over faded jeans. He peered through rimless glasses as he scanned an old leather text that was spread out on the table before him in a very familiar office.

Warren Landingham, Kevin's father, was one of the top experts on the paranormal and a senior professor at University of California Bayview. Nicknamed El Jefe, he'd been my mentor back in college, and my friend ever since—well, aside from a little blip when he had betrayed me to save his daughter. We were mostly past that, although sadly, things still weren't completely comfortable. But I couldn't think of anyone I'd rather have on my team for research into all things supernatural.

"Where are we?" I took a seat about halfway down the table, facing the video screen. I had to crane my neck a little to see Gordon, which was a bit uncomfortable, but I didn't complain. If everybody could come in at night to help out—including Gordon and El Jefe, who didn't even work for me—I wasn't about to grumble about a sore neck.

Dawna spoke up first. "El . . . Dr. Landingham and Mr. Waters have been giving us general information regarding ifrits and the djinn. I've been scouring the Internet to see if there are any news reports of break-ins like the one we're dealing with. I started with Indiana, since our client works at the University of Notre Dame. I checked the campus records too. So far, no luck."

"They probably didn't call the authorities."

"Probably not," she agreed. "But I figured I'd better check. Chris says that the Company wasn't called in at any point, so they don't have anything to give us." She nodded to Tim, who took the floor.

"I contacted Mr. Levy to see if he could give me a list of mages with enough power to manage astral projection. It's a very short list."

Kevin entered the conversation. "I'm working on finding out where each of them was at the approximate time of the break-in. I haven't gotten very far."

I tapped my fingers on the tabletop. Astral projection was a good guess. Rahim's recording showed absolutely no evidence that a corporeal being had busted into that vault. That was the smart way to do it. No physical being, no physical evidence.

Astral projection is not common, and it certainly isn't easy, but it's possible. Astral projection with physical exertion is even more difficult to do, but it's not unheard of. If that was how it had been done, the perpetrator would have been completely exhausted for two or three days—unable to even stand or walk. That would rule out each of the three mages who'd set the trap for Rahim. They had not only been up and about, they'd had power to burn.

So, either there was a fourth to their little party or the break-in had been done another way.

A ghost could have done it. In fact, that was one hell of a lot more likely than astral projection. But talk about your bad karma. Since ghosts are already dead, how much chance do they have of working off the bad already marking their souls? It wasn't like they had a big shot at redemption.

Of course, if they *knew* they were already bound for hell . . .

That thought led to another, even less pleasant notion.

"Abby, are you here?" I called.

Abby is the ghost of Abigail Andrews, aka Elena Santiago. Alive, she was the adoptive mother and biological aunt of Michelle Garza, known as Michelle Andrews. Abby had gotten murdered trying to protect her daughter from a ritual bloodline curse and had hired me from beyond the grave to save the young woman. I'd managed . . . sort of. Connor Finn hadn't killed her, but to keep the curse from working, I'd had to have her bitten by a werewolf—Kevin Landingham. Now he gets to mentor her in his not-so-copious free time.

Have I mentioned my life is weird?

Anyway, Abby is my "spirit Guardian" of the moment. I'd hoped her ghost would pass on to her eternal reward when I ended the feud and her daughter's life was saved. Nope. She was still here.

Apparently her raison d'être was to see every last Finn in hell, and there were two who weren't yet. At the suggestion of an ancient deity, I'd spared Jack Finn, Connor's son. And while Connor was undeniably dead, he wasn't gone. The elder Finn was every bit as powerful a ghost as Abby, and he hated me with an unholy passion. Even in death he was a dangerous villain. Maybe more dangerous than when he'd been alive. Because, really, what more could I do to him?

The temperature in my immediate area plummeted until

I could see my breath misting the air. A snowflake pattern of frost began to form on the tabletop. The overhead light flashed once, part of a very old code I'd developed with my dead sister. But what one ghost knows, they all do. So Abby knew that one flash was yes, two no.

"Are Finn and his buddies involved in this?"

One flash.

Oh, fuck a duck. Dammit, dammit, dammit. Well, that explained why *I* was involved. I'd thwarted them once—they'd be bound to hold a grudge.

"Are you *sure*?" I was grasping at straws. Ghosts know things we don't and they can't lie. It's not that they're super moral or anything. They're sort of beyond all of that. They just don't have the capacity.

Abby didn't bother with the light this time. Instead, she wrote her answer in frost on the surface of the table. "YES."

Hell.

Dawna's response was . . . colorful. Mostly blue. Everybody else stopped what they were doing and looked at me with varying degrees of alarm. Kevin was the most calm. But even he reached down to give Paulie a reassuring pat.

I was now officially terrified. Yeah, I was scared of the ifrit, but that was kind of an abstract fear. My terror of Connor Finn was deeply personal.

Even before Abby had hired me, a psychic had warned Finn that I was a danger to his plans. So he'd taken preemptive action. He'd had his men kidnap me, put me in a full-body bind, and leave me on the beach in my underwear in broad daylight.

Given my sensitivity to sunlight, that was not good. Very not good.

I wound up with second- and third-degree burns over most of my body. Recovery was excruciatingly painful. I'd had to call so heavily on my vampire healing to survive that the attack had put me back to square one in my fight to retain my humanity. It took me long months of hard work to get back to the point where I was today—where I could usually manage some baby food and other purees and didn't have to watch the clock like a hawk to be sure I ate every four hours to avoid blood lust.

I'd used those same months to work with my therapist on my brand-new, breathtaking fear of burns. With minimal success.

Frosty letters began forming across the tabletop. "He will see you dead."

Everybody gasped at once. Pandemonium broke out when everyone tried talking at once. When it became apparent that no one was going to stop and listen to the others, I raised my hand and they shut up, waiting for me to say something.

Okay, this was bad. No doubt about it. Connor Finn would see me dead. Ghosts can't lie; ergo, it was truth. But Abby hadn't said *when*—and that was a very important detail. It could be today, but it could also be when I was ninety-eight and in a nursing home. Granted, given the life I lead, the latter didn't seem likely. But, hey, I cling to hope where I can find it. And, since dwelling on my possible demise was counterproductive—and likely to distract me from the task at hand, thus leading to my possible demise—I pushed my fears aside and started issuing orders. Yeah, my voice was a little higher pitched than usual and might have been threaded with a little panic. My team ignored that entirely.

"Dawna, get online and get me all you can find on what happened at the Needle." I closed my eyes, taking a deep, calming breath. The government had clamped down hard on the situation rather than risk widespread panic, so information would be hard as hell to find. I knew more than most, since I'd been there, but there was much that I didn't know, like the names and abilities of the two dark mages who had escaped.

"Kevin, do you have any contacts who can look into what Jack Finn has been up to?"

"I'm on it."

I didn't like to leave Warren and Gordon hanging on the line, so I asked if they wanted me to call them back or if they'd rather hold. Warren stuck his head into camera range, right next to Gordon's. An older, more distinguished version of Kevin's, his handsome face was stern and serious. "We aren't going anywhere. We want to help."

"Thanks."

Warren gave a curt nod in acknowledgment.

There were three men who might have info I could use, but none of my team could reach out to them. I needed to be the one to call or they probably wouldn't talk. The hour would be damned inconvenient for all three of them. Still, life or death and all that happy crap.

Pulling my cell from my pocket, I dialed Dom Rizzoli first. Dom used to work for the FBI, in the Los Angeles branch. We'd met in the course of a couple of cases that were particularly hairy, helped each other out, and become friends.

Later, Dom sort of became my liaison with the bureau. He'd been promoted and moved, with his family, to Washington DC.

If anybody could get the sealed files on the Needle unsealed for me, it would be Dom Rizzoli. If I called now, in the middle of the night on the East Coast, I'd probably wake him up. He'd be grumpy. Then again, he'd probably be even more grumpy if I didn't ask for help and something bad happened.

Sometimes you can't win. I called his cell.

I got his voicemail. When I heard the beep I left a message. "Dom, it's me, Celia. I have a situation that involves the ghost of Connor Finn and I need information. It's important. Call me back . . . please."

Normally at this point I'd call Matty DeLuca and see what he could get me from his contacts with the Church. The militant arm of the Catholic Church is very well informed on anything that involves the demonic, and there had definitely been demons at the battle at the Needle. But Matty was, like Bruno, at his mother's deathbed. It didn't seem right to call, particularly in the middle of the night. Maybe I'd call tomorrow. More likely, when Bruno checked in I'd ask him to pass a message to his brother. Of course, then I'd have to give Bruno all the details, and he wouldn't be happy.

Well, neither were any of us. Bruno might as well join the club.

The third person I needed to speak to personally was Isaac Levy, my tailor, my friend, and a mage at the tippy top of the hierarchy of the local magical community. He's also pretty old, and I hated the idea of calling him this late, since he and his wife, Gilda, were sure to be in bed. On the other hand, he already knew something was brewing since Tim had spoken to him while I was out of it.

Isaac answered on the first ring, sounding less sleepy than I would've expected.

"Hi. Sorry to bother you so late, but . . ." I explained what was going on as succinctly as possible. By the time I was finished, any chance he'd had of falling asleep was long gone.

"I am glad you called. You need to be very careful, Celia. These are very deadly people, and they hold a grudge against you." Isaac sighed. "That Finn is involved in this, as a ghost, does not surprise me. He was a very willful and powerful man. He would not give up life easily. Do we know what his purpose for clinging to this plane is?"

"Abby says he will see me dead."

There was a long silence on the other end of the line: a long, ominous silence.

I broke it. "Do you know the identities of the other two mages in the working at the Needle?"

"Yes. Isabella recognized their magical signatures. Meredith Stanton was one. She was Harold's mistress and a nurse at the Needle. She's a very powerful witch and seriously deficient in ethics."

"She'd have to be, to be part of that crew."

"Indeed." He continued, "Bob Davis was the fourth."

Bob Davis had been the warden at the ultra high–security prison. He'd escaped in the confusion of the battle. He was way up at the top of the FBI's most-wanted list, had his picture in the post office and everything, but no trace of him had been found, as far as I knew.

He probably had nearly as big a hate-on for me as Connor Finn did, so if Finn's ghost was involved in this, the odds were good Davis was too. But why? What did they hope to gain? Like a lot of villains, I could see Davis not giving a rat's ass about collateral damage—but why risk setting loose a creature that would be nearly impossible to control? It didn't make sense. I said as much to Isaac.

"Power," he answered. "If they'd gained control of the node at the Needle and loosed whatever it was they were going to, they'd have had unlimited power with no constraints, ethical or otherwise. It is the same here."

"But why would they need that much power?"

"For some, it is an addiction."

I could get that, but it didn't feel like the right reason to me. Apparently Isaac agreed, because he said, "But I think there is more than that to this. Let me see what I can find."

"Thanks, Isaac. Call Dawna with your results, please. I'm liable to be unreachable, dealing with the client."

"Be careful, Celia. Be very careful."

"I plan to."

I disconnected and turned to the video screen.

"Okay, Gordon, Warren, what have you got for me?"

"Hasan's jar is in a pattern of flame and ash because of the primary disaster he was known to have caused," Gordon said.

"Which was?" Kevin shifted to stand beside me and slipped

me a note. I glanced at it: *Jack isn't involved. He's in a coma. Slipped on ice and fell down stairs. Abby?*

Could a ghost of Abby's power have coated steps with ice? Easily. Would she have, to kill the man who'd been part of her being tortured to death? Hell yeah.

Gordon's voice derailed that less-than-happy train of thought. "The eruption at Vesuvius."

"You just had to ask, didn't you," Tim complained.

Bubba started humming under his breath. Kevin glared at him, but the other man was unrepentant. It took me a minute to recognize the tune—I'd heard it on an oldies station: Carole King's "I Feel the Earth Move." Cute.

"So Hasan causes natural disasters?" Dawna asked.

"That seems to be his specialty," Gordon responded. "I can e-mail you a list."

"Please do. Any known weaknesses?" I asked.

"Not really," Warren answered. "It's true that the djinn are arrogant, but with good reason. There's not much regular humans can do to counter them. There's been a Guardian in every generation with special powers to deal with them since a couple of centuries BC, but not a lot is written about them or their abilities. The djinn generally stay away from both the angelic and the demonic, so we haven't found a lot that indicates either of those forces would be of help."

Not that I'd want to deal with the demonic, or even the angelic, if I didn't have to. But the rest wasn't helpful either.

Tim spoke up. "One of the prehistoric African creation myths has a pair of djinn fighting it out. They wound up killing each other, creating the great desert. But who knows whether that's true."

"It's true." Rahim's voice came from the covered walkway that connected the main building to the guest rooms. He appeared a moment later, seeming to materialize out of the shadows themselves. He looked better. In fact, if he hadn't still been wearing his flame-scorched shirt, I wouldn't have known that anything untoward had happened to him. That was definitely weird. I have vampire healing in my favor, which was why I was nearly entirely recovered after a few hours. Rahim didn't. He should still be down and out, not up and around and looking fresh as a daisy. I mean, Chris is good, but nobody's that good.

Dawna gave me a look that told me she'd noticed the same thing and was possibly even more suspicious than I was.

"Anything else we should know?" Dawna asked. Her tone was a little bit sharper than usual and I realized that she still didn't want me taking this case, regardless of what Dottie saw. I couldn't blame her. In fact, I would have heartily agreed— if I didn't trust Dottie so much. But I did.

Since Rahim had been very specific about not wanting us to do research, I more than half expected him to complain about our obvious information-gathering. Surprisingly, he didn't. Maybe the events in the circle had spooked him. Or, possibly, he was the type to pick his battles and had figured out this was one he wasn't going to win.

"I need to use magic to call the ifrit back to its jar. I am considering using another spell that will link my essence to Hasan's on the ethereal plane. I cannot do this if I am under magical attack. I need . . ." he paused, searching for the right word, "reinforcements."

Tim opened his mouth, but Rahim silenced him with a gesture. "I appreciate that you are willing to help, but the mages helping me must be of the line of the Guardians if the spells are to work. I called my grandfather in Florida a few minutes ago, before joining you. He has agreed to assist me and to obtain the—uh—some of the things we will need to do a more elaborate working. With his help I should be able to locate and perhaps trap Hasan. We fly out to meet with him. He is expecting us."

"Your enemies will expect you to go there," Dawna commented.

Rahim's tone was decidedly chilly. "Perhaps, but it is necessary. So we are going."

No "perhaps" about it, as far as I was concerned. If I were a bad guy and the only people capable of containing my monster were the Guardians, I'd have them all under close surveillance—video, audio, you name it.

It never pays to underestimate the enemy, so I always assume they're at least as bright and prepared as I am. Having gone up against Connor Finn and his buddies before, I knew they were very ruthless and very good at being bad. In fact, I'd never run into anyone better. I thought about saying so, but I knew that telling the client wouldn't do any good . . . and I knew that one more word and Dawna would insist we refuse the job.

"Any chance we could meet at a neutral location, some place the bad guys wouldn't expect?" I suggested. "That would give us a real advantage." I smiled, trying to take the sting from the words.

"We are going to Florida," Rahim answered, his tone one of absolute finality.

Apparently the djinn don't have a monopoly on arrogance.

7

It always takes longer to get ready for a trip than you think it will. Rahim wanted to leave as soon as possible, but that just wasn't practical. His grandfather would provide most of what we needed, but there were a few specialty items Rahim needed to pick up, and that would have to wait until morning, when the stores would reopen. PharMart was open twenty-four hours, but they didn't carry the really exotic stuff Rahim wanted.

I probably could've imposed on Isaac, but I didn't want to, and I wanted the extra time for my team's investigations. I also definitely wanted to consult Dottie again and in person. Clairvoyants don't have one-hundred-percent accuracy, but Dottie was damned good. Her visions had saved my bacon more than once. So, with ill grace, Rahim and Bubba went to the private airstrip where the Sparrowhawk was parked. Rahim's plan was to change clothes and do as much pre-flight stuff as he could while I packed and took care of some last minute things here.

We agreed to meet at the airstrip at ten o'clock. Take off would be at ten thirty.

Time flies, whether or not you're having fun. By the time I'd gone over everything one last time with Gordon and Warren, looked at the results of my staff's research, and packed a bag, it was seven thirty.

Dottie arrived then, and while the hot pink outfit she wore was cheery, her expression was grim. Giving me a nod in greeting, she moved slowly but steadily through the building until she reached the conference-room table. One of Dottie's scrying tools is a holy water–filled crystal bowl with a silver rim. Another is a *wadjeti*, an ancient Egyptian set of scarabs.

Today she used table salt and playing cards.

Sitting next to me at the center seat of the conference-room table, she poured the salt in a steady, even flow until she'd made a perfect circle about the size of a garbage-can lid. Peeling the plastic from a brand-new pack of playing cards, she shuffled them a few times and began setting out a pyramid pattern, starting at the top.

The first card represented me. The queen of hearts.

Next row, two cards. The ace and queen of spades. I didn't know what that meant until she spoke, her voice gone hollow the way it sometimes does when her power is riding her.

"The ace of spades is death or the dead. The queen is his tool. They stand between you and your goal, guarding the way against you."

She dealt the third level. Three cards: the jack of diamonds, the joker, and the king of hearts.

"The client thinks he is in control but the joker has the power. They threaten all that you hold dearest."

Fourth and last row: queen of clubs, ace of diamonds, jack of clubs, king of spades.

"Your enemies know you. For every move there is a counter; for every ally an opponent. They are your match in most ways. Ultimately you can prevail, but only if you embrace your hidden strengths."

Dottie shook herself, shedding the remnants of her vision like a dog shakes off water. Her expression wasn't panicked, but she definitely wasn't happy.

"Dottie, are you all right?"

"I'm fine." She didn't look fine. She looked exhausted and truly old. Usually she had a buoyancy that belied the walker and the calendar. Not now. Her skin was sagging, her expression deeply worried. "You need to go. But it is very, very dangerous."

I was lucky. Traffic was lighter than usual, and I made it to the airstrip on time. Rahim's jet was everything it had been advertised to be, and probably well worth the astronomical asking price, if you're into that sort of thing. I'm not. I am better about flying than I used to be, thanks to therapy, but I still don't enjoy the experience. Still, I couldn't fault Rahim for thoroughness. He performed his preflight check as impeccably and with the same attention to detail he'd given to his magic.

Once he'd given the jet a complete external inspection, we climbed on and he made his way to the cockpit. I went to the back and stowed my gear in the small luggage compartment across from the bathroom. Since it was a four-hour flight, I'd brought along reading material—research on the djinn. I set it onto the seat next to me and strapped myself into one of the four passenger seats that were arranged in pairs facing each other.

Either Rahim was a quick shopper, or he had talked someone into opening early. At ten o'clock, we were actually in the air. We would arrive at Midland, Texas, between two and three o'clock local time to refuel and get a late lunch, then fly from Midland to Treasure Island. And, since we were filing our flight plan like good little citizens, it would be spectacularly easy for our opponents to know precisely where we would be, and when.

Not that that bothered me or anything.

Sitting strapped into an admittedly luxurious leather seat in the passenger compartment of the jet, I tried to reassure and distract myself during takeoff by checking my weapons.

Since we were on a private jet, I didn't have to worry about what to pack—what I could legally take through airport security. I could go whole hog, and I had. My favorite gun, a Colt, was strapped in my shoulder holster; a Derringer backup piece was holstered on my ankle, my favorite knives were mounted in their wrist sheaths, and I'd filled my pockets with as many spell disks and balls as could comfortably fit. My jacket was stocked as well, with a stake, two One-Shot brand water pistols filled with holy water, and a garrote. I also had brought sunscreen, a hat, a little recorder similar to the one Rahim had used, my passport, and a couple of changes of clothes. I couldn't pin down Rahim as to how long we were likely to be gone, or what our destinations after Treasure Island might be, so I'd overpacked in hopes of having what I would need. Like the Scouts, I believe in being prepared.

We spent four uneventful hours in the air before landing in Midland. It was time for me to eat again and Rahim was hungry, so I slathered myself with sunscreen, slapped on my hat, and we walked the block and a half to the nearest fast-food roast beef restaurant.

We were too late for the lunch crowd and too early for dinner, so we had the place to ourselves except for the staff. Since solids are a problem for me, Rahim and I split a pair of French dip sandwiches. He got the sandwiches, and I got the dip, along with a large Pepsi and a chocolate shake. I lusted after his curly fries, because they smelled absolutely awesome, but didn't even bother trying to eat one. It is no fun having food get stuck in your esophagus.

Sitting in our little yellow and orange plastic booth, I drank my shake and sipped au jus from the little white plastic cup you're supposed to dip your sandwich in, all the while trying to pry more detailed information from the client.

"Okay, say we go. You and your grandfather do your thing. Then what?"

"If the spells succeed, we will be able to trap Hasan in Florida, and this will all be over."

"If you fail?"

"It *should* work." Rahim sounded supremely confident. His

body language, however, was less certain. Still, he plowed on, his voice firm. "At the very least, the spells will give me a link to Hasan and let me determine his location. In his current state, he will not be able to resist my spell binding him to his jar if I am physically in his presence."

I was persistent. "But if the spell doesn't work?"

He glared at me, dark eyes flashing. "I am the Guardian."

I didn't say a word, just stared, willing him to be forthcoming. Eventually, and with ill grace, he continued.

"Being the Guardian gives me access to certain . . . reserves of strength and magical power I can call upon in an emergency. I have access to enough power that trapping Hasan should be well within my capabilities."

"Even with the bad guys running interference?"

"Even so."

I didn't believe him, not after what I'd seen with my own eyes at the casting circle in my parking lot. Granted, his enemies had caught him by surprise. Next time he'd be prepared. But I didn't like it. Not one itty bitty bit.

Rahim could tell I was skeptical and that pissed him off, which put paid to my getting any additional information from him—and to any other topic of conversation, for that matter. We ate in record time, in less than amicable silence, and shared an equally quiet trudge back to the jet, where he repeated every step of the preflight inspection that he'd performed before we left California.

I probably should've been reassured when he found nothing wrong and we took off without incident. Instead, I got even more tense. The bad guys weren't stupid. They were bound to make a move. If they didn't strike at Midland, then Treasure Island was a safe bet. So I decided to rest up, and dozed for several hours. We were in Florida air space when we hit heavy turbulence. I bounced around in my seat despite the seat belt and had to swallow hard to keep the food I'd eaten from making a second appearance.

It was only spitting rain in Tampa, but there were heavy gusts of wind, which would make a smooth landing impossible for even the best pilot. Rahim brought us down safely and while I did not kiss the ground upon leaving the plane, I really did think about it. Rahim smirked about that.

Despite the rain, I made sure to slather myself with sunscreen before climbing down from the plane to check the area. Once that was done, Rahim passed our luggage down before joining me on the tarmac. He folded up the retracting steps, retriggered the latent security spells, and locked the plane in the private hangar he'd rented, while the wind drove the sprinkling of rain so hard that the drops stung as they struck my skin. I could smell the ocean in the distance, even over the scents of oil and gasoline, but didn't see any gulls dotting the leaden skies. Usually, if I was anywhere near the sea, I quickly accumulated a seagull or two, thanks to my siren heritage. Then again, they might have gone to ground due to the heavy winds.

Rahim was carrying a large-ish black duffel and his doctor's bag. I had a weapons bag and a pale blue, wheeled carry-on that had seen better days. It held toiletries, changes of underwear, a couple of fresh blouses, and a couple of pairs of pants. I'd packed a lot of sunscreen. Still, the weapons that really mattered to me were on my person: My guns, and more importantly, my knives.

Thinking of the knives reminded me of the man who made them. Even though we'd broken up after college, he'd sliced himself every day for five years, shedding blood and working magic, to create weapons that qualified as major magical artifacts. He did that because a clairvoyant had told him they would save my life. They were my most prized possessions and were capable of incredible things. Just a scratch from one of those knives could kill most magical creatures.

Bruno had put so much of himself into those knives that they were practically a part of him. He could sense when they needed a recharge without even looking at them.

The blades were beautiful and dangerous—just like the man.

I missed him. I was worried about him. A big part of me wished I'd insisted on going to New Jersey along with him. If I had, I'd know how he was taking things and I wouldn't be here, dealing with a case that was an obvious hairball. But when I'd offered, he'd turned me down. If I was being really honest with myself, I'd admit that had hurt more than a little. We were engaged, weren't we? No, I wasn't wearing a ring, but we'd been seriously talking marriage for a while now. Didn't that count? Didn't it make me part of the family?

I thought again about calling him. Of course, if he was at the hospital he'd have shut off his phone. And I didn't want to talk to his voice mail if I didn't have to.

Oh, hell. I hoped he was okay. Well, as okay as he could be, under the circumstances.

Life is awfully hard sometimes.

I closed my eyes, taking a second to send my thoughts in his direction. My grandfather had siren bloodlines and my great-aunt Lopaka was their high queen. I inherited not only my looks, but the siren "call," a type of telepathic ability. I'm not good at it, but I've been practicing, and my cousin gave me a ring that has given me better strength and range.

As I expected, he was at the hospital, at his mother's bedside, sitting vigil along with Matty and most of their other brothers. I carefully pulled my mind from his without interrupting.

So voice mail it was. I whipped out my cell phone, waited for the beep, and said, "Hi. It's me. I wound up taking a job and am going to be out of town for a few days. I'll try to stay in touch. Tell the family 'hi' for me. Love you. Call when you get a chance and let me know how your mom's doing, okay?"

It was kind of a lame message, but I didn't really know what to say. I was worried about him and his mom. I was even more worried about our relationship. I couldn't really apologize—I didn't think I'd done anything wrong. Then again, neither did he. I just wished . . . oh, hell, I wasn't sure what I wished. But it would have been good to talk to him, just to hear his voice. Corny as that sounds, it was the truth. But I knew I really didn't have time to chat—that might get me, or my client, killed.

I slid my phone back into my jacket pocket as Rahim, finished sealing the plane away, came up beside me. Hefting his duffel onto one shoulder, he took his magical bag in the other hand and led me toward the office. I stayed about half a pace

behind, keeping my eyes open, checking out the surroundings, looking for anything or anyone that seemed out of place.
There was nothing unusual going on. The private plane area
wasn't heavily populated at the moment and everybody
seemed to be busy going about mundane business. Still, I
kept an eye out as we passed through the automatic doors and
into the building.

At the desk, Rahim filed his paperwork, then pulled a
credit card out of his wallet to pay. I debated telling him to
use cash. Credit cards are so easy to trace. But what was the
point? We'd logged a flight plan and we were visiting a man
the villains would be expecting us to see.

Ever since 9/11 and the big threat of terrorism, it's hard for
a law-abiding person to go anywhere or do anything without
leaving tracks. I suppose that makes life harder for the crooks,
too, but I've never been sure it's worth the loss of civil liber-
ties to the rest of us.

"What are you thinking?" Rahim asked.

"Nothing important." I replied. For a second I thought
he'd argue with me, demand that I answer. I was getting the
impression he was way too used to getting his own way. Unfortunately, that's not an uncommon situation among the
type of folks who wind up needing my services. I gave him
the polite, shiny, and utterly meaningless smile I use to settle
clients down. As a result, while he compressed his lips in displeasure, he didn't argue, silently taking his receipt from the
attendant before leading me out a different set of doors.

The rain had stopped, which was nice. But the wind was
still gusty, tugging at my jacket, pulling it open. I didn't want

to flash my weapons at every passerby, so I took a moment to button up, reminding myself that it would cost me an extra couple of seconds on the draw.

My client seemed to have spotted his ride and was striding purposefully toward the passenger pickup area. Looking ahead, I saw a man waiting there who looked much like Rahim would should he be lucky enough to live another fifty or so years. The older man's hair had gone silver; his skin was leathered and worn with time. Wearing jeans and a light-weight canvas windbreaker, he stood next to a huge vintage Cadillac, a classic metal behemoth, complete with tail fins.

"Is that your grandfather?"

Rahim grinned, the expression taking a dozen years off his face. "Yes, it is." He waved vigorously and the old man responded in kind.

I sighed inwardly. That car might as well have had concentric circles painted on it. Fire-engine red, with tail fins and an abundance of polished chrome, it was beautiful, unique, and *noticeable*. No doubt it was properly registered, with the address of our destination listed in the DMV database. Damn it anyway.

"You're unhappy." Rahim spoke very softly, keeping a smile on his face as we strolled toward our ride.

"Even if they didn't anticipate us coming, it wouldn't take much to trace your plane from California to here, and the first thing they'll do is look at your relatives. Bad enough we're here. That car—"

"It's his pride and joy," Rahim hissed. "It will be fine."

I didn't believe that for a minute, and I was fairly sure he didn't either. Rahim could—possibly—afford to be more worried about the old man's feelings than his own safety. I couldn't.

"Trust me. The protections on the car are stellar." He was trying to reassure me, which was nice, but I wasn't buying it. I could accept that he needed to meet with the old man. I would have preferred we do it somewhere neutral and discreet. This was neither. Still, like it or not, we were doing this. Better to get it done with as quickly and cleanly as possible. And then Rahim and I were going to have a long, serious talk about listening to me, planning ahead, and taking appropriate precautions. Judging from what I'd seen so far, he wouldn't like it. He didn't have to. He just had to do it.

I very deliberately moved ahead of Rahim, greeting his grandfather with a smile and a handshake, using the hand I'd discreetly sprayed with holy water from one of the One-Shot water pistols tucked into my jacket. If he was the real grandpa, he might be offended by a soggy shake—but if this was a demon spawn, wearing Grandpa Patel as a disguise, the holy water would give it away.

Grandpa passed the test, eyes widening, then narrowing as he dried his hand on his pant leg. He muttered something under his breath in a language I didn't recognize. I didn't think it was Hindi, but I wasn't linguist enough to guess what it might be.

"Grandfather, you know she had to check. It is her job, after all." Rahim's voice was calm as he embraced the older man, but the look he gave me over his grandfather's shoulder was less than friendly.

When he stepped back, he said, "Grandfather, this is my

bodyguard, Celia Graves. Celia, this is my grandfather, Pradeep Patel."

I smiled. Pradeep didn't. He looked at me shrewdly and said, "You don't like my car."

"It's a very beautiful car," I countered, my tone professional and calm. "But it is also very noticeable, and probably properly registered to you. Rahim's enemies will be keeping an eye on you, since you are family and also an expert in matters related to the djinn," I continued. "I had a very noticeable car once. My enemies used it to find me. Despite my having the best protections available, they captured and tortured me."

Rahim winced. His grandfather didn't. There was a long moment of silence as the arrogant old man tried to stare me down. Finally, he said, "If you are right about this, I will eat my hat." Such an old-fashioned expression could have been funny, but wasn't—his words were precise, his tone crisp and bitter.

Rahim opened his mouth to say something, but I waved him to silence.

I counted to ten, biting my tongue until it bled so that I wouldn't say any of the snarktastic things that sprang to mind. When I had control of myself, I said, "Sir, I am not a seer. I don't know what will happen. I have to plan for what *could*. My job is to advise your grandson of risks as well as protect him from them."

He made a disgruntled *hmpf* sound, then grabbed my bags and put them in the trunk. Rahim joined him to stow his own bags. I stepped back until I had a better angle . . . and watched the two of them have a brief, discreet argument about me before getting into the car.

Rahim took the backseat, which left me riding next to Gramps. Oh freaking goody. I kept my expression neutral and reached for the door handle. The instant my fingers touched the metal, I got a jolt of pure magic like a hot ice-pick rammed through my hand.

Wow, the car really had *stellar* protections. Ow.

I didn't gasp, or swear, but it wasn't easy to just climb in and act like that hadn't hurt, and part of me was really annoyed at Grandpa Pradeep's smirk: annoyed enough that I began to notice the pulse point at the base of his neck, just a thin bit of skin, stretched tight over the arteries that held warm, salty blood.

Shit. "I need to eat. Now. Where's the nearest grocery?" I tore my gaze away from the old man's neck, resolutely looking out through the windshield. My jaw was clamped shut so tight that my words sounded odd.

The old man stared at me for a long moment. When he spoke, there was none of the previous hostility in his tone. "I can get you there in ten minutes. Will that be fast enough?"

"Do it." Rahim said, adding "please" as an afterthought.

Just as well. I wasn't sure I trusted myself to talk.

8

I was hungry enough to be blood-lusting. It had only been a bit over four hours since my last meal, but I had screwed up my mental calculations. I hadn't taken the time change into account. We'd headed east and I'd lost two hours in the air. That put us close to sundown.

Worse, I'd used my vamp powers for healing earlier in the day, and hitting the wards on Pradeep's car had pushed at my inner bat. Damn it. I should have anticipated at least some of all that. I felt stupid, embarrassed, and more than a little angry at myself. I was also unhappy with Grandpa Pradeep. Those protections of his had given the bat inside me a big shove and it wanted so badly to shove back. Still, I knew I could control myself long enough to get some food, provided it didn't take much longer than Pradeep's promised ten minutes.

The tension in the vehicle was palpable. We rode in silence.

We'd been driving for four or five minutes and had made it onto Central Avenue, the Treasure Island Causeway, when

I spotted them. They were very good, or I'd have caught sight of them sooner. There were three cars, working a tight pattern.

"We have a tail. It's a three-car team: the navy Buick, the silver Taurus, and the black SUV." I concentrated as I spoke, focusing to bring my vampire abilities to the fore. It was easy—too easy. My vision shifted, becoming more acute; I was able to see clearly into the blue sedan even though it was in the far lane and one car ahead. The rain had slowed to a mist, but the wind was heavy enough that I could hear it whistling around the car; it was keeping the mist from obscuring visibility.

The woman in the sedan's passenger seat wasn't pretty, but she was striking. More to the point, she held herself like an athlete or a fighter, and while I couldn't see most of the bulk of her body, I noticed where her jacket bulged under her seatbelt, probably bending around a weapon. Her dark hair was pulled back from a sharp-featured face with alert, hazel eyes. She was looking at us; a flicker of frustrated annoyance played across her features before she turned to say something to the driver.

"Are you sure?" Rahim's voice, behind me, was tense. He leaned forward, putting his head between his grandfather's and mine.

"Yes."

"I haven't noticed anything." Pradeep wasn't exactly arguing, more reserving judgment.

The cars were closing in. "We need to get off this road before we're forced onto the bridge."

There wasn't a lot of time to react. People were driving carefully on the wet roads. Traffic was heavy and we were in the left lane. There was a little grass island to our left, but it was filled with trees and street lamps placed at just the wrong intervals. Even if Pradeep jumped the curb, he wouldn't be able to run that obstacle course in this boat of a car. That meant turning right. The next section of Causeway Bridge was in sight, two blocks ahead.

Pradeep began to swear as the trio of vehicles closed in. I couldn't understand the words, but the tone was unmistakable. I guessed he believed me now. Our enemies knew they'd been spotted, so all pretense was gone. They were trying to surround us.

The older Patel hauled the big old Caddy into a hard right, forcing an opening, to the accompaniment of slamming brakes and blaring horns. Braking hard, Pradeep tried to cut onto the 80th Street exit, but the SUV beat us to the punch, positing itself diagonally across the lanes.

The Buick was right beside us on the left with its passenger-side window down. I shoved Rahim back behind the seat and down with my left hand as I fought the damned button of my jacket with my right, trying to draw my Colt.

Pradeep was no fool. He ducked, out of my line of fire, keeping his head only high enough to peek through the gap between the steering wheel and dash as he shouted, "No, don't! The protections will keep the bullet inside the car."

Well, hell. I put the gun back in its holster as the woman in the next car pulled a . . . paintball gun? What the hell was she doing?

I didn't have to wonder long. She fired three times in rapid succession—shots that splattered olive-green goo all over the windshield and the driver's side window, effectively blinding us to the road ahead.

I felt, not a surge of power, but a sucking sensation. The goo was eating the protections from the car. I wasn't the only one who realized what was happening. In the backseat, Rahim began swearing in a combination of English and something else.

Pradeep hit some buttons and switches, but the windshield wipers and washer fluid only smeared the green stuff around. The old man was effectively driving blind and he wasn't very good at it. The big car crunched into something with a screech of metal on metal and slewed right, bumping up onto the sidewalk.

Shots rang out over the sound of a loud clanging. I pulled a stake from its loop in my jacket, jammed it through the safety glass of the windshield in front of Pradeep, and yanked it sideways. The resulting tear wasn't large, but it let in day-light and gave the old man a peephole to see through. He hit the gas, racing up the sidewalk as bullets flew through the car.

No one was hit—the enemy was shooting blind. But our luck wouldn't hold forever. She kept shooting as water blurred past the bridge railing we were nearly scraping. Behind us the SUV had rejoined the chase and was gaining speed, working to get an angle. I knew the tactic. He planned to bump us, forcing us through the railing and into the water. Not that I could do a damned thing about it. I couldn't even shoot at them—the protection on the back windows was just fine.

"The SUV!" I shouted in warning as I dropped the stake and drew my gun again. I didn't dare shoot through the passenger-side window—there were noncombatants out there. But I had to do *something*.

"I know," Pradeep growled as the bigger vehicle slammed into our left rear bumper. He fought for control as the Caddy's front bumper screamed in protest as it scraped against the metal guardrail.

"Screw it!" I shouted to no one in particular. Rolling down my window, I climbed out until I was sitting on the window-sill, gun in hand, and began firing at our enemies. I managed to hit the driver of the SUV before I was jarred by a heavy thump that made me grab onto the Caddy's roof for balance, my body swaying high above open water. There was another huge crash. Red and white chunks of wood and fiberglass flew past, some slamming into my back and shoulders. I risked a glance backward, eyes widening in horror.

The drawbridge was up. We'd just slammed through the railing and were headed for open air.

9

I was screaming a warning as I slid back into the car. Not that it did any good. Pradeep slammed his foot on the accelerator until it was flat to the floor. The engine gave a throaty roar, like some huge, angry beast, and leapt forward, climbing the increasingly steep incline without slowing at all.

The wheels left the pavement and we were airborne, my stomach sinking to my feet as I clung frantically to the dashboard with the hand not holding a gun, screaming in terror. And then we just . . . stopped. The car was floating in midair, high above the open drawbridge. Pradeep was grinning as he took his foot from the accelerator, slammed the gearshift into park, and turned off the engine.

I couldn't help myself. Leaning out the window, I looked down. A large boat was navigating the passage directly beneath us. I could see cop cars converging on the bridge, where the SUV and the Buick sat abandoned. The bad guys were fleeing on foot to join the driver of the silver Taurus. By the time the cops got here through traffic they'd be long gone.

That was the first bit of bad news.

I got the second bit when I slid back into my seat. Pradeep was explaining things to Rahim.

"I knew about the levitation spells they have in place on the bridge. We will be stuck here for a couple of hours and I will have to pay a heavy fine—ten thousand dollars—but it is worth it. We are alive."

A couple of hours. With no food and me all vampity from adrenaline.

Could this day get any better?

I opened my mouth to ask what would happen if I got out of the car, but was interrupted by the simultaneous ringing of three cell phones and the noisy arrival of the 10News Chopper.

I slid lower in my seat. We were on the news. Of course we were. After all, we'd been involved in a public shootout and were trapped floating above a drawbridge. At this point we were probably the hit of YouTube.

I pulled my phone from my pocket. It was Bruno. I flipped it open, answering the call just as Pradeep and Rahim did the same. "Hi."

"What the *fuck?* You're in *Florida?* Floating above a *bridge?*" He wasn't exactly shouting, but it was close.

"You saw."

"I'm watching it live right now." He lowered his voice. I wasn't sure that was an improvement, since there was a hint of a growl under his next words. "What the hell happened?"

"It's a long story. I took a case this morning. It's gotten complicated." I could hear Pradeep and Rahim in the background, reassuring their respective wives that everything was fine.

"*Complicated.*" One word, but it held a world of meaning. I knew he was having to fight the urge to say more—to start up again about how I kept taking cases no one else would, hopeless, ridiculously dangerous cases that every other firm had the good sense to turn away. But he didn't say it. Didn't say anything, just waited; the very silence was somehow accusatory.

"Yesssss, complicated." Oh shit. I was lisping. The fangs were down and affecting my speech.

"Celia?" He made it a question.

"I need food, Bruno. But I'm sssstuck up here. Maybe for hourssss." My voice reflected the fear I couldn't quite contain.

I heard him take a deep breath and let it out slowly. When he spoke, his voice was soft, soothing, all anger set aside in the face of an obvious crisis. "Baby, listen to me. I need you to do something."

"What?" It was a little hard to talk; my mouth was watering. I didn't dare look at the men in the car with me. I could hear their pulses like thunder, smell their fear. It smelled so good. It would be so easy—

Bruno's voice came to me like a lifeline. "Celia, listen to me. We're going to hang up and you're going to e-mail me a picture of some empty space inside the car you're in. Can you do that?"

"Yesssss." I didn't ask why. I was hoping I knew.

"My aunt Connie is here. I'm going to have her send you some food. Just hang on, okay? *Hang on.*"

Aunt Connie was Sal's wife. I'd only met her once. We hadn't much liked each other. She was a teleporter. If she could get me food, I'd . . . hell, I didn't know what I'd do for her. But I'd do something. Something really, really, big.

The line was dead. Bruno had hung up. Fear and hope warred within me as, with shaking hands, I used my phone to snap a picture of the space in front of my lap and e-mail it to Bruno in Jersey.

A minute later there was a popping noise and a huge bowl of tomato sauce, fragrant with spices, appeared in my lap. Seconds later there was a series of three rapid pops and the floorboards in front of me were filled to overflowing with nutrition shakes and a wine bottle.

I was weeping with gratitude and relief as I guzzled my improvised meal. Chocolate diet shakes and tomato sauce may not sound like much of a meal, but to me it was pure heaven.

My phone rang while I was sucking down the third shake. Pradeep answered it. As if from a distance I heard him assuring Bruno that the food had arrived and we were going to be all right.

For the moment, anyway.

10

The police closed the bridge to all traffic, set up giant lights, and brought in CSI types to gather evidence. They left us hanging in the air while they did it. I got a beautiful view of the sunset. It was very pretty. I might even have enjoyed it in different company, and if I hadn't had to go to the bathroom. Only when the authorities were darned good and ready did they summon a group of uniform-clad mages. With the power of their combined magic, they gently lowered the Caddy onto the bridge. We were instructed to step out of the vehicle, slowly, and then to lie down on the pavement, putting our hands behind our heads.

We complied and I made myself lie absolutely still as a uniformed officer proceeded to thoroughly disarm me. I felt very naked and vulnerable, lying there under the bright police lights, knowing that there were any number of spots looking down on us from which a skilled sniper could take us out. But we were lucky; none did. Instead the three of us were escorted to separate vehicles for questioning as cheering bystanders watched, held back from the bridge by officers working crowd control.

I scanned the crowd as the cop pushed my head down, kindly making sure I didn't bash it while climbing into the car with my hands cuffed behind me. I was looking for familiar faces from the car chase, and for a moment I thought I spotted the woman. But the face was lost in the crowd in a flash, so I could have been wrong.

Even if she was there, it wasn't like I could do anything about it.

Looking through the window, I caught a glimpse of the Caddy. The car was trashed, completely totaled. The engine might be salvageable, but even that was questionable, given that it had taken a few direct hits. It broke my heart; remembering my own lost car, I could imagine how bad Pradeep felt. But when they helped him to his feet he didn't say a thing, just turned his back on the wreck and walked over to the waiting police cruiser. Rahim, too, ignored the vehicle, his face set in grim lines as they led him to a third car.

The police station wasn't far away. I was whisked through the back door, escorted into an interrogation room. I was lucky. The car chase had been all over the news; it was obvious I'd been acting in self-defense. Because of that, the cops were more generous than they might otherwise have been. They took off the handcuffs, for one thing. And while they sent a female officer in with me, they did let me visit the bathroom before they sat me down for questioning.

I was really grateful for the restroom break as the hours rolled on while I waiting in the interrogation room, mostly alone. Somewhere in there, the CSI folks asked for, and I gave them, permission to perform gunshot residue testing on my jacket. My attorney, Roberto, might get on me about it later, but I wanted their good will. Besides, I had no doubt there was video of the shootout circulating on the Internet already. No point in denying what they had actual evidence of.

Finally one of the local detectives deigned to grace me with his presence.

"Ms. Graves, I'm Detective Erik Allbright." He extended his hand, giving me a bright smile that wasn't particularly sincere. He was wearing black suit pants and a white shirt with its sleeves rolled up and the collar unfastened. I could see an anti-siren charm peeking out from his chest hairs.

Allbright was probably forty years old, with medium brown hair, brown eyes, and the kind of leathery skin that comes from spending a lot of time in the sun without much use of sunscreen. His features were pleasant, if unmemorable, and while he had a nice enough smile, it didn't quite reach his eyes.

"Detective Allbright." I shook his hand, firmly. Unlike a lot of guys I've met, he didn't feel the need to get aggressive and squeeze until it was uncomfortable. That was hard to do to me—my inner bat had great tolerance for pain—but I still didn't enjoy it.

"So, I have to ask. Why on earth would a college professor need a bodyguard to come visit his grandparents?" Allbright smiled more broadly.

"You'd have to ask him. But whatever the reasons, he did hire me. And it's a good thing he did."

"So what exactly happened?"

"I'm sure you have it on video."

He didn't deny that, just smiled and said, "I'd like to hear the story from your point of view."

Something in the way he said it made me wary. "I think maybe I should have an attorney present before I say anything else."

He wasn't happy about my request, but he didn't argue, just got up and opened the door.

The man who strode in had an alligator briefcase, a thousand-dollar suit, and a million-dollar smile. "Ms. Graves, my name is James Barber. I've been retained by Rahim Patel to represent your interests. I'm sorry it took me so long to get here."

I shook his hand, smiling broadly, and asked if I could have a copy of his business card and see his driver's license.

Yeah, I'm suspicious. So sue me.

Barber didn't bat an eye. Reaching into the inside pocket of his suit jacket, he drew out a business card, a stack of papers, and his wallet. The papers were the representation agreement, which verified what he'd told me.

"Could I have a moment alone with my client?" he asked Allbright, flashing another killer smile.

"Sure. Just knock on the door when you're ready." Allbright left the room, pulling the door closed behind him.

"All right. We'll be quick about this. Rahim Patel is paying me, but I represent you and only you. So you don't have to worry about a conflict of interest. The man you shot is in the ICU. He's alive—barely."

It was good he was alive, but bad that he was in ICU. If he was that badly injured, the cops wouldn't be able to interrogate him properly for days, by which time it might well be too late. Judging by the speed at which things had been moving since this morning, the situation with the ifrit would be coming to a head sooner rather than later.

Barber continued, "There's video all over the news and the Internet showing that you acted in self-defense."

"Did they get any good shots of the faces of the bad guys?"

"One or two people were able to get photos of the one you shot and there are a couple of blurry photos of one of the others. But whether the police will be able to enhance them enough to be usable is anyone's guess."

Crap. Having their pictures on the news would have put a lot of pressure on our opposition to go underground, might even have driven them away from Florida altogether, which would have been helpful. That there weren't any meant that the bad guys were still anonymous—and free to act.

"You've been cooperative, which is good. And since Treasure Island *is* an island, they have siren charms on hand, so there will be no accusation of mental tampering on your part. Also, you are a very public person with a known propensity for working on the side of the angels. So, while they could hold you for questioning for up to forty-eight hours, they probably won't."

"Good."

"They'll keep your gun as evidence. I'm working on getting them to return your other weapons."

"My knives," I said. Barber interrupted.

"Yes, I know. They're major artifacts, and very valuable. I'm fairly certain I'll be able to get them back to you shortly. I've contacted the district attorney. Under the circumstances, he's reluctant to press charges. On the other hand, he doesn't want it to look like he's going easy on you because you're a celebrity."

"I'm not a celebrity."

He gave me a disgusted look. "Of course you are. *I've* heard of you. I contacted your usual counsel, Roberto Santos, who confirmed for me that you have diplomatic immunity. If absolutely all else fails, we can use that—but only as a last resort. Now, let's get Detective Allbright back in here. Answer his questions honestly and *simply*. Don't volunteer any extra information. If for any reason I think you shouldn't answer, I'll let you know."

"Got it."

"Good." He got up, went to the door, and opened it. "We're ready now, detective."

The interview went about as well as I could have expected. Not great, but in the end the cops didn't arrest me and didn't hold me for forty-eight hours. They let me walk out with only the standard warning about it being an ongoing investigation. It was better than I had any right to expect, but I was too tired to rejoice. After all, I'd skimped on sleep because of the vampire case and the move. I was pooped. My attorney led me through the halls and out into a reception area where both Rahim and Pradeep were waiting.

"They are not keeping you?" Pradeep asked.

"No. But they've got my weapons. I have backup gear, but that's in my bag in the Caddy."

"Which is in impound. We won't be able to get to it until sometime tomorrow at the earliest," Rahim said. "That presents a problem." The way he said it made me think that I had missed part of an important conversation between the two Patels. Not unlikely. Since neither of them had actually shot anybody, their interrogations had probably been considerably shorter than mine.

"I can deal with that in the morning," Pradeep assured him. Turning to me, he said, "You're not hungry?"

I was, but not horribly. *Thank God for Connie*, I thought, but said, "I'll be fine for a little bit—'til we get where we're going. Where *are* we going anyway? I assume we'll be staying the night."

"My wife has arranged discreet accommodations for you. One of her friends from the bowling league manages a timeshare. There was a room available and I have made sure it is booked under another name. I have made arrangements regarding transportation as well."

I raised an eyebrow, but didn't say anything.

"I am an old man, but still capable of learning."

"Fair enough."

He wasn't lying about having learned from his earlier mistake. Our exit from the police station was managed like a Broadway stage show. Four cabs left simultaneously from the underground parking garage. Three contained spell disks magicked to project illusions that looked like Rahim and me.

One went to each of the local airports; the third was sent to the Tampa Marriott. We rode in the fourth, to a beach-front timeshare called Safe Harbor.

It was a pretty building, probably twelve stories tall, tan brick with lots of smoked glass. It was curiously built, with all sorts of angles, so that the balconies of every apartment would give at least a glimpse of the ocean. The parking lot was only half-full, and as we pulled up I could hear the sound of people frolicking in the swimming pool.

Pradeep left with the cab. Rahim and I rode a glass-fronted elevator to the third floor. I wasn't thrilled with that, but he told me that at this time of night both stairwells were locked. We only had to walk three or four feet to get to our apartment. Rahim unlocked the door, using an old-fashioned key on an oversized keychain shaped like a lighthouse.

I went through the door first. It was an efficiency apart-ment, scrupulously clean, and cute. Decorated in gray and tan, it had an ocean theme, with a mural painted on the walls, cream-colored tile floors, and a wall clock framed with ropes and sailors' knots. The windowless bedroom was tucked behind a set of sliding doors. The living area had an open floor plan that was furnished with comfortable beach-style furniture that would wear well and be easy to clean. The couch could fold out into a full-size bed. Open, it would take up most of the living area, butting right up against the two-seater dinette set that was less than a foot away from the galley kitchen. Sliding-glass doors across from the kitchen and beside the couch led out onto the balcony.

The bathroom was, if not precisely roomy, at least well

arranged, and had a cute little porthole-style window that was made with some kind of special glass that made the light coming through it look turquoise from one angle and pink from another.

"You take the bedroom. I'll use the couch," I suggested. It made sense. The way the apartment was laid out, anyone coming in the front door or from the balcony would have to go through the living room—and past the couch—to get to the bedroom and its occupant.

Rahim nodded and shambled into the bedroom, where he sank onto the bed and began sliding off his shoes.

"My grandmother stocked the pantry if you're hungry." His voice was listless, heavy with exhaustion. I knew exactly how he felt. It had been a long damned day. While I wasn't hungry, I needed to eat before sleeping, so I dragged my sorry heinie off the couch with a groan and walked the three steps to the galley kitchen.

"We should go to bed soon," Rahim said as I puttered around, looking for a pot and a can of soup. "The ceremony is at dawn tomorrow." His voice was muffled, and I could tell it was all he could do to stay awake.

I looked up at the clock and managed not to groan. We might be able to get a bit of sleep, but not much. Still, I didn't argue. "Ceremony?" I made the word a question.

"My grandfather has found evidence that Hasan may be hiding in one of the Temples of Atonement. He and I can work together to use magic to determine which of the temples it is. The best time to do this is at sunrise."

"Dawn. Right." I was so tired I couldn't imagine getting up

with the sun . . . and dawn was problematic for me for another reason as well. The vampire part of me doesn't like sunrise, not one itty bit. Sunsets are hard because the vamp wants to come out and hunt. Dawn is when it dies and tries to take me with it. It doesn't last—but until the sun is truly up, I am *not* at my best. I'd manage in the morning. I always do. But this wasn't happy news. I debated whether or not to say anything to Rahim about that now, then decided to break it to him in the morning rather than wake him. He was already snoring softly, lying fully clothed atop the covers.

When the soup was ready, I poured it into a large coffee mug and took it out onto the minuscule balcony. I closed the screen but not the glass. I needed to be able to hear what was going on inside in case of trouble.

I didn't bother to turn on any lights. My night vision is excellent, and being backlit isn't safe when you know bad guys are after you. I set my mug on the little table and settled into the lawn chair that was part of the set provided. Digging my cell phone out of my pants pocket, I hit speed dial. Late as it was, Bruno picked up on the first ring.

"You're okay?"

"Thanks to you and Connie, yes."

"The police statement went all right? No problems?"

It was obvious he'd been worrying: with good reason, really. I've had several run-ins with the authorities in the line of duty. Since I am one of the good guys, you'd think that wouldn't be a problem. You'd be wrong. I look like a monster. I have fangs and an über-pale complexion. It's very well known that I have siren abilities. The cops don't find any of these to be endearing qualities. A number of members of law enforcement have lobbied vigorously to have me locked up permanently. I shuddered at the memory of what those prisons were like.

"As well as can be expected. Bruno, thank you—and thank Connie for me. I know she doesn't like me . . ."

He gave a snort of amusement. "Yeah, well, Connie doesn't like anyone younger and blonder than she is, just on principle."

I laughed. That sounded about right. Connie was Sal's trophy wife. He'd married her after his first wife, Ida, passed away from breast cancer. It was no surprise that Connie worried that someone younger, and maybe blonder, would catch Sal's eye and he'd move on. I didn't know if she had reason to be insecure or not.

There was a moment of silence between us that wasn't quite as comfortable as it should have been. That hurt. I wanted things to be right again between us. I just wasn't sure how to make it happen.

"Bruno . . ." I started, but he cut me off.

"Celia, don't. Just . . . don't. I love you. And I know you love me. But I can't talk about us right now. I've got too much else on my plate. Mom's condition has gotten worse. Things here are insane. Sal's having problems with the Russians and everybody's on edge."

I took a sip of soup and tried to think what to say. Sal was the head of an old-school mob family. If he was having "trouble" with the Russians, it was probably damned dangerous for Bruno to be in Jersey at the moment. But he wouldn't leave, not with his mother ailing.

Isabella Rose DeLuca was matriarch of the family, a top-notch mage, and a force to be reckoned with. Normally I'd bet on her against all comers. But time and fate have a way of catching up with you. She had done what she had to do, and now she was paying the price, without hesitation or complaint. I might not like the old girl much, but I respect the hell out of her. And I knew for a fact that she'd do it again without hesitation if she were given the chance, if for no other reason than to protect the two sons who'd been part of the ceremony with her.

Isabella's mind and magic might be as powerful as ever. But her body was giving out. The node magic she'd channeled was causing her body to fail, one system at a time. The best doctors in the world were working on her, but they'd told the family there was only so much they could do. She was dying. It was that simple. And Bruno damned well intended to be by her side when she drew her last breath—screw the Russians and any danger they might pose.

"I'm so sorry. Tell your mom hi for me." I didn't say to get well. We all knew she wouldn't.

"I will." His sigh was so heavy it made *me* feel tired. "Look, I know you've got to do what you do."

That was a concession, but I didn't comment on it. He continued, "But do me a favor. Be careful. I love you so much."

"I love you, too. You be careful, too. It sounds like it could get hairy out there."

He didn't deny it, which from him was as much as an admission. And while there really didn't seem to be anything else to say, neither of us seemed willing to end the call.

I sipped more soup, staring across the parking lot at the strip of beach and patch of moonlit ocean visible from the balcony, wondering how we'd gotten to this point and worrying we wouldn't get past it. My heart ached. I knew we didn't mean to keep hurting each other, but we couldn't seem to help it.

Bruno finally broke the silence with, "I've gotta go."

"Yeah, me too. The client's doing some big ceremony at dawn."

"Dawn's not your best time." There was no judgment in his tone. He was just stating a fact.

"No," I sighed, "it's not."

"You'll be careful?"

"Much as I can." It was the best I could offer, and this time he accepted it without argument. "You too."

"As much as I can."

"Give my best to the family."

"I will."

We hung up after saying good-bye. I opened the screen door and leaned in. Rahim was still out of it, his breathing steady. Closing the screen again, I dialed Dawna. What with the time difference it actually wasn't too late for her.

We exchanged greetings and got straight to the point.

"Are you all right? I saw the shootout on TV."

"I'm fine. The client's fine. What have you got for me?"

"Nothing. Not a damned thing!" Dawna didn't bother trying to hide her frustration. "The good news is, there's been no sign of ifrit activity. None." She sighed. "*But*, there's also no clue as to who stole him or why. Most of the world experts on the djinn have taken 'leaves of absence' in the past few days.

The two who hadn't have both been murdered—and thanks to my stumbling into the middle of *that*, the FBI are on their way over to ask me a few questions."

I wasn't surprised about the leave-of-absence thing, and I'd bet dollars to donuts that the missing experts were probably involved in whatever action was keeping Hasan contained. But the deaths, and the lack of information on the thieves, were both seriously concerning.

"Has Dom returned my call?"

"No, he hasn't. I don't suppose you have his number handy?"

"It's in the Rolodex up in my office," I offered. I have an old-fashioned, paper Rolodex, with addresses and phone numbers of my contacts, clients, and so forth. I keep it up to date, too. I have a problem with phones. I lose them. Constantly. And while you can back up a phone, and even transfer information from phone to phone, I like having a paper copy. And a Rolodex doesn't ever lose its charge.

I wasn't entirely sure Dom would take Dawna's call, but hey, it was worth a shot.

"I'll try. How much information can I give him on the current situation?" Dawna asked.

That was a trickier question than it sounded. We're bodyguards, not private investigators or lawyers, so we don't have intrinsic protections or the client confidentiality rules that the police need to honor. On the other hand, we're not expected to protect more than the client's body.

"Just tell him I'm in the middle of a hairball that involves the djinn and that I have it on good authority that Connor

Finn's ghost and a couple of his buddies are involved. That should be enough to satisfy him, at least for a bit."

"He'll want to know more. He always does."

"Yeah, well, he can want what he wants. If he gives you too much trouble, have him call me."

"You're assuming you'll have a phone," she said, only half-joking.

"Yeah, yeah, cute. Whatever." I took the last gulp of my now-cold soup. "I need to get to bed. I've got an early day tomorrow. Let me know if you turn up anything else."

"I will. And Celia," she gave a meaningful pause. "Be careful."

God, I was getting tired of people saying that. I mean, seriously. I'm always careful. Or at least as careful as I can be while getting my job done. I might have said something to that effect, but she hung up before I could respond.

I went back into the apartment, trying to make as little noise as I could. Rahim was completely out, spread-eagled across the bed, snoring full out now. He hadn't closed the sliding door between the bedroom and the living room, for which I was glad. I would've had to slide the door open and check on him otherwise, and might have awakened him. As it was, I locked the balcony, double-checked the front door, set my dishes in the sink, and went about converting the fold-out couch into a bed. I took off my empty holster, draping it over the back of a kitchen chair. Next came the empty sheaths for my knives. Last, I undid my ankle holster, setting it onto the end table next to the bed. Since I didn't have a gun, I took one of the larger knives from the kitchen drawer and put it on the end table within easy reach. Then, taking off my shoes, I climbed into bed, switched off the light, and slept.

I woke to the sound of Rahim's phone playing reveille. I groaned. Apparently he was a morning person. It was enough to make me sick.

Seriously, 5:15 was just too early for anyone to be expected to rise, let alone shine and be chipper. Ugh. I *so* didn't want to get out of bed. The only thing that made the thought even close to bearable was that I could smell fresh coffee. Rahim's grandmother must have programmed the coffeemaker the night before.

I felt my way across the end table past the knife to switch on the light as Rahim edged awkwardly around the end of my bed on his way to the bathroom.

I rose. It only took a minute to convert my bed back to a couch. By then Rahim was out of the bathroom, so I picked up the knife and took my turn.

I don't like sleeping in my clothes much. I've done it before. I'll probably do it again, but I don't like it. Unfortunately my clean underwear was in the Caddy, which was in impound. I so did not want to put my dirty underwear back on after a shower. Yuck.

Then I had an idea. Quick as could be, I hand-washed my undies and dried them with the blow-dryer attached to the wall. It took less time than drying my hair had when it was long, and I felt much better about facing the morning. Silly? Probably. But true just the same.

I was putting the dryer away when Gordon contacted me mind-to-mind.

Princess Celia?

Gordon? What are you doing awake at—

Two thirty in the morning, he finished for me. *I haven't been to bed yet. I've been researching the Guardians and Rahim Patel.*

And obviously working hard at it. Oy. *Thank you.*

You're welcome. Ifrits are a bad business. I want to do all I can to help.

What did you find out? Obviously he'd found out something, or he wouldn't have bothered to contact me. But I couldn't hang out in the bathroom forever—Rahim would get suspicious—and I wasn't good enough at talking mind to mind to do it without the client noticing unless there was a lot going on around us.

Not much—some historic stuff that is interesting, but probably not germane. But there is some recent gossip I uncovered from someone at Notre Dame. The Guardians are chosen from a family line. It's an inherited talent. Usually there are two or three in a generation capable of stepping up to the position when the existing Guardian retires or dies. Pradeep Patel chose Rahim's father and Rahim's father chose Rahim.

Made sense.

Pradeep didn't approve of that. He thought the position should go to Rahim's cousin, Tarik. The two of them came to South Bend shortly after Rahim's father died, ten years ago. There was an argument. The secretary and professors I talked to said they weren't speaking English, but things got ugly

enough that security had to be called and Tarik and Pradeep
were escorted off campus. It might not mean anything . . .

Pradeep seemed to have worked things out with Rahim.
Maybe Tarik had, too. But if there was a traitor in the family,
Tarik would bear looking at. *Have you told Dawna?*

Yes. They're looking into both Tarik and Pradeep. Be careful.

I will. Thanks, Gordon. Now go get some sleep.

I am. Let me know if there's anything else I can do.

Of course. Thanks again.

Well, that was certainly interesting. I pulled on my clothes,
pondering whether or not I could trust Pradeep. Based on his
actions yesterday, probably—to a point. The old man struck
me as being totally devoted to his cause—and arrogant
enough to think that *he* was the only one who knew best. So
long as we did what he wanted, he'd support us. If we did
something he disagreed with, we'd have a problem.

I came out of the bathroom, clean, dressed, and smiling
as if nothing was wrong. Rahim gave me an odd look. I answered the implied question with two words, "Clean underwear," as I took a mug from the kitchen cabinet and began
filling it with coffee from the pot he'd left warming.

He grinned and the expression took years off his face, making him look much younger, less serious, less arrogant, and
almost attractive, despite the day-old, rumpled clothes he was
wearing.

I beat that thought down firmly. He was a client—and
married besides. If you think of a client as an attractive man,
your body language changes. That changes the relationship
subtly, and not in a good way. Maybe it's cultural, maybe it's

biological, but every time there's been sexual chemistry in the mix, the protectee has started becoming protective of me—which defeats the whole purpose and makes it impossible for me to do the job. Besides, I love Bruno. I've zero interest in anyone else.

Rahim's smile lost some of its wattage. Still, it didn't fade completely, and he took the chair opposite me at the small kitchen table amiably enough. "My grandparents will be here in a few minutes with suitable food, a gun for you, and the things we'll need for the ceremony."

"Tell me about what's going to happen."

The look he gave over the rim of his coffee mug spoke of his reluctance to talk about it.

"I need to know what's going on if I'm going to protect you adequately during the process," I explained. "It's not good for me to be surprised or get distracted by what you're doing. And while we're on the subject of 'not good,' you should probably know that I'm not at my best at sunrise. The first five minutes after the sun clears the horizon are really hard for me. I'll do my best, but you'll need to be particularly careful at that point. And I'll be carrying an unfamiliar weapon. That could cost me seconds when it counts."

"I see." He wasn't thrilled. All his bonhomie evaporated in an instant. Ah well, not much I could do about that. I drank my coffee with sublime calm and waited him out. Sure enough, a couple of minutes later he caved.

"I am the Guardian of the Djinn." I could actually hear the capitals in the way he emphasized the words. Rahim held up his wrist to show me the mark I'd caught a glimpse of the previous day. It looked like a cross between a curse mark and a tattoo: a darkened, shiny patch of skin about the size of an old silver dollar, with raised scarring in the shape of flame and smoke that were outlined in red and black. It was striking, almost pretty, and less obvious than it would have been on someone with lighter skin. "One of the gifts that comes with the responsibility is the ability to sense djinn. It helps me to hunt and trap the ifrits so that they do no harm. I *should* be able to find Hasan anywhere in the world. But I cannot. I *know* he is alive and active, but he is hidden from me."

"That sucks."

His mouth twitched with amusement, but his eyes quickly darkened. "My grandfather and I talked while you were being questioned yesterday. He believes that Hasan is hiding in one of the Temples of Atonement."

"You said that last night." I had no idea what or where a Temple of Atonement was or why Pradeep might think Hasan was hiding in one, so I sipped my coffee and tried to look interested.

Rahim's lips twitched again, his eyes sparkling. Still, his words when he continued were quite serious. "There are five temples, each built on a node by the djinn. The temples are in Cambodia, Mexico, Peru, Egypt, and here in America, in one of the ancient Anasazi ruins. At these spots, the world of the djinn intersects with ours, and it is through these temples that they transport their prisoners to our world. The residual djinn magic imbued in the temple stones, and the node magic beneath them, may be powerful enough to thwart my natural abilities."

I could buy that. I'd been around a node when it was accessed for magic. It was pretty impressive. Oh hell, who was I kidding? It was awe-inspiring and scary as hell. Djinn *and* a node. This case just kept getting better and better.

"Instead of the candles I used in the working in California, we will be using vostas from the five temples in the ceremony. If Hasan is hiding in one of the temples, the power of that stone will resonate differently and I will know."

"And you're doing it at dawn because . . ."

He began ticking off points on the fingers of his right hand. "First, the beach should be deserted, or nearly so, so there should be no threat to bystanders."

I approved of that. Collateral damage is never good.

"Second, the power of the rising sun will help with the magic." He sighed. "It would be better if it was closer to high tide—the rising water would wash away all traces of the magic. No one would even know the ceremony had taken place."

"No plan is ever perfect," I assured him. "Is this the best you can do?"

"Yes."

"Then we go with it."

He gave me a grateful smile and opened his mouth to say something, but I raised my hand and signaled him to be silent. He complied without argument. Trust at last?

I'd heard the elevator stop on our floor, then footsteps in the hall. They stopped outside our door. I smelled . . . well, heaven is probably too strong a word, but really, I do love bacon, and eggs, and fried potatoes, and I really, really, missed being able to eat them. My stomach began rumbling audibly.

"There's a blender in the cabinet," Rahim whispered, trying to hide his smile behind his coffee cup, but I saw it just the same. I couldn't help grinning back. I didn't know how he knew I couldn't eat solids. Maybe he'd noticed—after all, he'd seen me eat twice, three times if he was still awake last night when I was making soup. Maybe he'd done some research on me before we'd met. The latter would make sense, and was something I would've done. Research would also explain why neither he nor his grandfather had been affected by any siren issues. They'd probably been wearing anti-siren charms.

Whatever, I was getting breakfast. I'd have to blend the food and water it down with milk. But I'd be able to have a real breakfast, not just another nutrition shake. A small thing like that can make a huge difference at the end of the day.

There was a light tap on the door. I pointed and Rahim went into the bathroom. I slipped into my jacket and grabbed the knife, which I'd brought out of the bathroom with me and set on the table while we had coffee. As I opened the door to peer outside I wished mightily for at least a One-Shot with holy water—but mine was gone, along with my weapons. I had no way of checking to be sure that Pradeep and the older woman in traditional Indian garb who stood together in the hallway were actually Pradeep and his wife.

Her arms were filled with a pair of bags, one of which

smelled of food. He held what looked like Rahim's sports bag. There was no sign of my luggage.

I checked the hall in both directions to make sure no one was lurking and had forced them to get us to open up. Nothing.

Only when I was absolutely sure it was safe did I step aside to let them enter. By that time my stomach was tying itself in knots, wanting at that bacon.

"Rahim?" The woman pushed gently past me, setting her bags onto the kitchen table, and though I hadn't told him he could, Rahim emerged from the bathroom, his arms outstretched.

"Grandma." Pradeep was right behind her. I closed and locked the door.

The minute I did, Rahim uttered a series of soft words over his grandmother's shoulder and I felt a spell fall into place. The distant sounds of traffic and the ocean vanished and Rahim's voice took on a flat, almost hollow tone I recognized from past experience. We were under a privacy spell. No one would be able to overhear anything that was said until the spell was taken down.

"Good morning." I turned my attention to the bags on the table. The smell of food was coming from the one on the left. The one on the right smelled of gun oil and metal. Hungry as I was, I went for the bag on the right first. Inside was the weapon Pradeep had promised. An honest-to-God, Dirty Harry–style Magnum, and a box with extra ammo, in case I needed to take down a stray rhino or something. The thing probably kicked like a mule. But by God, it would do the job if any of the bad guys showed up to "make my day."

I took the gun from the bag and checked it. It was fully loaded and well cared for. I confirmed that the safety was on, then slid it into my holster. It was a snug fit—my Colt is a little smaller—but it wasn't too bad, and when I tried the draw, it didn't stick or slow me down. It would do.

I turned to Pradeep. "Thanks."

"No. Thank you for yesterday. I wouldn't have noticed the enemy until it was too late. Neither would have Rahim. You saved us."

"It's my job." That was the bald truth. "But you're welcome." None of us spoke about the problem I'd had afterward. Some things are better left unsaid.

Pradeep gestured to the woman with him. "This is my wife, Divya."

She was a tiny thing, no bigger than my own gran, who stood less than five feet. Her skin was darker than either Pradeep or Rahim's, and the hair in her long braid had more silver than black. Still, like my gran she was filled with energy and had a ton of personal charisma. Divya gave me a huge, if awkward, hug, tears filling her beautiful dark eyes as she thanked me profusely for saving "her men."

"It's my job, ma'am."

"I am so grateful!"

Rahim saved me from more embarrassment by announcing, "I smell breakfast!"

Divya released me with a laugh. "That one is *always* hungry." She shook a teasing finger at him, then set about unpacking food from the bags as Rahim fetched the blender and dishes from the kitchen cabinets.

Pradeep, meanwhile, moved the sports bag onto Rahim's bed.

By unspoken agreement, we put off discussing anything important until after we were all fed. I wasn't sorry. I was too busy reveling in the taste of real, if watered down and blended, food. It was glorious. Twenty-four hours of nothing but liquids and a jar of baby food had me close to the edge.

After the first few swallows, I felt the tension and irritability that had been building in me drain away. The bat always wants blood, but human food can keep *me* happy and sane. Besides, I *like* food. Back when I was first attacked, I'd been so excited when I had reached the point when I could eat baby food . . . and later, small amounts of regular food that had been run through a blender. It had all made me feel so much more human. Connor Finn and his thugs hadn't taken that away from me permanently, but getting back to it had been a long struggle. Overcoming my inner bat and living a normal life was an ongoing battle.

Only when the dishes were loaded in the dishwasher, with the machine's gentle hum providing background noise, did Rahim go into the bedroom.

"How did you get this?"

Pradeep replied, "After I left here last night, I went to the impound yard. I explained that it was an emergency, and that there were valuable magical artifacts—items they would not want to be responsible for—locked in the trunk of the vehicle. The officers in charge made a few calls, after which I was allowed to take my bag with the vosta. Nothing else." He looked apologetically at me at that. I hoped he was sincere and not covering a deliberate attempt to keep me away from my weapons.

Unzipping the black nylon sports bag, Rahim removed a carved box of ivory and fragrant sandalwood, which he carried through the tiny living room and set in the center of the kitchen table. About the size of a breadbox, it was old, so old the scent of the wood would have been unnoticed if not for my enhanced senses. It had a fitted lid, which Rahim lifted carefully and set aside.

The moment the box was open, magic hit me like a club. I jerked backward so hard my chair started to tip out from under me. Only my quick reflexes and Pradeep's instinctive grab kept me from falling to the ground.

"That one is still live." Rahim growled, pointing an accusing finger at a stone the size of my fist—the farthest right stone of a set of five. It was a topaz, golden in color, and pulsing with power, almost as if it had a heartbeat. It shone with an inner light that the other stones lacked. I could tell that all the stones were powerful, but the others were more . . . quiet about it.

Five vosta. Doing some quick math in my head, I figured that the contents of that sandalwood box had to be valued in the seven-or eight-figure range. Used to focus magic, a good vosta was worth more than your average house—in Los Angeles. No wonder the police hadn't wanted to be responsible for them.

Pradeep answered his grandson calmly. "You needed a vosta from each of the temples. This was the only Egyptian stone available. The last fully bled stone was that ruby that was destroyed a few months ago."

I tried not to flinch. *That* ruby—I'd been the one to destroy it. At the Needle. I suspected that Patel the elder would not be happy to know that.

Looking at me, Rahim explained, "One of these stones is from each of the temples I told you about. We will put a stone at each point of a pentagram, and I will stand at the center of the working. If, as we believe, Hasan is hiding in one of the temples, the stone from that location will resonate at a different pitch."

Rahim smiled and continued, "If we are lucky, the ifrit will come to the working and we will trap him. If not, we will at least know where he is and can hunt him down."

I worked hard to keep my face from showing the depth of my misgivings. In a few minutes we were going to try to locate or capture a being powerful enough to change the course of the universe. Why was I doing this, again? Oh yeah, right, because I'm a self-destructive idiot.

"But a live stone . . . the risk . . ." Divya's features were taut with barely controlled alarm.

"We have no choice," Pradeep answered, but I could tell from the look on his face that he wasn't any happier about it than she was.

"Why is it bad to use a live stone?" I felt stupid asking, but I figured I needed to know.

The three of them shared a silent look.

"Guys," I growled, "we're on the same team. I can't do my job blind."

Pradeep gave the tiniest of nods. Only then did Rahim explain.

"Ifrit absorb magic. It is . . . 'food' is too simple a word. A live stone, still filled with the magic of a disarmed ifrit, would be the perfect meal."

"For Hasan."

"Yes. But not just for Hasan, for every ifrit on the planet, and any other creature that is drawn to such things."

Holy crap. "So basically, to find Hasan we'll be ringing a dinner bell and shouting 'Come and get it' to every ifrit in existence?" That was so bad.

"There shouldn't be any free ifrit other than Hasan," Rahim said, but something in his voice made me suspicious of his soothing words.

"He's correct," Pradeep assured me, then added, "But there will be genies, and other noncorporeals, attracted to the ceremony. Most will be neutral. Some may not."

Great. That made me feel so much better. "And how many would that be?"

"Not so many," Rahim assured me with a smile. I wasn't fooled. He hadn't given me a number, which meant he probably didn't know.

Pradeep sighed. "It is a risk." He rubbed his hair with his right hand in an unconscious nervous gesture. "But a necessary one."

"When the spirits show their faces we will know their numbers, and perhaps we will even be able to mark them for later hunting." Rahim grinned at his grandfather.

Pradeep smiled as he nodded in return.

They hunted evil spirits . . . for fun. I suppose I shouldn't be surprised. After all, regular humans hunt big game and

vampires; some even hunt werewolves on the full moon—
totally illegal, but it happens. Thinking about it, it made
sense that the Guardians would hunt evil spirits. Probably
they considered it training, thought that it kept them sharp.

Divya looked sick, and that wonderful breakfast I'd enjoyed
so much was sloshing around uncomfortably in my stomach.
But I am a tough and intrepid bodyguard. I kept my misgivings to myself and my mouth shut.

"The others want to confer with you," Pradeep said to his
grandson.

The others? I wondered.

Rahim gave him a disgusted look. "Of course they do."

"They have the right." The old man's voice was severe. "You
have put them at risk and are using them and their powers."

"It is their sworn duty to assist me," Rahim snapped. "And
it is the thieves who put them at risk. Not me."

"And how did the thieves get past your defenses?"

The temperature in the room didn't actually drop, but there
was a definite chill in the air just the same. Apparently the rift
between the two men wasn't completely healed. And frankly,
Pradeep had a point. I didn't think that Rahim had been careless. He really wasn't the type. But anyone can make a mistake.
And the thieves had found the vault, and had known which jar
to take. The big question was how? Or, more likely in this
case—*who*.

"*Fine*." Rahim spat out the word. "We'll *confer*. I wouldn't
want the *others* to feel *used*."

Oh wow, there wasn't any bitterness there. No, not at all.

Rahim stalked the two or three steps into the kitchen and grabbed the saltshaker from the counter. He shoved the coffee table aside with just a little more force than was necessary, clearing space to work in the middle of the room. Pivoting in one spot, he poured a perfect circle of salt onto the floor around him, then held out an imperious hand to Pradeep. The older man's face was perfectly blank and impassive as he passed a pocketknife to his grandson. Divya sat silently at the kitchen table, her expression distressed.

Rahim opened the pocketknife and, without pause or hesitation, jabbed the tip of the blade into the Guardian mark on his wrist. Flinging drops of blood from the knife onto the salt circle, he spat out words I could not understand. As he did, power built until the air around him seemed to shimmer and thicken. One by one, faces appeared, floating in the air. All were male, some bearded, some not. They were old and young, handsome and ugly. Despite their differences, they bore enough similarity that I knew they were all branches of the same family tree.

I didn't understand the conversation; I don't even know what language they were speaking. When one of those not present spoke, his face enlarged, coming into clear focus as a three-dimensional, holographic head. Weird. Cool, but definitely weird. Most of the speakers only said a word or two, if that. One man, however, was determined to argue.

He was a little older than Rahim, with hard, sharp features that stood in stark contrast to Rahim's pretty-boy good looks. His dark eyes flashed, and there was no mistaking the sneer in some of his words.

I bet that's Tarik. Had to say, he looked like one tough cookie. Not a good enemy.

Five or ten minutes later, Rahim lost patience and snapped out one last retort before shutting the spell down with a gesture. Glaring at his grandfather, he said, "There. Satisfied?"

Pradeep was calm, unmoved in the face of his grandson's fury. "It needed to be done."

I saw Rahim draw breath to say something . . . and decide against it. Turning his back, he went into the bedroom to calm down. His grandfather packed up the vostas and sorted through a bunch of magical items from one of the sacks they'd brought. I guessed he was reassuring himself that he had everything needed for the ritual, even though he'd undoubtedly packed the supplies himself and checked them then. Finishing with a curt nod of satisfaction, Pradeep tucked the box of vostas into the sack. Meanwhile, Divya silently and efficiently used a broom and dustpan to clean up the mess.

I checked my weapons, such as they were: Pradeep's Magnum, the largest kitchen knives that would fit into my sheaths, and a wooden cooking spoon that could be broken off and used as a stake. Not exactly an impressive array, but it would have to do.

The handles of the kitchen knives were too thick to fit under my jacket sleeves, so Pradeep loaned me his windbreaker. I left it unzipped and adjusted the sleeves so that the handles of the knives stuck out just a little. The last thing I wanted was for a wardrobe malfunction to cost me seconds that would get us all killed.

I practiced drawing the gun, then practiced pulling the

knives. My moves weren't as smooth as with my usual jacket, but I thought it would be all right.

Looking up, I met Divya's gaze. The smile she gave me was more than a little sickly. Poor woman, she was absolutely terrified.

Couldn't say I blamed her.

Pradeep, Rahim, and I took the glass-fronted elevator to the ground floor. It was a short ride, but I felt hideously exposed the whole time and was grateful when we were reached the first floor and were able to exit. It was a short walk, across the paved parking lot and through a small gate, to the beach. This close to dawn that strand was the next best thing to deserted, and quiet enough that I could easily hear the sound of the ocean.

The scene was beautiful, lit by the fading rays of the pure, white light of a nearly full moon that reflected on the water, as well as by the orange glow of halogen lamps bouncing off more prosaic concrete. I could smell a sea breeze . . . and a drunk, sleeping it off near a footbridge a couple of condos down. I wouldn't have been surprised to find a vampire bite on him, lying exposed all night on the beach, but he was still alive—I could hear his soft breathing.

The local blood-suckers were hustling off to their nests to die for the day. My inner bat wanted desperately to do the same. I ignored it, moving despite the stiffness and pain in my joints that grew as the first hint of pink and orange backlit the belt of clouds on the eastern horizon, painting them in shades of blue and purple. The first delicate flickers of color danced atop the dark water.

We passed a large patch of tall grass and palm trees where sleepy birds made small sounds as they shifted around in the nests they'd made in the sandy ground. I suppose I shouldn't have been surprised at the color and texture of the sand, but I was, a little. I'd heard of white sand beaches, but in truth the color was a pale gray, particularly where it was wet. Other than the little scraps of broken shell and the occasional shell-covered ocean creature, the sand was incredibly fine. We kept walking until we were just short of the foam and debris at the water's edge.

I envied Divya, who had stayed at the condo. I'd have loved to go back to bed and get more sleep. Not that I thought she was resting—she was far too worried. More likely, she was standing on that postage stamp of a balcony, trying to catch a glimpse of what we were doing. I didn't check to see. Instead, I kept alert, my gaze raking the area as the two men began chanting. They dragged sharp sticks through sand that had been smoothed by the soft touch of the ocean, drawing the magical symbols they needed. I could feel the burning heat of the power building until it was like a bonfire at my back.

I gave a jaw-cracking yawn. I just couldn't help it. Shaking myself slightly, I fought to focus. At that precise moment, I heard a small, metallic click followed by a soft beeping. I turned and saw that the sleeping drunk was neither. He'd rolled onto his stomach and was aiming a rifle at Rahim. I shouted a warning as I drew the Magnum and moved into the line of fire. In the distance I heard the sound of motors on the water. The beeping was a homing beacon. The shooter and I fired almost simultaneously, in a roar of deafening sound and flashing light. We both hit our targets, my bullet tearing into his skull at the same instant a bolt of pure energy slammed into my chest.

My heart stopped, my body tumbled onto the wet sand. The pain was incredible. Indescribable. I couldn't breathe, couldn't do anything but feel my body failing and my brain shutting down.

It was nearly over when I saw a translucent image shimmer over the sand.

He was lovely—inhuman, made of smoke and the light of distant stars, a vision of terrible beauty. He smiled down at me, his expression beautiful but chillingly acquisitive. He moved forward slowly, with exquisite grace. As he did, I knew . . . knew who and what he was, what he intended to do.

Hasan intended to take over my body, and there wasn't a damned thing I could do about it.

11

The ifrit slid into me as easily as a hand slides into a glove. As he did, I felt my heart give a feeble thump, then another, my lungs expanding in a breath that felt like heaven, flooding my body with sweet, beautiful oxygen.

My body rose from where it had sprawled on the ground: rose with a fluid grace I could never have managed on my own. With that same liquid grace, he glided toward the circle and the Guardians.

Pradeep stood outside the circle, and I saw him, not as the old man I had gotten to know since yesterday, but as a fierce warrior. Whirling and slicing his own arm with a bloodied knife, he sprayed drops of blood in great arcs, splattering a shimmering, shifting cloud of spirits. The spirits screamed when the blood hit them, each drop burning like acid.

I knew then what Rahim had meant by "marking them." I also knew, instinctively, what Hasan wanted with my body. My flesh was the ifrit's shield. Pradeep's blood could hit me without doing damage. More, as a mortal, I could cross the ritual circle, disrupting it so that Hasan could kill the Guardians, steal the stone, and regain some small amount of the power he'd lost during his time of imprisonment.

No. I fought for control of my own body, forcing it to a stop just a fraction of an inch short of the circle.

That shocked him. *What are you?* Hasan was startled and beginning to be angry. *No mere human could fight me like this.*

I didn't answer, but I didn't have to. He was in my body and mind and could hear my thoughts. Every day, I fight to maintain my humanity in the face of the warring parts of my being that are anything but human. Now, in this moment, I needed to embrace the things that were different about me: the vampire strength, my siren heritage. Being human would not get me out of this. Being *inhuman* might.

The siren ring on my finger throbbed with power, making the ifrit riding me hiss with pain. His control of my body slipped just a fraction: enough that *I* was able to control that arm. I used that control to draw a knife.

You will do as I say. If you do not, I will leave and you will die.

Fuck you. As I said the words I used the knife to shallowly slice across the top of my hand.

It was a small cut, but the pain helped me focus. I pulled on my vampire nature, deliberately focusing on the smell of blood, so strong I could taste it like copper pennies on my tongue. At the same time I used my siren heritage to call on the power of the ocean and all its creatures. It was not high tide, but the water came, in a rushing wave that washed over the ritual circle and knocked me off my feet. I fell into the sea and

Hasan was forced out of me, his voice leaving my lips in a cry of frustrated fury.

The circle had been breached, by me and by water, the damage done. Hasan was not entirely corporeal, but damned if he couldn't interact with the physical just the same. He slammed into Rahim with bruising force, flattening him onto the sand. Rahim struggled, using words of power and physical strength, yet the ifrit wrenched the vosta from his grip. Hasan's howl of triumph mingled with Rahim's cry of rage as the shimmering form of the ifrit flew off over the ocean, the live vosta in his hand.

My vision was fading to black. My heart had stopped beating again. I couldn't seem to draw air into my burning lungs. I felt my spirit start to pull away from the body that anchored it to the world. Everything changed. Reality faded, becoming a pale, translucent watercolor, the edges blurring. I could see my body on the sand, but it wasn't *me*. The true me stood in the air a short distance away, slightly above the tableau. I watched Pradeep collapse to his knees, overcome by utter exhaustion; saw Rahim crawl toward my fallen form, his features drawn in a grimace of pained determination.

The air before me began to tremble, filling with dark, sparkling energy. In the blink of an eye, a familiar form appeared.

Connor Finn's ghost stood before me, solid and real. He looked almost exactly as I remembered him from my visit to the Needle, the high-security prison where he'd supposedly been a prisoner. His red hair was cropped close to his head, his expression ever so superior. Instead of the prison orange and accompanying shackles he'd worn then, he was clad, head to toe, in black: black raw silk shirt, black jeans, and the hooded black robe that he'd probably worn while performing the ceremony in which he died.

A grin split his face and he crowed with laughter. "It's true. You're really dead."

"Apparently so," I said, or thought I did, my voice sounding almost as tired as I felt. It was so weird. I probably should've been scared, hysterical even. But I wasn't. In fact, I didn't feel much of anything.

"No glowing white light, no angel to guide you along the passage to heaven. I'm so disappointed in you, Celia." He didn't sound disappointed, more delighted.

"Think how I must feel," I replied.

He chortled, blue eyes sparkling, the skin near his eyes crinkling with mirth. But only for a moment. He was still laughing when something changed. I felt pressure begin to build, the air becoming thick, almost liquid, swirling with darkness that moved like smoke made of black diamond glitter. The darkness grew, and with it rose a strong smell of brimstone—the scent of hell.

Now I was afraid. Was this it? Were the demons coming for me? I'm not a true believer and I sure as hell am not perfect. There are things I've done . . . terrible things. I didn't mean to. But . . .

Swirling black mist seemed to devour the very light as it formed a tornadic vortex with Finn at its eye, ever darkening, its spinning winds taking on hints of blood red.

Rushing winds roared, pressing my clothes against me, the pressure continuing to build until my virtual ears popped and my eyes streamed. Then, with a sound like a clap of thunder, an opening appeared, a rift in reality. For a split second I glimpsed something awful . . . something the human mind wasn't capable of fathoming. The scent of brimstone was so thick I could taste it clear down my throat, and I choked so hard I began to retch.

And then it was over. Nothing remained of Connor Finn or the storm that had swept him into hell.

Pain. I was in my body, lying on wet sand. My chest hurt. My lungs burned. I coughed weakly and heard someone sigh with relief.

"She's back." Rahim sounded as exhausted as I felt. I was so tired I couldn't even find the strength to open my eyes. I hurt absolutely everywhere; muscles I didn't even normally know I had burned in agony—but whether that was from lack of oxygen or an aftereffect of the djinn's occupation, I had no clue.

"You should not have saved her," Pradeep hissed. "She is not human. Hasan knows that now. He could use her as his vehicle."

I opened my eyes by dint of sheer willpower. Pradeep and Rahim were kneeling beside me in the sand. In the distance I saw lights strobing blue and red as uniformed officers swarmed onto the beach. They'd come in without sirens—or else my hearing had been offline. I didn't know, or care, which.

"We need an ambulance," Rahim shouted to the officers, not answering Pradeep.

"Facedown on the ground. Hands behind your head. *Now,*" the nearest cop commanded.

Pradeep and Rahim did as they were told. I didn't. I couldn't have moved that much to save my life. I was still having to concentrate just to keep on breathing. At least my heartbeat had steadied.

It looked as if I was going to live long enough to see the fallout from our failure after all.

Some girls have all the luck.

12

The EMT took one look at my ultra-pale skin and long canines and zapped me with a stunning spell. It must have been pretty strong, because when I opened my eyes, late afternoon sun was filtering through the drawn curtains of a hospital-room window. I was handcuffed to the bed and Bubba was sitting beside me. It was good to see him, big and burly, guarding me while I was out of it. I did wonder how he'd gotten to Florida so quickly—or had I been under longer than I thought?

I wasn't hungry. Then again, there were tubes running into my arm. One of them could've been giving me liquid nourishment.

"Hey." My voice sounded rough and scratchy.

"Welcome back." He gave me a smile. In my mind, I heard him say, *Don't say anything important. The cops have a listening spell on the room.*

"What are you doing here? How long have I been out?"

"Twelve hours, more or less. And before you ask, Kevin is guarding the client. Dawna sent us out and put us on twelve

on, twelve off until you're back on your feet." He reached
down by his feet. I couldn't see what he was doing, even moving to the extent the handcuffs would let me, but heard the
rattle of a plastic sack. When he straightened up, he held a
chocolate nutrition shake and a straw. "They've got fluids
going into you, but Dawna wanted to make sure you got
a couple of these in you, just in case."

Yay, Dawna! "Good idea." Bubba twisted the cap off of the
little plastic bottle and put the straw in, then held the bottle
for me while I gulped it down. I've grown tired of the shakes
over the years, but right now, this one tasted wonderful. The
scratchiness in my throat eased, as did a tension I hadn't realized had been building in me. By the end of the second bottle
I was feeling more myself again. I still hated the restraints, but
at least I wasn't having to deal with the vampire side of me
being so close to the surface.

Why am I handcuffed?

*You're under arrest for shooting a man on the beach. And
boss, there's more.*

Oh, shit.

*The man you shot in yesterday's firefight died in the
hospital—someone unplugged his life support. And two more
died in the ocean. They were on Jet Skis, armed to the teeth
with weapons that matched the ones the guy on the beach
had—and they drowned during the attack. You're a siren, so the
authorities are working on the theory that you're responsible.*

Holy shit. Four dead.

I wasn't at fault—at least I didn't think I was. Yeah, I'm a
siren, but I'm not much of one. I have to work hard even to

communicate telepathically. On the other hand, I've been known to do some weird shit when my adrenaline is flowing and lives are on the line.

Four dead. Wow. This was bad. This was *so* bad.

I've been in trouble before. More often than I'd like. But with this many bodies on my head, I was looking at life in prison. And not just any prison either: one of the monster hellholes.

The local guy the Patels hired has been hard at it and Roberto is flying in as co-counsel. But it doesn't look good.

I blinked several times to clear the blurriness from my vision. Roberto Santos is one of the top attorneys in the nation. He defends the famous and the infamous—so long as they pay their bills. I like him and I think he likes me. But more than that, I respect him. He's everything a great litigator can hope to be: handsome, cultured, and he has a brilliant mind and amazing courtroom skills. Sort of a modern Latino Perry Mason. I was glad he was coming, but that he felt he needed to meant that I was hip-deep in manure and sinking fast.

And boss, there's something weird, too.

Of course there was. My life was nothing if not *weird*.

What?

Your curse mark's gone.

"What?" I hadn't meant to speak out loud, but I was too shocked to keep silent. I've had a curse mark since early childhood, thanks to one of the siren queens, the late, unlamented Stephania. Her death curse hadn't succeeded in ending my life—though it had cost me my sister—but from my earliest childhood, I've had almost constant brushes with death and disaster. I was reliably informed that the mark had warped my life and career lines, so that I am drawn to deadly situations and have the urge to protect people from death.

I hadn't known it was there until I was an adult, when a piece of magical gear unexpectedly shattered the illusion spells that had concealed it. Since then, it had been visible, an irregularly shaped, reddish-black mark that covered most of my palm. The best experts in the world had been studying that curse for years now, and hadn't had a clue how to lift it.

I turned my head, straining to get a look at my palm. Sure enough, the mark was gone. I stared at the clean, clear flesh for long moments, stunned.

How the hell?

You died, boss. They had to do CPR to revive you and you crashed again on the way to the hospital. Dr. Sloan thinks that may have done it. He's practically ordered you to come see him the minute you get back home. He wanted to fly out here to see for himself but we talked him out of it because you're in the middle of a case. He'll never forgive you if you don't let him look you over, and soon.

My friend, Ram Aaron Sloan, was a retired professor from the University of California Bayview. He was the world's leading expert on curse marks and had been a little bit obsessed with mine since I'd first come to his attention.

I've technically died before, Bubba, and nothing changed. When they revived me, the curse mark was still there. Still, this time I'd seen Connor Finn, watched him being dragged to hell, as a matter of fact. And while it was terribly, terribly un-Christian of me, I felt more than a little satisfaction about that.

Maybe that vindictive streak of mine was why I hadn't seen the doorway to heaven? Then again, no one had tried to drag me to hell, either.

Rahim says Hasan could've removed the curse, but he doesn't know why the ifrit would.

Before I could digest that, thought, the door to my room burst open. The man who stood framed in the doorway was slender, with pale skin stretched taut over cheekbones sharp enough to slice bread. Below his tousled black curls, his eyes were a rather eerie green, more likely to be found on a cat than a human, and were framed by long black lashes. He was dressed in a very expensive, hand-tailored navy suit, but his attitude and body language screamed cop.

"What are you doing here?" he snarled at Bubba. "She wasn't to be allowed any visitors."

Bubba didn't respond, just turned in his seat. Something about that little shift in position was ominous enough that I decided to jump in before things went too far south to be salvaged.

"Hi. Celia Graves," I introduced myself, giving a cheery little wave of my cuffed right hand; the cuff rattled against the bed. "I just woke up a minute or so ago. And you are?"

"Special Agent Evan Morris. FBI." Morris moved his jacket aside so that I could see the badge case mounted on his belt. Since he was standing across the room, I couldn't see it in detail without going vampity, but it looked real enough, and he certainly had the attitude. In fact, he was so cold, I was risking frostbite just being in the room with him.

"FBI?" I made it a question.

"Two of the deaths took place in US territorial waters, under suspicious circumstances involving magic. That puts this under federal jurisdiction."

Crap. Not just local charges, federal, too. Fuck a duck. Twice.

Bubba, get my attorney in here. Now.

On my way, boss. Hang in there.

"Four people died last night. Five if we count you," Morris growled. "If you think you'll need an attorney to speak with me, I'll be happy to wait." He said the right words, but his eyes flashed with annoyance.

Bubba brushed past him on his way out the door. When the door closed, Morris turned to me. "So, what shall we talk about until your attorney arrives?"

"How 'bout them Marlins?"

He gave a snort of what might have been amusement as he settled himself carefully into the visitor's chair Bubba had vacated. "I don't follow baseball."

Of course not. We waited in a silence as thick and heavy, and about as comfortable, as a wet blanket.

Don't worry. You won't be charged, said a male voice in my head, in perfect American English, contractions and all. I knew that voice. I'd only heard it for a minute or so, but they'd been pretty damned memorable minutes.

Hasan.

The one and only. You will be released. I killed the men who would have killed you. Your curse mark is gone. You can thank me now.

"Who and what is Hasan?" Morris snapped, both audibly and in my mind.

You'll find out soon enough, little man, the very amused ifrit answered. And just like that, he was gone.

13

It happened just the way the bad djinn said it would, and it only took forty-eight hours for him to manage it.

The first day was hardest. I felt like hell, for one thing. My whole body ached. You know how, when you overwork your muscles, you get sore because they didn't get enough oxygen? Well, death is a non-oxygenized state. I hurt absolutely everywhere, including my eyeballs. My vampire-enhanced healing kicked in, but it took most of the day for me to recover. When I complained about pain, the nurse gave me a couple of aspirin, which helped for about five whole minutes before my enhanced metabolism burned it off.

It didn't help that I was cuffed to the bed. Tired and sore as I was, I simply could not get into a comfortable position . . . and the remote for the television was *just* out of reach.

No visitors, no flowers. No access to television, phone, or music. Since they were feeding me through tubes, I didn't even have meals to break up the hours. I had no contact with the outside world other than through the nurses, who would come in at the damnedest times to check on me and the machines. I'd finally begin to doze off and one would bustle in, and while they were all pleasant enough, they weren't chatty.

When the sun got really low, one of them closed the blinds. On the plus side, now I didn't have to worry about a sunburn, but I also couldn't enjoy the view. The only things to look at in the room after that were the machines and a clock whose hands crawled across its face with incredible slowness. When I tried to contact people telepathically I got absolutely nowhere.

No one has ever died of acute boredom, but if that were possible, that first day probably would've given me a close call. And I had way too much time to think about things like Hasan using my body as a puppet—the fact that he might be planning to do it again. And that it was likely I couldn't do a damned thing about that.

I was incredibly grateful when my attorney arrived to distract me.

Even though it was getting on toward evening, and he'd undoubtedly had a long day, Roberto Santos looked perfect. His black suit wasn't the least bit rumpled. His shirt was so white it practically glowed, and it had been starched to perfection. His tie was a vivid crimson, with black and gray diagonal stripes, the perfect amount of color and contrast.

"Hey, Roberto. Good to see you." It really was, and not just for the distraction. If he was on the case, I knew I was getting the best defense money could buy. A lot of money, mind you, but he was so worth it. Roberto and his firm—one of the premier firms in LA—have represented me for years. He knows all the details of all my various encounters with law enforcement, so no time was wasted bringing him up to speed.

"Celia." He smiled and pulled up the visitor's chair that had been vacant since Morris had left. Setting his briefcase onto the floor, he leaned back, trying to get comfortable. "I just got out of a pair of hearings with local and federal authorities regarding your cases. They haven't charged you with anything yet. Since you are restrained, you are considered to be in police custody, so the clock is running. They have a total of forty-eight hours before they have to either press charges or let you go."

"Unless they declare me a dangerous monster." I said it softly, because, frankly, the prospect scared me. In the past, someone had tried to do just that. They'd failed, but it had been a really close call. If anyone ever succeeded, I wouldn't have to be tried—or treated like a human being at all. They could just lock me away forever "for the safety of the public."

"That motion was heard and denied at both the federal and local levels this morning."

I gasped. I couldn't help it. "Thank you."

He gave a brisk nod. "Under the circumstances, it wasn't unexpected that they'd try that tactic. But they really didn't have any evidence to back the claim, and their own expert had to admit under questioning that it was highly unlikely you had the power to swamp the Jet Skis. Everything else involved purely human weaponry. Special Agent Morris testified that he heard the djinn admit responsibility for all the deaths, so they really didn't have a leg to stand on."

Maybe, but it was still scary that they'd tried.

"I've contacted your partner. She's sending appropriate clothing for you, in case you have to appear at a hearing. You'd need clothes anyway, since the ones you were wearing on the beach are currently being processed as evidence. Obviously, I don't want you talking to any of the authorities without me being present."

"The Patels hired James Barber for me as local counsel. He helped with the thing at the bridge."

Roberto nodded. "He's very good. But I'd still rather be there myself for any questioning, if you don't mind."

"No problem."

He picked up his briefcase and set it on his lap, then dialed a combination on the pair of old-fashioned physical locks before snapping the latches and lifting the lid. "Since you're in custody, only the police or your attorneys are allowed any contact with you. Your partner didn't want to send information to you through Mr. Barber, but she did ask me to pass on a few personal messages."

"Yes?"

He pulled out a yellow legal pad to refer to his notes. "Bruno has been trying to reach you. I decided to tell him what's going on and he's absolutely frantic despite my assurances that all will be well. He can't leave New Jersey right now. Isabella has lost consciousness, and it's only a matter of time. But he loves you and he's worried about you. So for God's sake, call him as soon as you get a chance." It was almost funny hearing Roberto relay Bruno's emotional message in his calm voice. Almost, but not really.

"Right." I'd actually intended to do that anyway. I didn't

like putting another worry on Bruno right now—he had more than enough on his plate—but he was my lover, and my friend, and he'd more than earned the right to know what was going on.

"Your great aunt says that if you need anything at all, let her know."

I nodded.

"And Dottie and Emma both say to be very, very careful, but they *aren't* saying anything else." He grinned thinly, as familiar with clairvoyants as I was.

He set the pad back in the case and snapped it closed.

"The doctors want to keep you for observation for at least another twenty-four hours, so there's no chance of you being transferred to a police holding cell or federal custody for at least that long. And while I know the cuffs and guards are a nuisance, they're actually working to our benefit. If you're cuffed, you're in custody. If you're not in custody, the clock stops running. So try to make the best of it. I'm staying on top of the legal aspects, but is there anything else you need?"

"There's one thing you could do that would be awesome."

He raised an eyebrow in inquiry. "Yes?"

"Can you pass me the remote?"

At seven the next morning, James Barber came into my room with the uniformed police officer who had been stationed outside the door. The officer didn't say a word, just unlocked the handcuff and walked out. It was obvious he wasn't happy.

That was all right. I was happy enough for both of us. The restraint had really been getting on my nerves.

"So, what's up?"

"Normally you would be taken to jail after the doctors cleared you, but that's not going to happen. Special Agent Morris heard the ifrit confess. So did the local police force; all of them, from the chief of police down to the newest recruit. Maybe even the janitor."

I blinked, stunned, and tried to think how that could have happened. I had no doubt the room had been bugged, but that would have had a limited audience. So, it had to have been magic, and magic with enough juice to overpower the spells set by local law enforcement and the feds. Hasan. Had to be. But why?

Barber ignored my stunned expression and continued talking. "While the district attorney and federal prosecutor are both displeased, neither one is willing to press charges at the moment. They do, however, want to meet with you at the Federal building this morning, at nine thirty. Your attendance is totally voluntary, but I strongly recommend you go and answer their questions. Roberto Santos has gotten them to agree to allow you to leave the jurisdiction, but that is contingent on your cooperating with the authorities."

"I have no problem with that."

"Good." He gave a brisk nod. "I have an eight o'clock hearing in District Court. I should be able to do that and reach the Federal building on time. Mr. Santos will pick you up here and take you to the meeting in his car. He's also assured me that you'll be appropriately dressed." He raised an eyebrow at that, as if wondering if I even possessed appropriate clothing. Not a surprise, given the circumstances under which he'd seen me.

"So, if there's nothing else you need until then," he concluded, the lilt in his voice making it a question.

"Nope. I'm good."

"Fine. Then I'll send in your associate." Barber nodded and left.

Unsurprisingly, my "associate" was Bubba. He dropped the black nylon duffel he was carrying onto the foot of the bed before taking a seat in the visitor's chair. He was a sight for sore eyes, dressed in highly pressed khaki trousers and a red, short-sleeved dress shirt. No jacket, but he'd probably left that in the car. After all, hospital regulations meant he couldn't come in armed, and why wear a jacket in the Florida heat if you don't have to conceal a holster and gun?

The very first thing I did was bum his phone and try to call Bruno. I'd been out of touch too long and I knew he would be worrying. He must've been at the hospital, though, because he didn't answer.

I was disappointed, but not surprised. Roberto had told me Isabella was doing worse. Of course Bruno would be with his mother. I left a voice mail saying I was fine, getting out of the hospital, and how much I loved him. That done, I gave the phone back to Bubba and turned my attention to the duffel bag. Dragging it to me by its strap, I unzipped it and immediately found myself grinning.

Okay, I'd known Roberto asked Dawna to send clothes. I'd expected her to go to my place and pick up something from my closet.

But that wasn't what she'd done. Nope. She'd gone shopping—high-end shopping at that. In the bag were two suits from Isaac Levy's shop: one in black and one in charcoal gray. The blazers were my favorite of Isaac's styles, and since he had my measurements on file, I knew they and the matching pants would fit perfectly. Both suits had been made from lightweight fabrics that would keep me from roasting in the heat; there was enough spell work on them that the power of the magic buzzed against my senses—not painful, but it was definitely noticeable. Digging farther into the duffel, I found a pair of silk blouses, one royal purple, the other a vivid crimson. Dawna had also included underclothes, socks, makeup, toiletries, some jewelry, and a pair of sensible black pumps. All of it top of the line. Thanks to my partner, whatever outfit I chose, I'd be looking *good*. Then again, that was no surprise. If Dawna ever decided to be a stylist to the stars, she'd make a killing at it. In the meantime, I'd reap the benefits.

I slid off the bed, grabbed the bag, and lugged it into the bathroom to get ready, leaving the door open just a crack so that Bubba and I could talk.

It was a huge relief to get out of that flimsy cotton, backless hospital gown. I pulled on plum-colored lingerie, then the black suit with the purple blouse. An amethyst and silver necklace and matching earrings completed the outfit. Looking in the mirror, I felt pretty good about my appearance.

Bubba's voice came to me clearly as I leaned over the sink

to apply just a hint of color. I have to be really careful with makeup. My vampire-pale complexion makes it really easy to overdo it and then I look like a clown.

"I'm supposed to tell you that Dawna got a text from Dom Rizzoli. He's trying to get the government to open the files on the incident at the Needle, but so far he isn't having much luck. Dawna's gotten a big fat zero trying to find any trace of any of Connor Finn's cronies—they all seem to have vanished. Meredith Stanton and Bob Davis are still at the top of the FBI's most-wanted list, but there haven't been any developments in terms of finding them, at least as far as she's been able to find."

That last bit didn't surprise me. Davis and Stanton were smart and powerful. If the feds hadn't found them, I'd be shocked if we were able to.

"What have the Patels been up to?" I called out.

"Nothing good," Bubba answered, clearly unhappy. "Pradeep and Rahim have been going at it pretty hard. The old man thinks Rahim should have let you die on the beach. A couple of other relatives have arrived and they've joined right in on giving Rahim a bad time. They blame him for everything. I don't know the language, so I can't tell you exactly what they're saying, but it's not hard to guess the basic thrust of the arguments, what with all the shouting and pointing of fingers."

That was no surprise either, not after what I'd seen the morning of the ceremony. Our failure on the beach wouldn't have improved things among the family members, just made it worse. I felt a little sorry for Rahim. Family drama sucks.

"Any word from Bruno or Matty?"

"Their mom is still hanging on. It's tough. Matty did check in with the Church. He's going through channels, so it may take a couple of days, but he thinks he can get you everything they have on the demons that were involved in the incident at the Needle. He'll try to get them to rush it if he has the chance, but he said something about 'the wheels of God.'"

I blotted my lipstick, dropping the tissue into the waste can. Zipping up the duffel, I returned to the main room. "They grind slowly, but exceedingly fine," I said as I tossed the duffel onto the bed and slid my feet into the pumps. I actually thought the original quote referred to the wheels of justice. But Matty's version worked as well. Maybe better.

Bubba checked his watch and winced. "I've got to go relieve Kevin. Are you going to be okay?"

"It's just a meeting. Roberto will be with me."

"Good. You need all the help you can get. This case is an even worse hairball than usual."

He wasn't wrong.

"I'll be fine." I tried to put as much conviction into the words as I could, but it sounded thin to my own ears. Bubba didn't call me on it. We said our good-byes. When he was gone, I sat on the edge of the bed and waited for my attorney.

As usual, Roberto was prompt. Today he wore a charcoal-gray suit, snow-white shirt, and a tie that had silver, white, charcoal, and black diagonal stripes. He was impeccably neat, and I suspected that if I were gauche enough to ask, he'd tell me that the suit had been hand-tailored on Savile Row and cost more than my first car.

Roberto was on time. The hospital wasn't. The wheels of God have nothing on those of hospital administration. It was nine forty-five when I was finally released. Roberto called to let the prosecutors know we'd be late, but I wasn't sure how much that helped reassure them.

The meeting wasn't a condition of my release—but it wasn't a request either. I knew that being late was going to piss everybody off. The authorities wanted answers. They also wanted to intimidate me. I didn't have the former, and they couldn't hold a candle to Hasan when it came to intimidation. But hey, let them take their best shot.

Roberto's driver dropped us in front of the federal building nearly an hour behind schedule. After being processed by security, we caught an elevator up and made our way to the conference room without trouble.

It was a pleasant enough space—an interior room, so there was no distracting view, but the prints on the wall, while bland, were attractive. Their frames were cherry, which matched the cherry veneer of the oval conference table, around which eight of us were seated in rolling black faux leather chairs that were actually pretty comfortable. The spells worked into the walls, floor, ceiling, and table were not. I could feel their power crawling across my skin like fire ant bites. It was unpleasant, but I've dealt with worse.

Going through with this meeting—"informal" as it was— would result in me getting my weapons back. Not the guns— the authorities weren't budging on those. Made sense, since they were part of an ongoing investigation. But I hadn't used my knives or any of my magical gear and I wanted them back.

After Special Agent Morris had heard Hasan admit that he'd killed the bad guys, he'd done some research on the ifrit. Today, he looked as good as ever, but even colder, in a gray suit the color of dirty ice with a snow-white shirt and a blue-and-gray striped tie. He introduced the others seated at the table. To his right sat the federal prosecutor, Jean Schulz. Despite the severe suit and the very obvious anti-siren charm she wore, I couldn't help but think she'd have been the perfect model for an Oktoberfest poster, or for selling schnitzel or strudel or anything else German.

Our hostess had reddish-blond hair, blue eyes, and fresh-faced good looks that probably disguised a brutal, focused ambition, given that she'd made it pretty far up in what was still, generally, a male-dominated field. Just past her sat the two local detectives assigned to the Patel cases, Erik Allbright and his partner, Joe Johnson. Johnson was new to me. He was tall, wiry, and black.

Allbright looked much as he had the other night. At his feet sat a large leather case, big and boxy, with runes worked into the leather. I could feel the power of it from clear across the room. Beyond them was the district attorney, a short, balding man with a large nose that looked as if it had been broken more than once. I tried to catch his name and somehow missed it.

I sat at the far end of the oval flanked by my attorneys, Barber having arrived before Roberto and me.

"If I could please have everyone's attention." Schulz's voice was a soft alto, but pitched to carry. The murmured conversation around the table ended and we all looked at her.

"Ms. Graves, I want to thank you and your counsel for agreeing to be here. It is absolutely voluntary, as under the circumstances, both my office and the district attorney have declined to press charges against you."

"How did you do that, anyway?" the DA asked.

"Do what?" I responded, although I was pretty sure I knew what he was referring to.

Within minutes of my being hauled off to the hospital from the beach, video from the morning's events was leaked to the press. Crystal-clear images showing that I was defending myself and the Patels appeared over and over again on every network newscast: locally, nationally, even on some of the international stations. Even when the stations decided to stop running it, it would still appear. The anchor would be talking about a bombing in Beirut, but instead of footage of that, my video would run. I'd seen it myself on the hospital television. Over and over . . . and over again.

"The video," he answered.

"Not me."

"I suppose you're going to tell us it was this . . ." Detective Allbright made a production of flipping out his notes and glancing at them, "Hasan?"

"No idea," I admitted, "but it seems the most likely explanation."

"Who and what is this Hasan?" the DA snarled at me. "How could he have done that? And why are you working for him?"

Special Agent Morris answered before I could. "Hasan is an ifrit. He was imprisoned in a djinn jar centuries ago by one of a special line of Guardians. I'm told that recently some humans engineered his escape, with assistance from the ghost of Connor Finn."

"An *ifrit*." Schulz glared at me, her voice a low hiss. "And you're *cooperating* with him."

"No. I am not." I said each word clearly, distinctly, and with more than a little heat.

"Then how do you explain this?" Schulz hit the button on the little recorder in front of her. It showed the familiar beach scene from a different angle, and it had been cued to the exact moment when Hasan had slipped into my body.

"Ifrits are well known to be able to inhabit the bodies of the recently dead." Roberto's voice was calm, but his hand had moved to rest lightly on mine in a silent warning for me not to lose it. He's worked with me often enough to know that I have a temper and to recognize that Schulz was deliberately trying to provoke it—to shake me up and see what popped out. "If you rewind your recorder approximately two minutes, you'll see my client getting shot in the chest with an experimental weapon that hasn't hit the open market yet.

"The blast was intended for her client, Rahim Patel. Ms. Graves placed herself in harm's way as part of her duties as Mr. Patel's bodyguard. Until this incident, these so-called 'heart attack' guns have been universally fatal, and, in fact, Celia Graves died. Hasan took over her body while she was helpless."

"So, did you see the white light at the end of the tunnel? Or something else?" Allbright was sneering again. You'd almost think he didn't like me, thought I was a villainous scumbag killer or something.

"Actually, I saw Connor Finn get sucked into hell."

That made them all blink.

"Really?" The DA asked, and I could tell he was both shocked and fascinated.

"Yep."

The temperature in the room began to drop abruptly. I shivered as my breath misted the air in front of me.

Joe Johnson shifted in his seat and crossed his legs in a casually feminine manner. "Really." The voice that came from his lips wasn't his—it was Abby's. Apparently she'd decided to manifest after hearing Finn's name.

Using Johnson's body, she continued, "Connor Finn's sole purpose for staying on this plane was to see Celia dead. She'd thwarted his plans, saved his enemies, and earned him the eternal displeasure of his master. When her body died, he was there to watch. He went to hell. She was revived thanks to the efforts of Rahim Patel."

"Abby, why are you here?" I asked.

"They assume you'll lie. I can't. So I figured I could answer their questions." She looked first at Schulz, then at the DA, with a sweet smile. "Ask away."

"What did you have against Connor Finn? Why have you attached yourself to Graves here?" Detective Allbright asked. His voice was surprisingly steady for someone who had just seen his partner taken over by a ghost. Of course, the fact that she had taken him over meant that Johnson was a channeler.

Perhaps this wasn't the first time this had happened in front of Allbright.

"Connor Finn slaughtered my extended family, tried to kill my daughter, and had me tortured to death. I'm here until the last Finn is dead—and working with Celia . . . well, perhaps it will give me the opportunity to work off some of my own bad karma. If not, at least it's never dull."

That was the God's honest truth. Frankly, I could use a little more dullness.

"Did Connor Finn kill the man in the hospital?" the DA asked.

"Yes. And Hasan killed the others. Well, all of them except the one Celia shot."

"Why did he kill them?" Schulz asked.

"I don't know," Abby responded. "Why do ifrits do anything they do?"

"Why is Celia Graves working with the ifrit?" Schulz again.

"She's not. But he intends to use her any way he can, whether she likes it or not."

While the others had been shooting out spontaneous questions, Special Agent Morris had been making notes. He spoke now, in carefully measured tones. "Give us the names of the humans who arranged Hasan's escape and the name and nature of the creature they're working for."

Abby had turned Johnson's body to face Morris and opened her mouth to answer him when, from nowhere, a howling wind tore through the room.

With an explosive *pop*, the power to the entire building failed. We were instantly thrust into total darkness that smelled strongly of brimstone. The air, which had been cold from the presence of the ghost, went hot, dry, and oppressive.

"Abby? Are you there?" I called. Nothing. No response. That couldn't be good.

"*Fuck.*" Allbright said what we all were thinking. There was the thud of a body hitting the floor. At the sound, Schulz called fire to her fingertips, giving us enough light to see Johnson sprawled out on the carpet.

Allbright leapt from his seat to kneel beside his partner, searching for a pulse, checking for breathing. Finding neither, he began doing CPR. Morris joined him, doing the compressions while Allbright did the breathing.

Roberto whipped his cell phone from his pocket. "No signal. Celia, can you use your powers to call for an ambulance?"

"Not from in here," Schulz interrupted. "The room's spelled against outside communications, including telepathy. Even with the power out. Go into the hall. Your cell phone will work there."

Roberto pushed away from the table and made his way out the door. I could hear him calling 911 as Johnson took his first unsteady breath. I heard his pulse stutter to life, unsteady at first, but gaining strength.

The men stopped CPR, but stayed at Johnson's side. Meanwhile I had risen to my feet and was using the sixth sense I have for magic to try to locate the source of the heat. It was no longer pitch black in the room, thanks to some light coming in through the open door. I was able to move around without tripping on anything or running into anyone.

When I reached the spot where Johnson had been sitting,

I felt a difference in the air, about two feet above the table. It was hotter there, and the smell of brimstone was stronger.

"Somebody pass me a gun with holy water." I ordered. "I need to patch the hole until we can get some warrior priests in here."

Morris was the only one who moved, drawing a One-Shot squirt gun from a holster at the small of his back. Instead of passing it to me, he took up a position beside me.

Allbright shook his head. "We don't carry holy water except on the night shift. We don't deal with the demonic—if anything like that comes up, we call for religious backup."

"Shit! Okay, my pair of One-Shots should be in the case. Get them." Here's hoping they were still loaded. If they weren't, we were screwed because the brimstone smell was getting stronger and I would have sworn I could hear booming hoofbeats coming closer.

Bless him, he didn't argue.

"Tell the EMTs we'll meet them in the lobby," Schulz called to Roberto as she went to the fallen man. Squatting down, she set about getting ready to put him into a fireman's carry. "We're getting out of here."

I didn't bother watching her and the others any longer; I shifted into vampire mode, using my enhanced vision to focus on the weak spot in reality. A demon shouldn't be able to come onto our plane without an invitation. Something was weird and wrong about this whole situation. I'd definitely talk to the experts about it later. Assuming we lived that long.

"Allbright—" I called.

"Got 'em." He came up on Morris's other side, passed me

one of the little squirt guns, and raised the other. "You do realize that this isn't going to do anything but piss him off," he snapped—then took a shooter's stance next to Morris, the little plastic water gun held steady with both hands.

"We're not shooting the demon. We're closing the hole. Which is . . ." I shifted, moving a little to my right until I found the perfect spot, "right *there*." I pulled the trigger.

Holy water sprayed in a steady stream from my water pistol. When the liquid hit the invisible wall of power, the opening in reality flashed into visibility for an instant: a ragged tear about a foot wide, its edges the burning red of embers. There was a loud hiss as the water steamed away; the smell of brimstone grew stronger. Through the opening I heard a furious bellow. The hoofbeats sped up, thundering toward us like a galloping horse that weighed several tons.

Allbright and Morris fired at the spot that had been revealed by my shot. When the breach flared to visibility this time, it was smaller and dimmer. The holy water was working. As the last drop from our guns hit, I felt the rip close.

"Is it shut?" Allbright asked me as he lowered the now-empty squirt gun.

"We've patched it. But the seal won't hold long. We need to get out of here right now, and evacuate the building."

I wasn't kidding. There was no time to waste. The heat in the room hadn't abated at all. If anything, it was getting warmer, and there was a growing *presence* in the air, a sentience that made my heart thunder in my ears.

A mighty blow hit the patch with a boom like the clap of thunder at the point of a lightning strike. Then another.

"Oh shit." Morris and Allbright both looked at me with wide eyes. Glancing at them, I realized we were the last ones in the room. Everyone else had left.

"Time to go." I announced.

"Ya think?" Morris was out the door in an instant, with me right at his heels and Allbright close behind. As we dashed down the hall, we passed firemen and a pair of warrior religious running toward the conference room. The warriors were wearing orange robes that bore no resemblance to Matty DeLuca's Catholic raiment. Whatever religion they represented, as they passed us, the holy items they clutched started glowing like magnesium flares with the power of their faith. I wondered if I should go back and show them exactly where the problem had been, but then decided to take a different tack.

"There was a weak spot two feet above the table on the right side. We patched it with holy water, but it won't hold long," I yelled to them.

The last priest in line gave me a curt nod of acknowledgment. The first fireman to reach the door shouted, "Right. Go!"

I hesitated, still uncertain.

"Come on, Graves. Let's go! They've got it." Allbright was holding the door to the emergency stairs open for me. Behind him I could see a steady stream of federal workers evacuating the building. Morris was nowhere in sight; I assumed he was already on the way down.

He was right. It was the priests' job, not mine. And I can't tell you how glad I was about that.

I took a deep breath of air that didn't reek of brimstone and we stepped through the door together. It was only once we were in the stairwell, descending with the rest of the crowd, that I noticed the calm, female voice transmitting everywhere, like a magical public-address system.

"Evacuation protocol in effect. This is not a drill. Proceed to your assigned exit and report."

"Everybody seems pretty calm," I observed to Allbright.

"Ever since 9/11, every government office has been required to do monthly evacuation drills. People find them annoying, but they are effective," he explained.

Of course, they don't know we're running away from pissed-off demons, I thought to myself.

Demons and *an ifrit.* Morris's grim voice sounded in my head. *What the fuck have you gotten yourself into, Graves?*

His mental voice didn't feel snide or judgmental. Maybe standing side by side, sealing the breach, had changed his opinion of me. Still, the question wasn't one to be taken lightly. And I needed to answer it if I wanted to stay both alive and in possession of my soul.

14

Allbright and I exited the staircase into the atrium. I'd had to pass through it coming in, but I'd been in such a hurry I hadn't really noticed it. Now that the space was full of federal employees who continued to stream down from the upper floors, I couldn't speed through it, and the place made an impact on me. Three stories tall, it had towering windows on all four sides, which let in brilliant sunlight that shone off the marble floors and made the water in the burbling fountain sparkle like diamonds.

There were big marble planters, their wide edges forming seating, scattered at convenient intervals throughout the atrium. Some were square, others circular. Each planter was filled with full-sized trees and tropical flowers. I even saw a few birds flying around. Presumably they'd gotten in through the revolving doors and had found life inside comfortable enough to want to stay.

Crowds of suited men and women shuffled forward in a steady river toward all the available exits—except for a small one that the firefighters, police, and other emergency personnel were using.

Standing on tiptoe I saw our group, tucked in a corner away from the main flow of traffic. A couple of EMTs had a vigorously protesting Johnson strapped to a gurney and connected to some equipment.

Schulz waved to get our attention. I tapped Allbright on the shoulder and pointed. It took a little effort, but we managed to shove our way through the crowd and over to them. Roberto moved aside on the planter where he was sitting, clearing a seat for me. I was glad. All the adrenaline from what had happened upstairs was draining away, leaving me shaky and weak.

I sat down a little abruptly, resting my elbows on my knees, my head drooping a little.

"Well, that ended badly," Schulz observed.

"Not nearly as badly as it could have," Allbright answered. "Good thinking, Graves."

The prosecutor glared at him.

"I'd suggest you bring in an exorcist to clean that room once the priests have cleared the building for occupancy," Morris said.

"Yes, we will. Although how I'm supposed to pay for that with the budget cuts . . ." She shook her head.

"The church might do it as a freebie," I offered. "If you need me to, I can make some calls. I know a couple of people."

She gave me a look that told me she planned to hold me responsible for this mess. Totally unfair, but there you go. Some people need to assign blame.

"I'll manage," she said, her tone arid. "Frankly, I'd rather you left. The sooner the better."

I didn't say a word. I didn't trust myself to be diplomatic.

"Detective Allbright," Schulz called, "do you have the paperwork for Ms. Graves to sign?"

Allbright was still standing by the gurney, one hand resting on his partner's arm. I heard him tell Johnson, "I'll meet you at the hospital," before he trotted over to us. Behind him, the EMTs began wheeling the gurney through the rapidly thinning crowd, toward the main entrance.

Coming up to me, the detective reached into his pocket and drew out a stack of folded paper and a pen. Passing the pages to me, he bent down over the case, which was sitting on the floor at Roberto's feet. I had no idea who had carried the case out of the conference room, or when, but it made me happy to see it. Allbright didn't bother with a key, but I heard him chanting a spell to release magical protections.

I raised an eyebrow at him.

"It's bio-keyed. Johnson and I are the only ones who could touch anything in here until the spells were released," he explained.

He flipped the lid open, letting me see the contents. My holsters, knives, and spell disks were all there. When I'd checked everything over and seen that all was in order, I used the bench beside me as a writing surface and signed off on the forms. I handed the pen and papers back to Allbright, waiting politely as he tore off the yellow copy and gave it to me.

I handed the receipts to Roberto and took off my jacket. Schulz turned to me. Her blue eyes burned bright with barely contained rage, but she kept her voice deceptively pleasant.

"I would remind you that there is no statute of limitations on murder."

I knew that.

"And while your attorneys keep assuring me that you are working hard to protect your client and innocent bystanders, I must tell you I have some serious doubts about you. I have never before, in my entire life, been exposed to the demonic. Nor, I wager, have any of the others who attended this meeting.

"You have been involved in situations with the nefarious multiple times. Your file states that you have even been the subject of an exorcism. Either you are singularly unlucky," she didn't bother to hide her skepticism, "or you are working in concert with the demonic. If that is the case—" she left the sentence unfinished, an unspoken threat.

Roberto opened his mouth to respond, but I signaled him to silence. "Ms. Schulz, you've left off a third possibility—and it's the one that's the most accurate."

"Oh?" Her voice was frosty.

"I've been responsible for blocking major demon infestations not just once, but twice. In doing that, I've not only made them aware of my existence, I've made them my enemies."

Allbright gave me a sick look. Morris winced.

Schulz glared at me, spots of bright color appearing on her cheeks. "If that is the case, how are you still alive?"

"Pure, dumb luck and powerful friends."

She gave a derisive snort. Her next words were delivered

in a honeyed, overly pleasant tone that no one could possibly believe was sincere, "Ms. Graves, should you ever return to Florida, I would recommend you vacation elsewhere. Miami, Orlando, perhaps—you could take in Disney. Don't come back to Tampa."

I decided not to comment. Really, what could I say that wouldn't be hideously offensive? Instead, I turned away and spread my blazer out on the bench, then reached into the leather case and began arming up. I slid stakes into a pair of loops, then did the same for the empty One-Shot water guns. Next I dropped spell disks and balls into the jacket's left pocket. The recorder went into the right. I put on my holsters. I didn't have any guns, but I'd be getting some as soon as possible. And frankly, wearing the holsters was easier than carrying them. Next I strapped on the sheaths for my knives—over the sleeves of my blouse—and slid the blades into place. Then I put the jacket back on. It fit without a bulge or bump, perfectly balanced, the weapons invisible to the casual eye.

Schulz stared at me the whole time, brow furrowed. I pretended not to notice.

Morris looked thoughtful.

I shuddered, haunted by the sense of presence in that conference room, knowing that the stench of brimstone was clinging to my hair and clothing, and more, knowing that what I'd told Schulz was the absolute truth. Major demons knew my name, knew me, and wanted me dead—and preferably damned.

Compared to that, Schulz's dislike was nothing.

Still, it wouldn't pay to be impolite. "We got interrupted

and you didn't get to ask me your questions. Do we need to reschedule?" I asked. I looked from Schulz, to Roberto, to Morris, keeping my expression pleasantly cooperative.

"My client is scheduled to leave the city this afternoon," Roberto said.

I was? That was news to me. Although, come to think of it, the Patels probably wanted to get back to business. Not to mention that if they couldn't lock me up, the authorities would probably want me out of their jurisdiction—easily accessible, mind you, but out of their hair.

"We could do a video conference." I suggested. "Maybe next week?" I looked at Roberto, who nodded.

"I can have my assistant get in touch," he told Schulz.

She looked as if she'd bitten something sour, but answered politely. "Please do."

Morris moved to stand directly in front of me. I was surprised when he extended his hand to shake. I looked at him with raised eyebrows, but took it.

"That was good work upstairs," he said. "Thanks."

I managed not to blink stupidly. Generally, professional law enforcement consider amateurs like me to be dangerous nuisances. For Morris to thank me was the ultimate compliment. It also signaled a real change in his attitude toward me. I appreciated that more than I could say.

"You're welcome," I managed to respond.

"Good luck with the ifrit and the demons."

"Thanks. I'm going to need it."

15

I spent a few minutes at the curb with my attorneys, waiting for the limo to arrive. Roberto thanked Barber for his help.

"Happy to oblige." He turned to me and added, "Be sure to give the Patels my regards."

"I will."

The long, black Caddy pulled smoothly to the curb beside us. The driver came to open the door. I had a brief flash of memory—another time, another limo had driven me into an ambush. Still, I couldn't just stand at the curb like an idiot. Roberto was already climbing inside.

"Is there a problem?" Barber asked, looking at me closely.

"No, just a hint of a flashback."

"You seem to live a very . . . tumultuous life."

"Yeah, I do." It sucked. Big time. And it made me think that maybe, just maybe, I needed to do some serious thinking. I like protecting people and I'm good at it. But in the past five years I'd had more direct clashes with the demonic than most warrior priests have in a lifetime. Thus far I'd survived—thanks to luck, skill, and some badass help. But I know the statistics. There are reasons the Catholic Church offers a stellar retirement and disability package to its warriors. Few live to see the former. Most use the latter.

I climbed into the limo to save myself having to say anything more to Barber.

He bent at the waist to look me straight in the eye. "Take care, Ms. Graves, and good luck."

"Thanks . . . for everything."

"You're welcome." Straightening, he stepped back, allowing the driver to close the door.

Moments later, we pulled away from the curb and into traffic so smoothly that it was hard to tell we were even moving. Nice.

Roberto told the driver to drop him at the airport's main terminal before taking me to the area for private planes. Then he pulled out his cell and passed it to me. "Rahim Patel asked that you call as soon as the meeting ended. He's waiting for you at his jet. He's anxious to get moving as soon as possible."

"Of course he is." It made sense; I'd even thought of the possibility myself. But I would have liked at least a couple of minutes to relax and recover. Yes, technically I'd gotten plenty of down time in the hospital. But anyone who's been in one can tell you that hospitals aren't restful, and they sure as hell aren't relaxing.

"Celia." Roberto's voice brought me back into the moment. He met my gaze, his expression grave. "I'm your attorney. It's my job to give you advice." He paused, picking his words carefully. "This case is an even worse mess than what you usually bring me. If the ifrit hadn't intervened, I'm fairly certain I couldn't have kept you from being imprisoned, probably for life. As your counsel, I have to advise you that continuing this assignment is not in your best interests." He sighed, and looked away. "But as a man, I have to say that I'm more afraid of what will happen to the rest of us if you don't."

I opened my mouth to say something, but he waved me to silence. "I know a lot of the stories about you are just stories, exaggerations. But I've seen the reports and the pictures. I know what really happened. When it comes to fighting the monsters, demons, and what have you, you and your team *are* the A Team."

The scariest part was that I wasn't sure how it had happened. I'd started out as a regular bodyguard—and that was a dangerous enough profession all by itself. I had no idea how my job had morphed into this, or how to change it back.

Since I didn't have any clue how to respond, I changed the subject. "Before I call Patel, I want to check in with my office."

"Feel free."

I settled back into the plush leather seat, dialing the office number from memory, watching the scenery go past. We were near enough to the airport that I saw billboards advertising long-term parking lots and giving directions to the rental car return area. I also spotted our escort. Two unmarked cars, no-nonsense Ford sedans with unassuming exteriors that masked kick-ass engines—probably local police—and a single federal vehicle with Morris behind the wheel. Apparently the authorities were going to make sure I really did leave.

"Graves Personal Protection." Dawna's voice was on the other end of the line.

"Hey, Dawna. What're you doing answering the phones?"

"Dottie's making a deposit at the bank. How did the meeting go?"

"Not great," I admitted. "But they're letting me go, so it's over for now. We're going to have to teleconference next week, but I'm on my way to the airport. Thanks for sending the clothes, by the way. They're great!"

"Well, I wasn't sure whether the Patels had been allowed to get your suitcase out of the car in impound or if the police were going to return your clothes from the beach. You needed to look good for that meeting."

She was right. First impressions make a huge difference, whether people like to admit it or not. Looking good also gives a person a psychological edge and confidence that can really help in tense social situations.

She was also right about my suitcase. I had no idea whether the Patels had retrieved my bags, which meant I didn't have my passport or my phone charger. The fact that I hadn't even noticed that until Dawna mentioned it was beyond careless. Although, in my defense, the whole demon attack had been a bit distracting. "Hang on, Dawna."

I turned to Roberto, saying, "Do you know whether anyone has been able to get my luggage from the car in impound? In addition to my clothes, my passport's in that bag. And what happened to my phone?"

"Rahim Patel has the luggage that was in the Cadillac," Roberto assured me. "As for your phone, I suspect it's in the hands of the authorities. They have the clothing you were wearing that day and are processing it as evidence. That's going to take some time, and in all honesty, I'm not sure you'll ever get them back. I can push them on it if you want me to, but considering the circumstances, I'm not sure that would be wise."

"You're probably right. Thanks." Given that my phone had been with me on the beach, it was now considered evidence and I wouldn't be seeing it for a while, if ever. Sheesh. Sighing inwardly, I went back to my call.

"Dawna, I'm down a phone again. Was this one insured?"

"Yes. I'll process the claim. In the meantime, I don't want you out of touch. Take Bubba's or Kevin's when you get to the airport."

"Okay." I hoped the guys wouldn't mind. Nobody likes being out of touch, even temporarily. On the other hand, everybody on staff knows about me and phones. It's becoming legendary, to the point where they sometimes run an office pool when I'm on a case, to see who can come closest to guessing when I'll lose or destroy one. I find it embarrassing, but my shrink assures me that it's probably a great morale-and-team-building exercise. So I try to maintain my sense of humor. Sometimes I even succeed.

"I'm going to need Dottie to check things out for me again. A demon tried to interrupt the meeting—"

"How? They can't manifest without a human creating an opening for them." Dawna didn't bother to hide her alarm. Couldn't say I blamed her. The situation was pretty damned alarming. I shivered from a chill that had nothing to do with the ambient temperature. "I don't know, and I'd love to find out."

"I'll call Warren. By the way, I do have some news, although I'm not sure what to make of it."

"Shoot."

"Some guy from the Company called a little bit ago. I'm supposed to tell you and Kevin that Jack Finn died this morning, at eight a.m. California time."

Eight o'clock back home would be eleven here in Florida—which was almost exactly when Abby had disappeared. Since I knew her reason for staying on the earthly plane had been to see every Finn dead, it seemed likely the two events were connected. But did those things also connect to the demon's appearance?

Hell if I knew, but it seemed likely.

"Thanks. And please pass my thanks to the Company."

"Will do, next time I talk to Chris." She paused for a moment, probably running a pencil down a list of notes, making sure she'd told me everything she thought I needed to know. Dawna always double-checked before ending a conversation with me when I was on a case, since it was never clear when we'd have the chance to speak again. "I haven't heard any more from Dom Rizzoli. Do you want me to nag him?"

"Nah. If he can't get the information, he can't get it, and pushing him on it won't do any good. If he has anything for us, he'll pass it on."

"I hate not knowing more."

"Me, too."

"Oh, Dottie just walked in. Let me put her on."

The limo slowed as we pulled onto the airport exit ramp. Traffic had thickened and we were stuck. Roberto had busied himself going through papers from his briefcase and making notes on one of those yellow legal pads. He glanced at me and smiled, in no obvious hurry to get his phone back. I was glad. I really wanted to get Dottie's take on things.

"Hello, Celia." Dottie sounded unusually frail, with that little quaver in her voice you sometimes hear when talking to the elderly. That bothered me. She's usually so vibrant and energetic that it's easy to forget how old she is . . . and when her age shows, it's usually because she's not feeling well or has been working too hard. Or both. "I've been using my bowl to check on your situation. You still need to work with Rahim, but you need to be very, *very* careful."

"Dottie, are you okay?"

"I'm fine," she assured me. "Just a little tired."

"Maybe you should go home and rest."

"Don't worry about me, Celia," she said firmly, with a hint of aggravation in her voice. It made me wonder if others had been fretting over her: probably Fred, her husband; maybe Dawna.

"Yeah, well, we worry because we care. You mean a lot to us, Dottie."

I could actually hear the smile in her voice when she said, "I care about you, too. And I'd tell you to drop this case like a bad habit if I could, but it really is necessary that you finish. Just remember that you can't trust Rahim.

"It's too late to back out—the stakes are too high." Her voice got the familiar singsong quality it has when she's getting a vision. "You're in terrible danger. Hasan believes he can use you. The only way out of the maze is through it."

There was about a thirty-second pause, then Dawna picked up. "Sorry about that. Dottie went into a trance. I'll let you know if she has anything else when she's herself again."

We said our good-byes and I hung up, then handed Roberto his phone. Yes, I'd been supposed to call the client, but we were almost to the airport. I didn't see where a minute or two would make that much difference. And I wanted to think about what Dottie'd told me before I spoke with either of the Patels.

Roberto took the phone without comment, tucking it into his pocket with a nod of acknowledgment and began packing his papers and notes back into his briefcase.

"I'm on my way back to California to get ready for a big trial. I won't be available for the next two weeks. Try to stay out of trouble," he said.

"If I do that, how will you pay the rent?" I teased.

His smile was fleeting. "I'll manage somehow." He paused. "Seriously, Celia, you need to be careful. The feds have very long memories, and they'll be watching you very closely from now on."

"I know." I did know. I didn't know what to do about it. Hell, I wasn't sure there was anything I *could* do about it. Dom Rizzoli was a fed and we'd become friends. But Schulz . . . well, that glare she'd given me promised trouble if I ever found myself back in Tampa, which, God willing, I wouldn't.

Roberto shook his head, "I know you do what you have to, and I believe you always try to do what's right. But this . . . this is a clusterfuck."

I blinked in surprise. In all the years he'd represented me, I'd never heard Roberto swear like that. Not that he was wrong, far from it. But his language brought me up short, made me think; which was probably exactly what he intended.

"I'll be careful."

"Do that."

There was no time to say anything further—the driver had pulled the limo to the curb. Roberto snapped his briefcase closed and locked it, then climbed out of the car.

"Bye, Roberto," I said.

"Good-bye, Celia. Take care."

The driver came up then with Roberto's bags. My attorney closed the limo door with a solid thunk. I watched him wheel his luggage across the pavement and through the terminal doors, where he disappeared into the crowd of flyers.

A couple of minutes later, after navigating the airport's maze of interior roadways, the limo dropped me off by the front door of the private airfield entrance. I didn't have any cash on me, so I asked for the driver's business card, intending to send him a tip later, but he assured me that Roberto had taken care of it. I grinned, knowing I'd see the charge on my next bill. The driver handed me my duffel, which he'd retrieved from the trunk.

Squaring my shoulders, I crossed the concrete to the door, feeling my exposed skin heat as the sun baked it painfully even across that short distance. Through the glass doors

I could see Bubba, Kevin, and the client waiting in the lobby, a grim, quiet group. Though the men were nicely dressed, they looked imposing enough that most people avoided the area around them, as if they were surrounded by an invisible moat.

Discreet it wasn't, but it was probably useful. My guys had plenty of visibility to see any enemy coming. Not that there were any, at least none that I could see. That was a little surprising, really. They were out in the open and lined up like ducks on the range in one of those video games.

Of course, Hasan and I had thinned the ranks of the enemy considerably here in Tampa. Maybe they were out recruiting? Whatever the reason, I'd take the quiet for the gift it was. Without my guns I felt naked. My knives are good for close-in work, and dear to my heart besides. Magic disks and spells are great. I was even glad to have the little recorder and my other tech toys. But for distance work, nothing really compares to a gun.

"Hi, guys," I said, striding up to the trio.

"Hey, boss." Bubba smiled at me. "Guess they decided not to keep you."

Kevin gave a long sniff, his expression darkening. "Why do you smell like brimstone?"

"It's a long story. I'll tell you on the plane."

"No," Rahim said firmly, "you won't. Your men have impressed me with their skills, but they are not coming with us."

I gave him a withering look. He could not seriously be pulling this shit again.

"Mr. Patel, you've faced multiple attackers—twice now. We

were lucky on the beach. If the bad guys had been just a bit quicker and if Hasan had not intervened, you'd be dead."

An ugly flush crept up from his neck, his eyes darkening until they were almost black.

"I do not owe Hasan my life." His voice was a deep, ugly growl—ugly enough that Kevin instinctively moved to position himself between us.

"No, you owe *me* your life. And I'm telling you that you need more than one guard."

"I saved your life as well," Rahim noted dourly.

"Yes, you did, and I'm grateful. But that doesn't change the facts of the larger situation. My death left you unprotected."

He gave me a haughty look down the length of his nose. "The terms of our agreement have not changed." We stared at each other in a long, charged, silence.

I counted to ten, then a hundred. The client was being an idiot. The question was whether I was going to go along with his idiocy. I'd died once already on this case. I wasn't eager to do it again. Next time, Rahim might decide Gramps was right and not revive me.

Kevin broke the tension. "Bubba, can you go with Mr. Patel to do the preflight check? I want to brief the boss on what happened while she was in the hospital."

"Right." Bubba turned to Rahim with his most winning smile. "After you," he said, gesturing in the direction of the doors to the tarmac. I could tell from the look on Rahim's face that he was considering arguing some more before he stomped off with ill grace. Bubba had to hustle a little to stay within easy protection range.

"Okay, Kev, what's up?"

"First, Dawna called, asked me to give you my phone." He pulled it from a pocket and handed it over. "Both Dom and the Church came through. The file's saved here." He pointed to an icon on the phone's screen. "Also, I think the client's up to something."

"How so?"

"He's got that look," Kevin said. "Plus, I overheard him fighting with Pradeep earlier this morning. Couldn't understand a word, but it was easy to tell the old man was raising hell with him. That's probably part of why Rahim is in such a foul mood."

"Bubba said he's been having family issues." I sighed. "I wish I could just tell him to go to hell, but Dottie says 'the only way out of the maze is through it.'"

"How poetic." He gave an annoyed snort. "Seers." He'd know; his sister was one.

I tapped my upper lip with the tip of my index finger as I thought about how to handle everything. "All right, Rahim's being an ass, but according to Dottie and your sister, I need to go along with him." I paused for effect. "The minute we're in the air, get a copy of our flight plan. Follow as quickly as you can. Be discreet, but I want you guys to have my back."

"Got it," he said, then gave me a meaningful look. "You do realize the full moon is coming soon?"

Crap. It was. "Do you need to go back to California?"

He thought about it for a long moment, then shook his head. "Nah. Like I told Dawna, I should be okay if I take steps. But it's going to be hard to protect you from a distance."

I shifted my duffel to a more comfortable position and started across the lobby, toward security and the tarmac. "Do the best you can. I trust you. But Kev, if you need to go, go. Bubba can watch my back."

"Not like I can."

I wasn't going to argue the point. I trust him and Bubba implicitly. But Kevin's monster side and his experience in black ops give him what Liam Neeson would refer to as a "particular set of skills." Which reminded me: "Do you have a backup gun? The cops kept mine."

Reaching under his jacket, he retrieved a Glock 9mm from a holster, checked the safety, and passed it to me. I'm not a huge fan of Glocks—just a personal preference. But it was a gun, and I knew it would have been perfectly maintained. I put it in my empty shoulder rig. It wasn't a perfect fit, since the holster had been designed for my Colt. My draw would be a little slower than normal and I'd have to compensate for that. But I had a gun again. Which made me feel both more secure and more able to do my job. Kevin handed me a spare clip, which I dropped into a jacket pocket.

"This is your main weapon?" That he trusted me with it said a lot about our relationship.

"Yeah, but you're on duty. And I've got more in the car."

"Thanks, Kevin."

"Just don't get yourself killed."

Kevin was right about one thing: Rahim was in a foul mood. He sat behind the controls of the plane, sullen and silent, waiting for permission to take off. I was in the passenger compartment, but though the door was open and we could've chatted, I really didn't want to talk to him. Anything I was liable to say at this point would just make things worse.

The case was a disaster.

Not only had we not captured the ifrit, we'd given Hasan a live vosta to chow down on—which he'd probably already consumed. That meant he'd be much stronger next time we went up against him. Rahim had a traitor in his organization—I was sure of that. I couldn't trust my client, either, given Dottie and Emma's warnings. And while I was trying hard to ignore what had happened, the fact was, I was completely and totally freaked out about the ifrit being able to take over my body.

I shuddered at the memory. One of my main goals (maybe not number one, but definitely way up there) was to make sure that I never went through that again. Rahim might be a bit of a demanding ass, but he was the single best bet I had to put the djinn back in the bottle.

Next were the humans—a group in which the ghost of the late, unlamented Connor Finn had fit right in. Finn had been a psychopathic, mass-murdering SOB with both brains and power, quite possibly the single scariest human being I'd ever encountered—and he was one of the freaking *crew.* They had a boss.

A boss who shed heat and smelled of brimstone.

There are people who claim they aren't afraid of the demonic. There are even some people who worship demons.

I'm pretty sure they're idiots.

My hand went instinctively to a set of scars burned into the skin not far from my heart.

"What are you thinking?" Rahim asked from the pilot's seat.

"That I don't have enough information about what's going on," I admitted. "Anything you want to tell me? Like maybe, where we're going? What the plan is?"

"South Bend, Indiana," Rahim answered. "I still need to locate Hasan."

"The ceremony didn't work?"

"No, we were interrupted too soon."

"And you haven't been able to get a bead on him since? Even with your family's help?"

"No." His answer was curt, the flat tone meant to discourage me from probing further.

There was more to that story. There had to be. I'd been down for two days. He wouldn't have spent the entire time arguing with his family.

So I waited.

Silence can be a very effective tool in negotiations. It takes on a weight and power of its own. When you talk, people can argue, make points, talk over you, or talk you down. When you wait in perfect, calm, silence, most people feel compelled to break it. The tactic doesn't always work, but it's effective enough to make it always worth trying.

I sat there, perfectly pleasant, but implacable.

He pretended to busy himself with the controls.

I waited.

Finally, with a grimace, Rahim twisted in his seat to face me.

"We are going to South Bend so that I can retrieve texts and equipment from my office at Notre Dame. My grandfather has withdrawn his support, as have most of my relatives. One or two cousins have agreed to work with me. Otherwise, I am on my own."

Shit. That was bad.

"This does not change my responsibility, but it requires a change in my approach." He turned back toward the controls, but not before I caught a glimpse of the pain, sorrow, and rage in his eyes.

"Are you going to be able to do what's necessary?"

He was saved from answering by the call from the control tower. We were cleared for takeoff.

I settled back into the cushiony leather seat and closed my eyes. Takeoff is not my happy time. I'm better about flying than I used to be, but I doubt I'll ever enjoy the experience.

We made it into the air without incident, climbing until we were skimming through fluffy, cotton-candy clouds. When the jet flattened out at cruising altitude, I pulled Kevin's phone from my jacket pocket and tapped the icon for the research Dawna had sent.

"What are you doing?" Rahim didn't turn, so I met his eyes in the mirror.

"Catching up on my e-mail," I lied, smiling sweetly. "I've got it running in spell-protected mode, so it won't interfere with the jet. I won't be able to make calls or text, but at least I can cruise the Internet."

"Good." He didn't sound like he thought it was good. In fact, I got the distinct impression he'd intended to tell me to turn off the phone, something I had zero intention of doing. To distract him, I tried a change of subject. "I meant to ask you earlier, is my bag on board?"

"Yes. It's in the storage compartment."

"Oh, good. My passport's in it, and my phone charger. The phone battery goes fast in protected mode." Luckily Kevin and I had the same make and model at the moment, so I could use my charger with his phone.

Rahim gave a grunt of acknowledgment and shifted his attention back to flying.

I started reading.

It took quite a while. I took a break about an hour in to use the restroom and drink one of the nutrition shakes Rahim had been kind enough to stock in the jet's mini-fridge. While I was up, I took my duffel out from beneath the seat and shifted it to the little storage compartment across from the bathroom. Opening the door, I was glad to see my suitcase in there, along with the medical bag Rahim used for his magical gear. Beside them was a navy duffel that I assumed held Rahim's clothes and personal effects. I stowed my duffel and removed my case. Setting in on the little counter above the fridge, I unzipped it and began sifting through its contents, looking for the charger.

There was no sign of it. And, more suspiciously, I could tell from the moment I opened the bag that my belongings had been repacked. I didn't sense hostile magic. More to the point, I didn't sense any magic at all. And I should have. Like a lot of people who travel a lot, I keep a stock of spell disks that have been designed to let you overfill your suitcase while preventing anything inside from getting wrinkled. They dissipate as soon as you unpack a bag.

Since my suitcase had been stuck in the Caddy, those spells should've still been working. They weren't. That pissed me off mightily. Zipping the case closed, I stowed it away again and stomped back to the sitting area. I debated confronting Rahim and decided against it for now. But a knot of painful tension tightened between my shoulder blades.

I went back to my reading. Dom had done the best he could, but a lot of information had been redacted from the reports he'd given Dawna. Surprisingly, the wheels of God had also gotten rolling at a good clip. The Catholic Church had provided the name of the specific demon that had been in the center of the battle at the Needle. It was long and unpronounceable—to me anyway. Even if I could have said it aloud, I wouldn't have. I didn't want to risk getting his attention. His position in the nefarious hierarchy was literally way the hell up there and he had more strengths than weaknesses.

I read and reread the information, trying to figure out how it all fit together. Again and again I came up blank. Frustrated and feeling stupid, I decided to take a break.

I closed my eyes, intending to concentrate on Bruno's face. Even if he was at his mom's bedside, I should be able to reach him telepathically. I needed him so badly, his calm, his confidence. Years of working with dangerous magic had toughened him. He never panicked, no matter the situation. He'd trained himself not to. I needed that from him now. There was also a chance that he'd see the connection I was missing.

Taking deep breaths, the way I'd been trained, I began deliberately relaxing my muscles, starting with my toes and working my way up until I was in a light trance. When I was absolutely in control of myself and my power, I pictured Bruno's handsome features, a face I knew as well as I knew my own. I felt a connection start to form; then something big and powerful smashed into me, grabbing my magic and dragging it somewhere else entirely. I tried to break free, but whoever or whatever it was was simply too strong for me. I had no choice in the matter and all of my panic and fighting were to no avail.

I was in darkness so complete that there was no sense of depth, no contrast between lighter and darker shadow, only utter blackness and oppressive heat, heavy with the stench of brimstone.

"Is the djinn cooperating?"

I didn't recognize that pleasant, melodic voice, but I knew it wasn't human. I'd heard a voice much like it coming from the mouth of a greater demon as he'd taunted me while attacking. A wave of pure panic swept over me. I tried to wake myself, to convince myself this was just a dream. But it didn't feel like a dream and I didn't wake.

"Yes, master. And that concerns me. He's being too coopera-

tive. He's up to something." I knew that voice. It belonged to Bob Davis.

My mouth went dry, my pulse raced. I'd suspected Davis was part of this—after all, he'd been working with Finn at the Needle. But suspecting and knowing are two very different things.

"Djinn are always up to something. It is their nature."

The voice was smooth, cultured, sweet as honey in your mouth. No human possessed a voice with that richness of timbre, that pure, seductive warmth that promised . . . anything, everything you could possibly desire. Again, a greater demon had used that exact tone on me when he'd been trying to seduce me.

"You know the tale of the scorpion and the horse."

"I do."

"Good. Learn from it. Use Hasan. Do not trust him. And leave no opening for him to exploit. I will not tolerate failure."

"Yes, master."

"What of the traitor among the Guardians?"

"He has had a change of heart."

"Not surprising, I suppose, but disappointing nonetheless. Kill him when you get the chance."

"Of course."

"The damaged siren?"

"She was dead, but they revived her."

"So Connor Finn has advised me. Next time, make it permanent."

"I may only have to wait. Her own allies are planning to kill her. Pradeep Patel has hired assassins."

"Just so long as it gets done, and soon. She has been a thorn

*in our side for too long." There was a slight pause before he
continued, "Besides, my brother has plans for her."*

Total panic gripped me, and the rush of adrenaline gave me
the strength to break free of the dream, vision, whatever it
was. I opened my eyes, my breath coming in shallow pants,
my hands white-knuckled where they held the armrests in
a death grip.

16

"Celia, are you awake? I'm getting ready to start our descent."

"I'm awake." My voice sounded rough and raw. I swallowed convulsively. Though I had started the vision relaxed, now I was rigid with terror. I was actually a little surprised I hadn't wet myself. It's one thing to know intellectually that greater demons are interested in you. It's another thing entirely to hear one of them talk about it. His brother had *plans* for me? Oh, no. So no.

I tried to force myself to relax, one muscle at a time. Deep breaths, slow, in and out. It helped, but not as much as I would've liked. I felt . . . odd. Spacey, like something important was missing inside me. It was somewhat similar to times when I was really sure I'd forgotten something really important, but couldn't put my finger on what it was.

Then it hit me.

We were in Indiana, heart of the Midwest, miles and miles from any ocean. That wasn't good for a siren, even someone like me who is only part siren. I'd been to a landlocked country before—Rusland in central Europe. I hadn't felt like this then, but Rusland is a tiny country and Europe is relatively small compared to the United States. Being so far from salt water was going to be a problem; the questions were, how big a problem, and what could I do about it?

"Are you okay?" Rahim gave me a worried glance over his right shoulder.

I shuddered. "Fine," I lied.

He didn't look like he believed me, but he didn't argue. He was too busy landing the plane. Just as well. I needed to get a grip—couldn't have the client seeing me a total wreck.

By the time we were on the ground, I'd regained enough self-control to at least put on a good front. When we were safely parked and unloading the luggage, I asked Rahim, "So, what is the plan?"

"I believe that doing a spell similar to the ceremony we tried the other night, but with the stone from his jar as the focus, should give me enough of a link to him. I don't doubt Hasan has ingested the power from the vosta; his heightened magic will make him harder to control, but it will also make it more difficult for him to hide." Rahim gave me a searching look. "There is a better way, but I cannot ask it of you."

Uh-oh. "What way?"

"Hasan possessed your body. You *were* him. There is no better link than that." His expression had become speculative. He might not ask me to act as the focus for his spell, but he was sure as hell hoping I'd volunteer.

Shit. Heaping, stinking mounds of shit.

I so did not want to do this. But we needed to find Hasan. The odds of using the gem from his jar probably weren't good or they'd have tried it before. I didn't doubt that I really was the best bet. Even without Rahim working any magic, I could almost feel the ifrit out there, lurking at the fringes of my consciousness.

Then I had a really horrible thought. What if my nightmare had come to me through that connection with Hasan?

You're not as stupid as you look. Hasan spoke in my mind, condescending and amused as always. It terrified me. It also pissed me off.

Get the fuck out of my head. I mentally enunciated every single word.

No. There was no give in the word. *They want you dead. You need me if you are to survive until I need you.*

Why? What do you want from me?

That's for me to know and you to wonder.

I blinked. I mean, seriously, that was so childish, a phrase right from a playground memory.

Where do you think I learned it? There is nothing about you, no thought, no memory, I don't know intimately. I know you better than you know yourself.

Then you know I'd rather die than let you have my body.

Yes, but I also know you won't allow them to kill you if there's any hope of stopping me. And you always hope.

He was right. And my best hope was standing right in front of me, no matter how little I trusted the bastard. "How long would you need to keep the spell going to find him?" I asked Rahim.

"Not long, particularly with a human link—one minute, maybe two."

You don't want to do that, Hasan said.

One minute doesn't sound long—but a lot can happen in that amount of time, particularly when you're dealing with supernatural beings.

I want you out of my head, I insisted.

That's not going to happen.

Oh yes, it was. It so was. I wasn't sure how, but I would get every last bit of Hasan out of me or die trying. If I needed to cooperate with Rahim Patel to do it, so be it. Still, if I was going to do that, I wanted a trick or two up my sleeve. Because ultimately I knew, absolutely and without question, that Rahim would sacrifice me in a heartbeat if he thought it would help him capture Hasan. And while I might be willing to risk my life to accomplish that, *I* wanted to be the one making the choice.

17

I **was getting** tired of travel in general and airstrips in particular. The one in Indiana was nice, clean, and pretty much indistinguishable from the ones in California, Texas, and Florida. Once again I watched the bags while Rahim put security spells on the plane. Then we hiked over to the parking lot where a silver Honda was waiting. I wasn't surprised by Rahim's choice of ride. It was small and practical, but probably fairly comfortable.

Because he'd left it parked right in the open, Rahim got to stand around while I checked for mundane physical threats like bombs and the like. Then I got to stand around while he released all the magical protections on the vehicle. He minded waiting. I didn't. Because when he was fully occupied, working mojo on the car, he wasn't able to spare attention for me. I took full advantage of the freedom.

Calling to mind the image of my business partner looking frustrated and worried, I reached out. It was harder than usual to contact her, but at last the connection with Dawna clicked into place. I spoke mentally as quickly as I could, in case Rahim figured out what was happening and shut me down.

Dawna, it's me. I may only have a minute or two. Tell Kevin and Bubba I'm going to Rahim's office at the University of Notre Dame. They need to get to me ASAP.

They're on their way now—they caught the first flight they could.

Rahim wants to use me as a link to Hasan in some ceremony.

Don't do it! You can't trust him.

I know. I know. But I need Hasan out of my head soonest.

We'll find another way. I don't trust Rahim.

Neither do I.

Keeping an eye on Rahim, I knew I didn't have much more time and I wanted to get in touch with Bruno. A lot had happened in the last couple of days and I knew he had to be seriously worried about me, just as I was worried about him and his mother. So I ended the conversation with Dawna and concentrated on my lover.

This time the connection snapped into place so quickly, it was almost painful. I saw his face as clearly as if he stood right in front of me. His eyes were dark with worry, his body poised as if he'd been pacing. He probably had. He does that when he's upset.

Celia! Thank God! Are you all right? How did the meeting with the feds go? Where are you? Did you get my message? He fired questions at me faster than I could possibly answer them, even mentally.

I'm fine, I assured him. It was even mostly true. *The meeting* went sideways, but they're not charging me. I'm back on the case and I'm in Indiana.

What the hell is in Indiana?

Rahim's office. He's lost the backing of most of his family because of the way things went in Florida, so he has to get some things from his office here. He says he has a plan.

You don't sound very sure about this.

I'm not. I don't trust him. I think he's the only one who can trap Hasan, and I owe him my life . . . but . . .

Trust your instincts. If you think he's up to something, he probably is. Are you okay? Indiana's a helluva long way from the ocean.

Well, it's not great. But I think I'll be okay. I sighed. There was one more thing I had to tell Bruno that I knew he wasn't going to like. *The meeting with the feds was interrupted when a demon tried to manifest.*

How was that possible? Did somebody summon it?

No, which makes no sense. It tried to come through a weak spot in reality. We sealed the hole with holy water from my One-Shots, but it was a really close call. I added, *Bruno, it was a major demon.*

Ah. I think I may know what happened. I'll have to do a little research to be sure. In the meantime, Celie, you need to be more careful. A demon and an ifrit is a bit much, even for you.

Tell me about it! I paused, taking a deep breath. *How's your mom doing?*

A little bit better, actually. She regained consciousness for a while yesterday, even managed to say a couple of words. He sighed. *We all know it's only a matter of time, and the doctors have her pretty heavily sedated, but at least she's not in any pain.*

I'm glad for that. Are you doing okay?

Not really, he admitted. *There's a lot going on. Sal's dealing with some bad business, on top of the usual family stuff.*

Bruno's family is big, close, and has more past issues than *National Geographic.* I wasn't surprised he was having to deal with "stuff" in addition to his mom's illness.

I love you, I told him. *I miss you so bad.*

I love you too. Did Dawna give you my message?

What message?

He swore, then said, *Sal heard through the grapevine there's been a high-money hit contracted on you. It got picked up by a couple that usually works out of Europe. They're real pros. You need to be careful.*

My thoughts about that were colorful to say the least. The vision had been a warning. Pradeep really was trying to kill me. Why?

Then it hit me, and I felt like an absolute idiot for not seeing it sooner.

If I died, Hasan could take over my body, just like he'd done on the beach, but only for a few minutes. But I'm an abomination. I'm not fully alive any more, even though I'm breathing and have a heartbeat. Which might mean that so long as I'm not fully dead either he could inhabit me for as long as he wanted. Why he'd want to, I had no clue. Still, I was betting there was a reason—it was the only thing that made sense.

I had to fight not to throw up, I was that horrified and sickened by my thoughts. But that would explain why Hasan was so determined to keep me alive—and why Pradeep had been furious with Rahim for reviving me.

My connection with Bruno was severed as neatly and abruptly as a surgeon cuts flesh. In my head, instead of my lover's voice, I heard Hasan.

Ah, so you've figured it out. But that doesn't change anything.

Why do you need a body?

You'll find out soon enough. In the meantime, do be careful. I'd prefer my vehicle didn't sustain any unnecessary damage.

By the time I'd finished my mental swearing, Rahim had finished with the car. The absolute instant he wasn't working other magic a blank white wall of mental shielding slammed into place around me. While it was a relief to end the contact with Hasan, I didn't like the fact that Rahim was high-handedly interfering in my communications.

"Hey!" I glared at Rahim.

"You are on duty. I need your *full* attention."

He wasn't wrong, but I was pretty damned sure that wasn't why he'd cut me off. Saying so wouldn't be productive or diplomatic, so I remained silent and on guard while Rahim stowed my suitcase and my black duffel along with his own duffel and his medical bag. I guarded him until he was in the car, then walked around to join him—all the while very obviously scanning the area for outside threats.

The drive from the airstrip to the campus was quite pretty. The weather was cool and crisp, the sky a cloudless, china blue. A gentle breeze fluttered leaves that were all the brilliant colors autumn in the Midwest has to offer. Rahim stopped at a PharMart that had gas pumps to fuel up the Honda, and reluctantly agreed to go inside with me so I could pick up some sunscreen and quick nutrition in the form of baby food. I'd had a diet shake on the plane, but that had only taken the edge off my hunger. A tube of sweet-potato/applesauce mix, combined with a little tub of turkey puree, washed down with a can of soda, and I was good to go. While I ate, I tried to use my telepathy to contact Bruno and Dawna and got nada. Just what I'd expected, but unhappy news nonetheless.

We drove from PharMart straight to Rahim's office.

Like most universities, Notre Dame has a problem with parking. There's not enough of it. It was four in the afternoon, so you'd think that there'd be less of a problem. You'd be wrong. Rahim had a faculty sticker, so he could go into any of the reserved faculty lots. But the covered parking lot was full. So was the open lot closest to his office building. As he circled around, looking for a spot, I slathered every bit of exposed skin with sunscreen. When we finally did find a place to park I was able to walk with him to the building without burning . . . much.

The Magic and Metaphysics Department was housed in Richards Hall. It was a huge, beautiful Redbrick building with big white columns and large windows with white trim and black shutters. Passing through the halls, I found out just how popular Rahim was. Students, faculty, and staff all waved, and more than a few tried to stop him to talk about how glad they were he was okay after "that thing in Florida."

Rahim was pleasant and polite, but firm, keeping us moving forward until we reached the central staircase. The three flights of stairs we climbed were easily as steep as the ones in my old office, but both of us arrived at the top in good time and not the least bit out of breath.

The wards on the building itself hadn't bothered me much. The ones on Rahim's office door were an education in agony.

"Ow, oh, *ow*." I automatically followed him into his office. That was a mistake. I found myself standing just inside Rahim's not terribly large and hideously cluttered professorial office with tears streaming down my face. "Are those wards even legal?"

"They're sub-lethal," Rahim assured me.

"Barely."

He didn't argue. "They are only triggered if someone actually enters the doorway. So long as my office is undisturbed, no one is harmed. It's a new process, one I devised myself. The magic affects all of the surface nerves of the body, aggravating the pain centers. It's keyed to recognize my bloodline. Anyone else gets the full treatment."

I suspect the glare I gave him was less than effective, what with all the crying I was doing.

"I can't risk the artifacts I have stored here. Everyone in the department knows that my office has strong protections." He sounded a little defensive. "Why don't you wait out in the hall? I won't be long."

I didn't really trust him, but I was useless inside that room. The second I stepped back over the threshold, the pain eased. "How do you meet with students?" I asked as I wiped tears from my face and scanned the hall for threats. There were none that I could see, so I watched Rahim through the doorway, staying alert to my surroundings. The walls were thin enough that bits of several nearby conversations would have been audible even without my enhanced hearing.

"I use one of the small conference rooms on the first floor for office hours and appointments." He bent down to pull open a cabinet door, revealing a small safe. He turned his body slightly, so I couldn't see what he was doing as he opened the safe, but I suspected that was due to an excess of caution. I was pretty sure that, like my own safe, Rahim's had magical and bio-keyed controls rather than a mundane lock. I wouldn't have been able to break into it even if I'd wanted to. And why would I want to?

Setting his bag of magical gear down nearby, he flipped it open. While I watched he transferred several items from the safe to the case, beginning with Hasan's djinn jar and a large gem, both of which he set carefully into his bag. Next came an antique knife and a small, worn, leather-bound book. Once all had been loaded, he snapped the bag shut, then closed the safe and the cabinet door.

I moved aside as Rahim stepped out of the office, carrying the medical bag. He pulled the door closed and reset the wards with one hand.

"We'll use the staff spell room for the working," he said. "It's close at hand."

"We're doing this *now*? Right now?"

"I don't dare waste time. Every moment we wait gives Hasan more of an advantage."

When he put it that way, it sounded oh so reasonable. I was beginning to think that perhaps he specialized in that—perfect rationalizations for any occasion.

Perhaps I was misjudging him, but I didn't think so. First, there was the whole thing with Rahim blocking my siren ability; then there was Hasan's warning; and finally, the professor's body language was just a teeny bit off. I couldn't have said exactly what the tells were—it was too subtle for that. But he was not acting and moving the way he had the other day. Pradeep might be the one who had hired the assassins, but Rahim was up to something—something involving yours truly. I really, really, wished I felt less mentally foggy. I needed to be at my best right now and I just wasn't.

Rahim and I took the elevator down to the first floor in silence almost as absolute as that of a spell disk. We walked in similar silence down a hall, through an open area divided into cubicles and rimmed with copiers and other shared office equipment. The secretarial staff smiled and greeted him by name, looking up from whatever end-of-the-day tasks they were trying to complete. He smiled in acknowledgment, but didn't slow his pace, hurrying around a corner and down another hallway, this one lined with classrooms, until we finally arrived at a pair of metal double doors with a sensor lock similar to the one on my safe.

When Rahim placed his palm against the reader, a small drawer sprang open to reveal a needlelike protrusion. Without hesitation, Rahim jabbed his finger, drawing blood. Only after the machine had a chance to confirm his identity did I hear the locks click open.

We stepped through the double doors into a room that was awash with magic, absolutely beautiful, and so sunny I could feel my skin start to heat the instant I cleared the doorway.

The space was the size of a large auditorium, and opened up the full five floors of the building to a skylight that took up the entire ceiling. The floor was polished hardwood stained a dark mahogany and polished to a warm glow that matched the paneled walls, on which elegant Art Deco light fixtures were spaced at regular intervals. The room's understated elegance was completely overwhelmed by the casting circle affixed to the floor. It was huge, the biggest active circle I'd ever seen.

The outer edge was gold, the center six inches silver, and the inner edge, copper. The metal was deeply etched with runes in various languages and from assorted schools of magic, and gems had been set in its surface at regular intervals. They were angled to catch the light, sending forth flares of color that formed patterns in the air of the room.

"I can't stay in here without better sunscreen." Since it was fall, and this was Indiana, there hadn't been much summer stock left on the shelves. The SPF 15 that had gotten me from the car to the office building wouldn't be up to protecting me from prolonged exposure to the light in this room.

"Hang on a second," Rahim said. Setting down the medical bag, he closed the doors, then hurried across the room to a control panel set into the far wall. As he did, I discreetly pulled the recorder from my pocket and set it on the floor in a shadowed area just inside the door. As cover, I slipped off my shoe, pretending to shake a stone out of it before sliding it back on.

Rahim flicked a switch and the glass of the skylight tinted until it was the dark gray of expensive sunglasses. The pain of the sunlight faded as the glass darkened. While I could no longer see the play of colored light cast by the gemstones, I felt it in painful flares of blistering heat against my skin. It was fascinating and more than a little scary. If the circle had this much latent energy, it was hard to calculate how much juice it would give an active working.

"So," Rahim said, giving me an eager and somewhat calculating look, "are you willing to assist me?"

I stayed right where I was, near the wall, outside the circle.

"I think you should try it the other way first." I smiled at him sweetly. "With the power in this circle, you may have enough magic that you won't need me." The circle was that amazing.

He didn't bother to hide his disappointment. "As you wish." Retrieving his bag, Rahim moved to the center of the circle, where he took out the jar, the gem, and a rondel dagger.

The knife looked old, as if it had actually been made back in the Middle Ages when that style of blade was popular. The hilt was round—hence the name—and made of carved wood, well worn from use and dark from the oils of the many hands that had undoubtedly wielded it over the centuries. The blade was a little over a foot long, tapering to a needle point, and was coated with some sort of green paste—I didn't know what, but I was guessing it was poisonous. It smelled bitter.

Rahim repeated the preparations he'd made on my new

casting circle back in California. When he'd finished, he returned salt and holy water to the bag, leaving it outside the circle and not far from the door, where it would be handy to grab when it was time to leave.

Finally, he moved to the center of the circle, picked up the dagger, and began to chant.

I should have seen it coming. Seriously. I knew I couldn't trust him. I knew there was a link between me and Hasan and that Rahim wanted to exploit that link. But I didn't think that he'd be able to use Hasan's jar on *me*.

I was wrong.

Power hit me like a club, staggering me. I stumbled one step closer to the circle's outer edge before I could stop myself. Bracing my legs, I fought hard not to move, not to lose consciousness. I was sick and dizzy from the magical blow, but I wasn't giving in. With more effort than was pretty, I managed to pull Kevin's Glock from my holster, training the gun onto the center of Rahim's mass. "Stop it, now."

Rahim snarled, his face growing ugly with anger and strain. He shouted words in a language I didn't recognize and made a throwing gesture with his right arm.

The gun melted from my hand; just turned to liquid and slid through my fingers to form a puddle of goo on the floor at my feet.

What the *fuck?*

I didn't have time to think about it. In an eyeblink I felt as if a rope had been flung around me, pinning my arms to my sides, and dragging my body off balance like I was a lassoed calf. I was yanked forward, closer and closer to the edge of a circle that had come to life.

The air around me was thick with power. The circle began to heat and flashes of light, like miniature bolts of colored lightning, began zipping around its edges in a dizzying array that grew faster and more frenetic with every word Rahim uttered.

I fought hard, screaming with rage and betrayal. The bat within me came rising to the surface like a whale breaching the water. It was not enough. When I crossed the circle, a sound like rushing wind drowned out all other noise and the colored lights all went to a brilliant, near blinding, white.

The flare of power was agonizing. I felt as though my entire body was aflame. But it wasn't all bad news, because I felt Rahim's control slip in that moment. The shift lasted only an instant, but that was all I needed. Moving with vampire speed, I pulled one of my knives from its sheath and used it to slice at my invisible bonds.

Rahim shrieked in surprise and pain. He shouted and made the same throwing gesture as before, this time aiming at the knife in my hands. I felt the flare of heat as the spell hit . . . and then felt the spell shatter against the magic the blade contained. Invisible, burning shards of power zoomed in all directions, like glass from a cup dropped on the floor.

I staggered to my feet, and found myself isolated in an eerily silent dome of light. Directly in front of my face, the air blurred and rippled, parting to give me a plate-sized porthole, through which I could see and hear another location, presumably the one where Hasan was hiding.

The window was directly between me and Rahim, blocking my view of whatever my "client" was up to. I took a pair of quick steps to one side, which turned out to be a very good move, because that meant that I wasn't where Rahim expected me to be when he swiped at me with the dagger.

Rahim's movements were inhumanly fast and his eyes were glowing red—more magic at work, or was he not as human as he'd seemed? I could smell the paste on the dagger's tip. Whatever it was, I didn't want it touching me, and I sure as hell didn't want to get stabbed.

With my bat in the driver's seat, everything was in hyperfocus; my hearing intensified, as did my sense of smell. Best of all, my strength and speed went off the charts. I was able to drop and roll under Rahim's attack and immediately get to my feet, using the single, fluid motion I'd practiced so many times during training. Rahim spun to face me, but not before my leg shot out in a kick that caught the outside of his knee, driving it sideways with a sickening pop and wet tearing sounds as the joint separated and soft tissue tore.

He screamed and, while it was inevitable that he'd fall, he threw the weight of his body forward, trying to close the gap between us and catch me with his blade. He missed, but only by a fraction of an inch. I danced out of the way and was brought up short by the electric heat of the spell circle. I smelled my hair burning and felt blisters rise on the exposed skin closest to the barrier.

He'd locked the circle! I wouldn't be able to leave, couldn't pass the perimeter until Rahim released the magic, crossed it himself, or died.

We were effectively fighting a cage match.

Hissing in surprise, I shuffled away from the edge of the circle, moving on the balls of my feet, keeping my body at an angle so as to present the smallest possible target to the Guardian. At the same time, I drew my second knife. I held the blades ready, one high, one low, potentially both weapons and shields against his attack.

Rahim lurched to his feet. Gasping in pain, he managed to stay upright, keeping most of his weight on his good leg.

I knew this was going to be a dirty fight. I had him on reach, but Rahim's blade was longer than mine and poisoned. Then again, if he wasn't fully human, perhaps the magic in my knives would be toxic to him, as it was to other magical beings. I could only hope.

I circled him, gliding, moving quickly but with care, trying to draw him off balance. Watching carefully, I saw that he was desperate—which makes most people careless in a fight—and while he wasn't unskilled, I could tell that he didn't practice regularly. I do. I train hard, particularly with my knives, since they're my favored weapon.

The circle gave me another advantage. Keeping it up and locked was a huge power drain, and all that power was coming from Rahim. The longer our battle lasted, the better off I'd be. I could see the strain telling on him more with every passing second.

"Why are you doing this?" I asked.

It was Hasan who answered, audibly, through the window,

while Rahim panted for breath. "He hoped to use our bond to tie me to you permanently. Then he'd kill you. The human sacrifice would power the spell that would drag us both into the jar for eternity.

"Failing that, giving you true death would make you useless to me after a few minutes." Hasan's voice echoed, ringing like a gong off the walls of the circle. "This plan will fail."

Beads of sweat broke out on Rahim's face. "You cannot enter this circle. You can do nothing to stop me," Rahim snarled.

"*I don't have to. She's better than you are.*" This time Hasan said the words both in my mind and aloud. Again the circle rang with his voice, loud enough to give me an instant, intense headache. I blinked back tears that blurred my vision. Rahim saw his opening and lunged; I sidestepped the attack, slashing at his arm with the knife in my left hand and simultaneously executing a leg sweep that took his good leg out from under him.

Rahim shrieked in pain, twisting as he fell. He swept the dagger toward my outstretched leg and I heard the sound of fabric ripping as the razor edge of the blade tore through my pants. I danced away, waiting for but not feeling the sting of injury. Nor did I smell blood.

The dagger had missed my flesh. I almost sighed in relief.

My erstwhile murderer hit the floor, screaming in frustration and agony.

KILL HIM!

"No."

I looked down at Rahim. He was done. That last attack had

taken it all out of him. He lay on the floor, panting, his face gray with fatigue and running with sweat. I knew I could kill him easily, and a big part of me wanted to. But sad to say, the world's best hope rested in Rahim's knowledge.

"He would see you dead." Hasan tried to reason with me. "He is a danger to you."

"Not right now he isn't."

I stepped away from the fallen man, keeping him in my peripheral vision as I moved to look through the magical porthole that still hung in midair near the circle's center. It was wavering now, in time with the beats of Rahim's heart. It would close when he lost consciousness—which I suspected would be soon—and I wanted to make sure I got a good look at what was on the other side before it did. I peered through the opening at an underground cavern, carved more by nature than by man and magic, with seeming passages leading beyond it, into shadowed depths.

The space was lit by balls of mage light as well as by more prosaic electric lanterns. Huge stalactites in shades of variegated brown and gray stabbed down from a cavernous ceiling like the fangs of some huge carnivorous beast, their white tips dripping the mineral-filled water that formed them. The floor was bare stone, with some areas blasted smooth by magic and swept clear and others left natural, covered with stalagmites, dirt, and loose stone.

In the largest open space was a casting circle almost identical to the one in which I stood, down to the placement of the gemstones. I focused my vision on it and the only difference I could see was that the runes were all written in a single language. I was surprised that I didn't at least recognize the writing, since El Jefe had made us cover all the current and ancient magical languages in his courses. I should have known what it was, but I didn't. On the other hand, the markings looked somewhat familiar, enough to tell me I'd seen similar runes before. I cudgeled my brain, trying to remember where, but came up empty.

In the distance I heard a man and a woman, speaking quite softly. Their words had an odd, echoing quality, probably because of the cave's acoustics. Her voice was waspish. Again, I felt I should recognize it, but damned if I did.

"She's not dead. How can she not be dead? Finn's gone. His ghost was here to see her dead, and now he's gone and she's *not*."

"Ah, the miracles of modern medicine. Apparently they managed to revive her."

Bob Davis, again. I was really beginning to hate hearing his voice.

"It doesn't affect the bigger picture," Davis continued in a reassuring tone.

"I don't give a damn about the bigger picture. I want her *dead*."

"Be careful what you say, Meredith. Our master would be none too pleased to hear you talking like that."

Meredith, as in nurse Meredith Stanton, one of the two survivors from the black ceremony at the Needle. Well, well.

Stanton's voice grew sullen. "I serve the master. You know that. But that *thing* has thwarted us at every turn."

"That's not why you want her gone."

"No. She murdered Harold. She should pay for that."

Okay, that wasn't fair. I had not "murdered" Harold Halston. When I disrupted the ceremony at the Needle and shot the vosta they'd been using as a focus, the backlash had killed Halston. It was not my fault that he couldn't shield in time. Well, all right, maybe I bore some indirect responsibility for his death, and I certainly couldn't say I was sorry it happened. But it wasn't murder.

"She will," Davis told Stanton. "Just as painfully as I can manage."

Oh, great. *Just* what I needed to hear.

Actually, it is. You have enemies before you—can you really afford to leave one at your back?

He had a point. I stared through the porthole, memorizing details of the cavern. Davis and Stanton were both wanted by federal authorities. If I could get enough information on their hideout, I might be able to call in an anonymous tip and let the Feds take some preemptive action for me.

That would just leave Rahim for me to deal with, an enemy I was going to keep a very close eye on, and whom I knew I could take. Besides, call me suspicious, but it seemed to me that the more Hasan wanted Rahim dead, the more I needed to keep the Guardian alive. Preferably far, far away from me, but still, alive.

Hasan laughed and the sound of it chilled my blood. *I want your body. I can't reach you in that circle. That is unacceptable.*

Not to me.

You're not the one whose opinion matters. I am. You see, I've ingested the power of the stone. I am strong enough now that

I have broken the bonds the Guardians placed on me, all those years ago. I am free now, free to do as I choose.

My choice is this: If you don't do exactly as I say, I will exact retribution on a scale that beggars the imagination. I will make it hideously, painfully personal. To keep me from doing that, you are going to present yourself to me at the Temple of Atonement in southern Colorado. In my mind I saw a map, with a location circled in blood red. *Be here by nine o'clock tomorrow morning.*

And if I'm not?

First, I will kill everyone you care for, starting with your dear old gran. Then, my eye will move outward, to the general public.

To prove that I can—and will—I will give you a small show of power. To give you . . . incentive.

The image in the porthole shifted. Instead of the cavern I saw an oil-drilling platform somewhere in the middle of an ocean.

Watch.

With sick fascination I did: A huge explosion rocked the facility; a fireball consumed men who swarmed over the platform's surface like ants; oil pumped from the burst pipes like blood from a severed artery, black fluid slicking the surface of everything it touched, covering the water below in an ever-expanding pool.

I will see you at nine. Don't be late.

18

WAS STILL staring at the flaming oil rig when the porthole winked out as Rahim lost consciousness. One second it was there. The next it wasn't.

He wasn't dead—the circle was still up. It wouldn't be if he were gone. I approached the body sprawled across the floor cautiously just the same. He could be playing possum.

I kicked his knife to the other side of the circle before bending down to check his pulse. It was weak, but there. His color was bad, his breathing ragged. He needed help, now. While part of me was angry enough to think it served him right to let the circle drain him to death, another, larger part thought better of it. So I dragged him right up to the circle's edge, then rolled him over it. The circle collapsed as soon as Rahim was on the other side.

With the pressure of the circle's magic gone, I felt much better. Moving quickly, I grabbed the rondel dagger and my recorder. I needed to hide them, and fast. Thinking quickly, I slid off my right shoe and stripped off my sock. I thrust the blade of the knife into the sock, then slid the bundle through one of the loops in my jacket, where I normally stowed a stake for killing vampires. Not a perfect solution, but the best I could come up with on short notice. At least the sock was long enough to cover the entire blade—I wasn't sure how much of the metal had been tainted by the poison and I didn't want to risk even casual contact with that toxin. The dagger felt awkward and lumpy beneath my jacket and I was painfully aware of the need to be careful not to do anything that would cause the blade to jab through the protective fabric. I slid my shoe back on and dropped the recording device into my pocket. Only then did I open the door to the casting room and yell for help.

People came from all directions, and more quickly than I expected. Then again, this was the part of the building where people worked difficult experimental magic. Probably this wasn't the first emergency they'd had to deal with. Nor was it likely to be the last.

A bear of a man with grizzled hair and beard, wearing gray dress slacks and a charcoal sweater, shouldered me easily aside. Squatting down beside Rahim, he searched for a pulse and shouted for a woman standing in the hall to call an ambulance. I thought I recognized her as one of the secretaries I'd passed in the hall on the way to the workroom, but I could have been wrong.

A crowd was gathering, peering in through the doorway.

"Good God, what happened to his leg?" the man trying to help Rahim asked.

"We were sparring and there was an accident," I lied. As I spoke, I pushed a little with my siren abilities. They weren't in top form this far from the water, but anything I could manage would be better than nothing. I needed Rahim to get help without anyone thinking too hard about what had happened to cause his injuries. The big problem was the magical strain. That was what would kill Rahim—and pretty quickly if it wasn't treated soon.

The grizzled man—probably another professor—shook his head, waving a hand in front of his face as if to shoo away a buzzing fly. But his next words let me know that my push had hit home. "He's overstrained his magic, but he's breathing and his pulse is good. We need to get him to the hospital as fast as possible, but he should pull through."

There were murmurs of relief and some of the watchers—mostly those who looked older than the average college student, so presumably teachers—began shepherding others away from the scene.

The woman I thought was a secretary glared at me as she pulled out a cell phone and called 911.

Oops. Using my siren abilities on the man had set off aggression in the woman.

Time to disappear. I tucked myself into a group of three or four others who'd been bold enough to come into the workroom as they—we—all filed out. I didn't have time to waste dealing with the police investigation, and, call me crazy, I figured the attempted murder terminated my contract with Rahim.

The secretary was still staring after me as I scuttled through the doors to the nearest classroom. It was empty, which was fine by me. I needed a little privacy to calm down and catch my breath. With a press of the button I set my watch to run a countdown to Hasan's deadline. Though I knew it'd just stress me out more, seeing the numbers ticking steadily down, I needed to know how much time I had.

Reaching into my pocket, I pulled out Kevin's cell phone. The battery was dead. Crap. I opened the door and peered out. The coast was clear. The woman I'd pissed off was gone.

I needed a phone. Probably my best bet would be the secretarial area. If I was lucky, most of the staff would still be away from their desks, dealing with the crisis. Luck was with me; when I got to the cubicles, it was easy to find an empty desk and help myself to a landline. On a hunch, I dialed 9 for an outside line. I smiled at the next dial tone and called my office.

"Graves Personal Protection."

"Dottie, it's me. Can you use your gift to tell me anything? I need help." I didn't say anything specific since there were people at some of the nearby desks, pretending not to listen. Besides, knowing Dottie, she'd been keeping tabs on me via her gift.

"Yes, you do. Badly. But I don't dare tell you much, the situation's too delicate." She thought for a long moment, the silence dragging on the line between us. Finally, she said, "You should know, you need to meet with Mrs. Patel and her son at the hospital before you leave Indiana. It's critical. They have something you'll need."

"What?"

I shouldn't have bothered asking. She'd already put me on hold. A moment later Dawna picked up.

"Celia, are you all right? Dottie's been worried sick but

won't tell me *anything.*" It sounded as if Dawna was about to tear her hair out with frustration. It's not an uncommon sentiment for people who regularly deal with clairvoyants.

"For the moment, but the job's gone to hell in a handbasket," I said aloud. In my mind I projected, *Rahim tried to kill me.*

"He *what?* Why?"

The ifrit wants my body—permanently. Apparently Rahim thought killing me was the best way to keep him from getting it. It's the same reason his grandpa hired the hit men. I projected while saying something boring and mundane.

Dawna started swearing. She was surprisingly good at it for someone who doesn't do it often. Well, hadn't done often, until we took this case. "Did you kill him?"

No. We need him to get the ifrit back in the jar. I didn't want the staff members wondering about my long silence, so I said, "The client overstrained his magic. They're taking him to the hospital." *I need you to hire somebody to take over protecting Rahim. Someone who will report to us. I'm not turning Rahim in for trying to kill me—he has to be free to try to deal with Hasan, and he needs to be protected, but I want to know what he's up to.*

This was a risky path to take. If the Patels stiffed us, we'd be out not only our labor, but the cost of whomever we hired as well. But my life was at stake and that was worth more than a few bucks.

"I'm on it. Should I call the Company or Miller & Creede?"

"Doesn't matter to me. Long as they know they're working for us and report to us."

"The Company then. Creede would ask too many awkward questions."

I winced. She was right. The Company is a quasi-military organization with independent contracts with governments all over the world. They also have other, less savory, dealings. If you've got the money, they'll do whatever, no questions asked. I sighed. This was going to cost a *lot* of money. If Rahim didn't pay his bill, we might not be able to hire a medic after all.

"Bubba and Kevin are at the South Bend airport right now, getting a rental car. Where should I have them pick you up?"

I was happy to know that my guys weren't too far away. They must have gotten a flight pretty soon after Rahim and I left Tampa.

"I'll be at the hospital. I'll get you the address."

Dottie told me I need to meet with Mrs. Patel and her son at the hospital, but we've got to move fast. The ifrit gave me a deadline to get to this cave in Colorado. If I don't go there and give him what he wants, he'll start killing people, starting with Gran, you, Bruno, everyone I love.

"And what he wants is you? Celia, you can't—"

No, but I can't risk everybody either. He said he couldn't reach me when I was standing inside an active casting circle. Maybe it was just that particular circle. I mean, it was pretty elaborate, with jewels and everything. But it could be that I can be safe in any circle. After all, he'd needed my body to cross the one on the beach. Then again, that one had had jewels, too—the vostas. Crap. "I want you to get hold of everybody. I want every single one of you to get into a circle and wait this out. Hasan specifically mentioned Gran, so I really need you to make sure she's protected."

"*Everyone?* Celia, that's a lot of people. Where do I draw the line?"

She was right, of course. I have a lot of friends. Normally that's a good thing. But it did give Hasan a ridiculous number of possible targets. Damn it. "Don't. Just call everyone in the inner circle, and tell them to call everyone they can think of, and on out. Better for too many people to know than not enough."

"I'll do it. I promise."

"Thanks, Dawna."

I need guns and ammo.

I thought Kevin gave you his Glock.

Rahim destroyed it.

"What? How?"

Magic.

"Good luck telling Kevin. I'm sure he's going to be as happy to hear that as he is when he learns you want everyone to hide."

I snorted a laugh into the phone. Dawna was right. I could just imagine how well Bubba and Kevin would take that advice.

"You do realize that if everyone is hiding in casting circles, we won't be able help you. You won't have any backup." She took a breath. "I assume the phone you got from Kevin is either gone or dead? You need to get a new one, soonest. We can't afford for you to be out of touch right now."

"I know." I hung up without saying good-bye. Yeah, it was

rude. But there was nothing else she could say that I wanted to hear. Besides, the secretary whose desk I was using had just arrived. Wouldn't you know, it was the same one who'd glared daggers at me in the hallway. Now she was looming in the entrance to her cubicle, her expression set in hard lines of annoyed disapproval.

"Sorry. My cell battery was dead. I just need to make one more call. I need a cab to the hospital."

Frowning, she stepped into the cubicle. I stood up and she took her seat; if I hadn't stepped aside quickly, she'd have plowed into me. Turning her back in dismissal, she said, "I'll have one meet you out front."

19

Memorial hospital of South Bend is on North Michigan Street. It seemed nice and well run. I caught a glimpse of Rahim in one of the curtained-off areas of the emergency room. He was conscious, with IVs in each arm. I started toward him, but was stopped by a woman in scrubs who, while pleasant, was very firm.

"Let her in." Rahim's words were a little slurred. "She is with me."

The woman stepped aside, but the look she gave me was unfriendly.

I stepped close to his bed. The circumstances didn't allow for privacy, but the place was busy enough that there was plenty of background noise. Plus there was a fair amount of whirring and beeping from the machines Rahim was hooked up to, the ones that kept track of his vitals.

"You had them call an ambulance. Why? You could have left me to die." He kept his voice barely above a whisper.

"Don't think that didn't occur to me," I answered. "But,

like it or not, you're the Guardian. I want Hasan back in the jar. You're my best bet for seeing that happen."

He nodded.

"But, for the record, I quit. My replacement should be here soon."

"One of your men?"

Seriously? Did he really think that my guys were going to look after him after what he'd done? Hell, he'd be lucky if they didn't try to take him out themselves.

"Nope. We're done." I started to walk away. I'd only gone two or three steps when his voice stopped me.

"Celia, I can't say that I'm sorry. I genuinely like you, but Hasan cannot be allowed to take over a body on a permanent basis."

I turned, meeting his gaze. "Believe me, I don't intend to let him. But why?"

He seemed to consider answering me for a moment, then closed his mouth firmly and turned away, facing the wall.

Fine. So be it. I walked down the hall to the ER lobby. There was a television, but it was muted, and magazines, but none of them really caught my fancy. There were plenty of people milling around. I wasn't exactly guarding Rahim, but I did keep an eye on the people who were coming and going.

Coming soon included the representative from the Company. He arrived quickly enough that he must have been in the area—though why, and doing what, I had no clue. The name he'd used when I'd known him was John Jones, and while he looked utterly ordinary, he was one of the most dangerous men I've ever met.

He greeted me with a nod of acknowledgment. "Graves, I see you're still among the living." He meant it as a joke. He'd been the one to break the news to me about being an abomination—someone partially, but not completely, turned by a vampire. He'd been sure at the time that I'd either be killed by my sire or take the last step and wind up feeding on people. So far, I'd proved him wrong. But it hadn't been easy.

"More or less." I couldn't match his light tone, and seeing that, Jones stopped smiling.

"Where's the client?" he asked soberly.

"I'm the client. Rahim Patel is the protectee. He's in the ER, being treated for overstraining his magic. He might need surgery on his knee." I reached into my jacket and pulled out one of the One-Shots. Spraying a trickle of holy water into my palm, I extended my damp hand to Jones.

We shook.

It was him. Not that I'd expected a switch, but you can't be too careful.

I sent him down the hall, but didn't accompany him to make introductions. I was sick to death of Rahim Patel.

Irritable and restless, I wandered outside. Across the parking lot I saw a trio of people in scrubs, smoking just off hospital property. A little way to the right was a stone bench, set next to a flowerbed filled with yellow and orange fall mums. Making my way to the bench, I sat down, concentrated, and focused on reaching Bruno. Like before, it was a strain, but I managed. Still, with all the effort the mental conversations were taking, I was starting to get one hell of a headache—then again, maybe that was just the natural result of having to deal with the Patels.

Hi, I said in Bruno's mind.

Thank God! The way our last conversation ended, I was afraid . . . He didn't say what he'd been afraid of. Then again, he didn't have to. I was beginning to understand why he hated my job. It had to be hard for him, wondering every day if I'd make it back alive and unharmed. It's the same thing the spouses of cops, firefighters, and members of the armed forces go through, and it costs a lot of them their relationships. Would it cost me Bruno? Would I have to give up my job—my business—to keep him? Would I be willing to? He had never actually asked . . . yet.

This case is awful. I can't wait for it to be over. And I can't wait to see you again.

Tell me about it. His mental voice held exhaustion, frustration, and worry. Before my most recent bout of training with my great-aunt, I wouldn't have known that, wouldn't have been able to "hear" emotion. Now that I could, I got to worry even more about the people I talked to this way. I'd known things were bad, but hearing his voice I wanted desperately to put my arms around him and give him a hug, to be there for him. That I couldn't sucked rocks.

Are you okay? How's your mom doing?

Not well. He answered the last question first. *And I'm not okay,* he admitted. *You?*

Nope. Did Dawna talk to you?

No. I've got a missed call from her. Is it important?

Only life or death.

The ifrit gave me a deadline to get to a cave in southern Colorado. If I'm not there on time, he's going to start killing people, starting with everyone I love.

Bruno is a master of colorful invective, but I was still impressed by his reaction. I would never have thought of some of those combinations.

There's this special magic circle at the University of Notre Dame. It has gems at the compass points. Hasan couldn't reach me in it when it was active. I'm hoping something like that will work for you guys too.

I pictured the circle in my mind, projecting the image as clearly as I possibly could.

Got it. I'm at Sal's. He's got a circle I can use, and Connie has plenty of jewelry.

Why are you at Sal's? I didn't mean to sound suspicious but apparently learning to hear emotional nuances brought with it the ability to project them as well.

I like Sal, I really do, but I have no illusions about what he does for a living, and I'm always nervous when Bruno spends too much time around his uncle.

In spite of everything, they're having a birthday party for one of Joey's kids later today. I said I'd help out with the magical protections. The boys are already here. Joey and Roxanne went to pick up the food.

It was hard to imagine the party being anything but a disaster under the circumstances. Nor could I fathom why a kid's birthday party needed magical protections that required a mage of Bruno's level. How bad had things gotten out there? I might have asked, but Bruno changed the subject.

A Mrs. Patel called—I assume that's your client's wife? She said it was a matter of life or death and she offered a good price, so we sold her the vosta we used at the Needle. Any idea what they plan to use it for?

I had an idea, all right. At a guess, the Patels needed to replace the stone that Hasan had stolen when he'd disrupted the ceremony on the beach. But I had no proof and I didn't want to alarm Bruno any more. *Look, I've got to go. Don't wait until the last minute to get in the circle. I don't trust the ifrit to keep his word.*

I can take care of myself, Celie, he grumbled.

I know. I know. But I'd never forgive myself if something happened to you and it was my fault.

He gave a huge mental sigh and I could picture him shaking his head. *Baby, this is not yours. If anything happens, and I don't think it will, it's not your fault. It's Hasan's. All his. You can't be blaming yourself for everything bad that happens to us. Yeah, that curse mark . . .*

Oh! I hadn't meant to interrupt him, but his words had reminded me. I looked down at my hand, once again marveling at the fact that the mark that had been there most of my life had vanished.

What?

My curse mark's gone.

What?!

It's gone. Disappeared. Hasan removed it.

Why would an ifrit do something good? That doesn't make sense.

I couldn't blame him for being suspicious. I mean, seriously, the man's not an idiot.

For the same reason he took out a couple of the assassins and warned me about Connor Finn's buddies. He wants me alive.

Why?

He plans to use me. I don't know for what.

Shit! He paused. *Be careful, Celie. That the curse mark's gone is a great thing. Really great. We might even have a chance at a normal life. But you can't trust an ifrit. They're pure evil.*

I know. I know. A normal life? Like with kids and a house in the suburbs? Eep. I've always known that's what Bruno wanted, but it had never quite seemed *real* before. Just the thought of it scared the crap out of me. *Gotta go. Love you.*

You too. Be careful!

You too.

I cut the connection between us before he could glimpse what I was thinking and feeling.

The rush of panic I felt had nothing to do with ifrits, magic, or demons. Bruno wanted a "normal" life. Did I? Was I even capable of one? After all, my own childhood hadn't exactly been normal. And what about kids? Did I want one? A bunch? Could I even have them, given that I wasn't entirely alive? If I couldn't, did I want to adopt?

A whole world of possibilities I'd never truly considered seemed to open up in front of me, scaring the living crap out of me.

I really couldn't afford to let thoughts like that distract me at a time like this. But, sadly, much of my life is made up of times like this . . . which might be a big fat clue. Then again, maybe I could change. Did I want to?

Maybe. Maybe not.

I was still turning all that over in my mind when Kevin and Bubba pulled up in a midsized rental car. Bubba hit the button to roll down the passenger-side window and I got to my feet, glad to see them and glad for the distraction.

"Hi, guys."

"Hey, boss. Glad to see you up and around." Bubba grinned at me.

"Good to see you, too." I meant it.

"How come you're not on the client?" Kevin cut to the chase. "Are you having trouble being in the hospital?"

"No." I wasn't, which was good. It had been some time since I'd eaten, and hospitals in general—and ERs in particular—could be a real problem for me if my bat was close enough to the surface to be aroused by the blood. But the whole time I'd been inside, I hadn't felt so much as a twitch. "I'm good. Did Dawna get hold of you?"

"I've got a missed call. Is it important?"

Jeez. Hadn't she been able to reach *anybody*?

I was about to get into the car when I remembered Dottie's warning about Abha Patel. Dammit.

"Park the car," I told Bubba. "We need to talk."

I waited on the bench, trying to figure out the best way to break the news to them. There wasn't one. So when they walked up to me, I just cut to the chase.

"Rahim tried to kill me."

"He *what?*" Bubba was outraged. Kevin just blinked. I could actually see him making connections in his head.

When he spoke his voice was even, almost flat. "Hasan can inhabit your body. You're alive, but part of you is also dead. You're the perfect vessel. He can use you for a lifetime, do all the things he couldn't without a physical presence."

This was some of what I liked best about Kevin—he's got experience, a background in metaphysics, and the brains to figure things out on the fly.

"That's my guess, yeah," I confirmed.

"Oh, *fuck*. Celia—" Bubba's eyes were wide enough that the whites were showing all around. "This is so bad."

"I know. And it gets worse."

"It can get worse?" Bubba sounded astonished.

I opened my mouth to give them the rest of the bad news, but said nothing. Two people were coming toward us from the ER entrance.

They were an interesting pair. The woman was beautiful. She wore a traditional Indian sari in pink and turquoise, edged in gold, the bright colors emphasizing her warm brown skin and liquid brown eyes. Over one shoulder she carried a large pink bag that was meant to be a purse, but was the size of a tote. With her was a boy of about ten, wearing a striped T-shirt over blue jeans. He looked like a younger version of Rahim, down to the mark on his wrist.

"You are Celia Graves," the woman said, her voice soft and lilting, with a bit of a British accent. There wasn't the least bit of hesitation in her manner.

I nodded.

"I am Abha Patel. This is my son, Ujala." She extended her hand. I shook it, but only after spraying mine with a bit of holy water. Ujala and I repeated the gesture and I got a jolt of magical energy for my trouble. He was a mage, and already a powerful one despite his youth. My natural magic reacts to mages. With Bruno and John Creede, the reaction definitely included a sexual element. This was just pain. I managed not to flinch, but wasn't sorry when the boy released his grip.

"These are my associates, Kevin Landingham and Bubba Conner."

Everybody shook hands. When we were all done with the polite greeting ritual, Abha spoke. "I am a seer. I know what my husband did. I know that you have the evidence that would convict him—the dagger and your recording."

Kevin's eyebrows shot up, but he didn't say anything. Bubba just stood there, never taking his eyes off of Ujala. It was clear to me that he didn't trust the boy. I didn't know what Bubba had sensed, but I trusted his instincts.

"I am here to offer you a deal," Abha continued.

"What deal?" I kept my voice even, calm.

She didn't answer directly. "Ujala is very powerful. He will be an excellent Guardian when fully trained. But he has just begun his training. Pradeep was a powerful Guardian, but he is old and is more feeble than pride would let him admit. Tarik is too ambitious to be trusted. Rahim is needed, whether his family believes it or not.

"So I offer you a trade: information and protection in exchange for your evidence."

"And how do I know he won't just try again? Holding that evidence protects me from future attempts."

"No. It does not. Because to perform his duties, Rahim is willing to go to prison or to die. At the start, he did not want to kill you, but Pradeep convinced him that it was the only way, that you are too much of a risk left alive." She broke off, her eyes filling with tears.

Ujala picked up the tale. "Great-grandfather and Tarik have accused my father of incompetence and have turned many of the members of our family against him. Great-grandfather claims my father is incapable of doing what is necessary, and that he and Tarik are now our only hope."

I said to Abha, "You're helping me because—"

"I've seen the various futures. We have little chance, but what hope there is lies with you. Ujala," she added, turning to her son. He reached into the back pocket of his jeans and withdrew a drawstring bag made of black velvet.

Loosening the string, he poured its contents into his palm. The gold of the chains and charms shone brightly. The gemstones set into each of the three circular charms sparkled and the air around us buzzed with magic. It felt like I was breathing power rather than oxygen. Normally, magic burns across my senses. Not this. This was cold, cold enough that goosebumps broke out over every inch of my exposed flesh and my breath misted the air.

"I am not fully trained yet," Ujala said softly. His voice still had a childlike pitch, but the tone and emotion behind it were eerily adult. "But I know enough to make the *sujay*, the protection amulets worn by those of our family who are not Guardians. While these are around your necks, Hasan cannot use magic against you, cannot control your mind or possess you." Ujala held out the necklaces with their sparkling charms, offering them to us . . . to me.

Abha said, "When you are thus protected, though Hasan cannot harm you, or act directly against you, he can, and will, attack indirectly—using humans he can influence or control, nature, or even objects."

"So he can't take my body, but he can have his minions shoot me?" I said.

"Or make the earth swallow you whole, or—"

"Got it," I interrupted, not really wanting to hear a more extensive list. My imagination could supply enough horrific possibilities without help, and the memory of what had happened on that oil rig was still fresh in my mind.

"Will you take our deal? Will you accept these and leave my husband free to do what he must?"

I looked from the glittering gold in Ujala's hand to Bubba and Kevin. What we were being given wasn't complete protection, but it was the best we were going to get. And since I didn't have time to deal with the authorities right now, I figured, why not? Reaching into my jacket, I removed the sock-wrapped dagger and passed it to her. I took the recorder out of my pocket and, while the Patels watched, hit the delete button to erase the scene I'd recorded earlier.

"Good." Abha gave a short, satisfied nod. "Now you must go. Rahim should be in surgery for one hour. I will wait another thirty minutes after that before reviving him, to give you a head start."

With a low bow to each man, Ujala carefully handed one necklace to Kevin and one to Bubba. Last, he turned to me. Bowing, he said, "May the *sujay* protect you in your quest. May you be blessed with courage and insight to do what is right, and good to protect all others."

"Thank you," I said.

"No. Thank you," the boy said sincerely.

Mother and son moved away, reentering the hospital as we put on our *sujay*.

The metal was quite cold when I first put it around my neck, but soon warmed to my body temperature. The circular charm fell gently against my breastbone. I felt a warm tingling and the gemstones flashed brightly, once, before returning to normal. If the same thing happened with Bubba and Kevin's necklaces, I didn't see it.

Bubba looked me straight in the eye and said, "So, now what?"

20

Kevin and Bubba are my friends, my employees, and damned good at their jobs, but they have different skill sets and training. For one thing, Kevin has an affinity for covert work that Bubba doesn't. Of course, Kevin also has to deal with being one of the monthly furry, and tomorrow was the full moon. Whether his condition would be an asset or detriment was a coin flip at this time, but I wanted him free to handle it.

Explaining that Jones had been hired to protect Rahim, I asked Kevin to covertly keep an eye on them. "I need to know what they're up to and I want advance warning if Rahim plans another attack."

"Got it."

"Bubba, you're with me." I stood between the two men, looking from one to the other. "Do either of you have a spare gun?"

Kevin gave me a long look. "What happened to my Glock?"

"Rahim used magic to melt it. I don't know how he managed it—the spell didn't even burn my hands, yet the gun is a puddle of goo on the floor of the casting room at Notre Dame."

"Damn." Kevin's voice held equal parts admiration and irritation. "That was one of my favorite guns."

"Sorry. I'll replace it when we get home. In the meantime . . ."

"I've got another nine you can use," Kevin said. "It's locked in an airport case in the trunk of the rental car. He turned to Bubba. "Give us a minute?"

"Sure," Bubba said, but he didn't sound happy about it and his body language made it abundantly clear that he didn't like being left out of the loop. He dug the car keys from his jeans pocket and passed them to Kevin. "Don't dawdle."

Kevin and I crossing the parking lot quickly. My skin heated almost immediately in the late afternoon sun and I remembered, belatedly, that it had been a while since I'd put on sunscreen. The package labels claimed the stuff lasted four hours, but it never did.

My skin had reddened by the time we reached the silver rental Honda. I kept a close eye out for anything suspicious, but saw nothing unusual. It was unnerving, knowing that somewhere out there, people were waiting to kill me: skilled, determined people.

Kevin hit the button to unlock the car doors. "Get in, out of the sun."

I climbed into the passenger seat, leaving the door open so we could talk. He went around to the back of the car. I heard him pop the trunk.

"I've got your back, boss," Kevin said, his voice raised slightly. "So does Bubba."

"I know, and I appreciate it." I glanced over my shoulder, looking through the rear window. My view was blocked by the trunk lid, but I kept looking back there anyway.

"You're still nervous."

"Yep."

"Good. That'll keep you alert. The people they hired to hit you are good—a team from Europe, a man and a woman. They specialize in making things look like medical accidents, using spell-poisons that cause heart attacks, strokes, that sort of thing."

"How do they get needles—" I started, but he cut me off.

"No needles needed. He creates a distraction. She taps the victim in the confusion; she wears a ring equipped with a biodegradable spike that has the curse on it. I'm told it's no more painful than a mosquito bite."

That was appalling, disturbing, and very scary. I mean, seriously, I would never look at a crowd the same way again. "How do you know—"

"Jones called me."

Kevin took Jones's call, but let Dawna go to voice mail? Interesting.

"I'd heard of them back when I was working for the Company. They're top of the line." I couldn't see him, but I could hear the concern in his voice.

"You think I should keep you with me instead?" I asked, scanning the parking lot. No sign of trouble other than an ambulance driving up to the ER, siren wailing and lights flashing. I saw that Bubba was watching it closely; he didn't relax until the EMTs and their patient had gone inside.

"No. Bubba's no good at covert. You need someone who can operate in the background, and that's me. And you need Rahim alive until the ifrit is back in the bottle."

"I do."

I heard him shuffling things around in the trunk, felt the shift of energies when he found the gun carrier and started releasing the protections on it.

Taking a deep breath, I said, "Kev, I . . . I'm in way over my head. The crew from the Needle job are behind this; there's the ifrit; and something demonic showed up during the interview with the Feds."

"I know." His voice was calm. "Dawna briefed me. So did Emma."

Emma Landingham DeLuca, his sister and one of my best buddies, wasn't as powerful a clairvoyant as Dottie, but I'd given her some magical tools that let her make the most of the gift she has.

"What did Emma say?"

I heard the sound of a zipper sliding open, then the sound of a weapon being checked. It's hard to describe if you've never heard it, but the sound is unmistakable. A moment later, Kevin appeared at my open door. In his hands was the Glock he'd promised, along with a box of ammo.

Even though I'd heard him check the gun seconds earlier, I went through the usual routine as well. Partly from habit, but mostly to get a feel for it before sliding the weapon into the empty holster under my jacket. He walked back to the trunk and I listened as he zipped the bag shut and reactivated the spells. He rummaged in the trunk for a few more seconds; then the weight of the car shifted as he lifted something out. There was a slight crunch of loose gravel as he set whatever it was on the ground before slamming the trunk lid.

I waited for him to answer my question.

"I can't tell you anything," he finally said, frowning. "It's too dicey. I might screw things up, make the situation worse."

"It can get *worse?*" My joke had a hint of hysteria around the edges.

Kevin grunted in acknowledgment. "It can *always* get worse. But I've got your back and you'll have Bubba with you. He's a good man. You do whatever you have to and we'll cover you."

"Thanks."

He snorted, saying, "Gotta protect the old paycheck." He added, "We'd better get moving. The clock's ticking."

For a second, I debated whether or not to ask my next question, before deciding that, while it wasn't a particularly diplomatic question, the situation was dire enough that it had to be asked.

"Is this going to be too much for you? What with the PTSD—"

"We're at the full moon. I'll be fine. Stress doesn't bother the wolf in me. It's the human part that has problems."

I'd seen Kevin with his wolf on once—it had been scary as hell, and I'm no cupcake. If he couldn't control his beast, there'd be all sorts of trouble. "And the wolf?"

"He'll be fine too. I've got this, boss. Really."

I heard the conviction in his voice, but I wasn't finished. "Michelle?"

He smiled at the mention of her name, a smile of relief more than fondness. Michelle was the client he'd had to turn wolfy to save. Doing so had made him responsible for mentoring her into her new life. Unfortunately, she'd shown every sign of having a huge crush on Kevin, while he was not at all interested in her in that way.

"Michelle now has enough self-control that I felt able to introduce her to a friend of mine who runs with a secret pack. She's hunting with them this month and with any luck at all, that'll be that."

"There are packs?"

"I mentioned it before. I know I did."

He probably had—maybe in the middle of some battle or other, because I truly didn't remember. I suppose having a pack was a good thing for the shifters, but for me, it was a little frightening to think about. Kevin alone in wolf form was scary. Kevin with Michelle was terrifying. A *pack?* Holy shit! Made me think seriously about locking myself inside, somewhere really secure, during every full moon from now on.

"It's going to be fine." He met my eyes, his expression calm and earnest, and I believed him . . . mostly. And really, there wasn't a damned thing I could do about it. I needed him to do this if I had any hope of success, and the mission was too damned important for us to fail. But it was a huge risk, and one I didn't much like taking.

"I've *got* this," he said again. This time, I heard the barest hint of a growl.

Yeah, it was the full moon all right.

"Fine." I forced myself to smile up at him. "Thanks for the gun."

"Just make sure you live to give it back to me."

Bubba and I decided to take the car from South Bend to O'Hare airport in Chicago. I let him drive. The trip is a little over two hours if you obey the speed limit, and driving rather than flying meant that we could stop to get me fed . . . and I could bounce ideas off Bubba without having to worry about who might be listening from the next seats. Plus, I had access to phone and the Internet. In any case, I wasn't sure that flying would have been any faster, even assuming there was a flight leaving right away and that we could get through ticketing and security at the local airport in record time.

We stopped at a PharMart so I could pick up a few things—a particularly good idea since I was beginning to feel more than a little irritable. I'd been under a lot of stress, had recently been in a fight that brought the vamp in me to the surface, and it was getting on toward sunset. This was not a good combination. I thought about having Bubba go shopping for me, but it would have taken longer to tell him what I needed than to take care of it myself.

The guy behind the cash register was in his early twenties, with dark brown hair that curled over the collar of his white uniform polo and eyes that were just a little bit lighter shade of blue than his vest. I tried to smile at him as I grabbed a cart and ducked down the nearest aisle. I didn't feel like smiling. Not in the least.

I found an inexpensive bag in aisle four I could use to replace the duffel Dawna had sent me. Unfortunately, the lovely new clothes Dawna had provided, along with the bag, were in Rahim's car, as was my original suitcase.

So I needed to start from nothing. I grabbed sunscreen, toiletries, socks, a six-pack of cheap cotton underwear, and a pair of T-shirts. Yeah, they'd look a little weird with the dress pants and jacket, but at least they'd be clean. After a moment's thought, I grabbed a pair of sweatpants as well. For all I knew, something would happen to what was I was wearing and I'd be out of clothes again.

Down another aisle, I loaded up on nutrition shakes and baby food.

I told myself to relax, but I couldn't seem to manage it. This case was getting to me in a big way. And there was a real chance that it would all be for nothing. After all, whether the Patels would pay the bill without a fight, now that they'd tried to kill me and I'd quit, was anybody's guess. Assuming Hasan could be returned to his jar and one of the Patels survived.

The light in the store was beginning to hurt my eyes, and I could now hear the throbbing pulse of the woman standing in front of me in the checkout line. She was older, maybe seventy. Slow enough that she'd be easy prey.

I shuddered at the realization that my vampire nature was starting to rise to the hunt.

No. Absolutely not.

Closing my eyes, I took deep, slow breaths while counting to one hundred. When I heard movement I opened my eyes long enough to shuffle forward with the group. Two more people in front of me. I could make it. Just a couple more minutes.

A teenager finished buying condoms. It was the old woman's turn.

She had coupons—expired coupons—and was counting up change to make the price, in *pennies*.

I found myself growling in irritation. That startled and frightened both the woman and the checker. I could hear their breathing go shallow, their pulses quickening.

Saliva filled my mouth. I was so *hungry*. I took a deep breath: in, three count, out. Slowly. Then I grabbed the biggest, gaudiest holy item from the display at the checkout. *See folks, no vampires here. I'm just a little ol' human with a pale complexion. Nothing to worry about.* I'd have forced a smile, but I could tell my fangs were down.

My clutching the giant holy object settled the two of them a little, but not much. Nobody tried to stake me or spray me with holy water, but they sure as hell didn't dawdle.

Finally the old woman paid. The checker sped me through the process and I swiped my card, grabbed my bag, and strode briskly to the exit. As I stepped through the sliding glass doors, the sunset hit me like a club. My inner bat tried to rise full out, teeth down, skin glowing, eyes shifting to hyperfocus. My own pulse raced as I smelled sweet fear drifting toward me on the light breeze. The old woman was trying not to stare at me as she loaded her purchases into the back of a battered midsized sedan a row or two away. I could still get her. Easy.

The window of a nearby car rolled partly down.

"Boss . . . *Celia.*"

I turned at the sound of my name and saw a familiar face, lined deeply with worry.

Bubba. It was Bubba, and he was my friend. He was not food. People were not *food*.

The sight of Bubba's concern brought me to myself a little: enough that I could reach into one of the bags looped over my wrist. I pulled out one of the little glass jars of baby food and twisted off the cap without even trying to read what I'd be eating. Anything would help, and I wouldn't have really seen it anyway. I was crying.

That, more than the pureed peaches I was swallowing, drove the bat off. Emotions disgust and confuse the vampire. It has about as much understanding of friendship as I do of nuclear physics, and to it, pain is something to be dealt, not endured.

When I could trust myself, I walked over to the rental car. The glow of my skin had faded enough that I looked almost normal—normal enough that Bubba was willing to unlock the doors and let me climb in with him.

He drove off as I strapped myself in—and just in time, too. Someone had called the cops. They passed us going down the main drag, lights flashing, but sans siren.

"You okay?" Bubba asked.

I didn't look at him. I didn't dare. Instead, I focused completely on the food I'd bought.

"Yeah, I'm jusssst ducky," I lied. I *so* wasn't. But that didn't matter. Life wasn't going to stop to give me time for a little breakdown. So I needed to suck it up . . . change that . . . pull myself together. "I jussst need to eat, maybe take a quick nap. It's been a long day." I was still lisping around my fangs—not good.

"I get that. Eat. Sleep. I've got GPS, I can get us there."

"Fine," I said as I dug a chocolate nutrition shake out of one of the PharMart bags and chugged it. Then I took a swig of liquid vitamins, followed by a jar of pureed turkey and yams. Only when I was full enough to relax did I glance at him. "Thanks, Bubba." No hint of a lisp that time. Yippee.

"*De nada*. Now sleep."

"Okay, but wake me up in an hour. I need to make some calls." I closed my eyes and let the movement of the car and the sounds of the road lull me to slumber.

I dreamed of angels and demons.

Seriously.

I was floating in the vacuum of space, the universe stretched out before me in a shimmering carpet, colorful jewels scattered on midnight velvet. I knew there were other universes, but I couldn't see them. My whole attention was caught by the scene before me. Michael the archangel was battling a demon in the form of a bat-winged, multi-headed serpent. Its claws raked at his armor; his blows rained down on its scaly hide. With each sweep of the creature's tail stars were swept from the sky; the wind from his wings sent meteors sailing off into space.

It was breathtaking and awe-inspiring. The sheer breadth of the titanic battle was almost impossible to fathom, spanning, as it did, not just three dimensions, but five or more. For they fought in more than the three dimensions of normal reality: on the ethereal plane, and through time.

Far, far in the distance I glimpsed a familiar configuration of planets. Our solar system was tiny, and just one of an uncountable number of habitable systems.

It felt like maybe ten seconds later that I heard Bubba say my name.

"Celia. Celia." A strong hand shook my shoulder. I blinked stupidly up at Bubba, trying to gather my wits.

"Time to get up, boss."

I clung to the remnants of the dream. It was important. I knew it. But why?

"Right." I swallowed a little convulsively. My mouth was dry. I'd probably been snoring. Glancing at the read-out on the dash I saw that I'd slept longer than an hour, closer to two. Looking around, I saw that we were in one of the big truck stops on the highway near O'Hare. It was a busy place, well lit, and close enough to the road that I could hear the traffic whooshing past. "You were supposed to wake me in an hour," I scolded him.

"You needed your rest. It's harder for you to control your vamp side when you're tired."

I couldn't argue with that, so I didn't bother trying. "I'm going inside to use the bathroom, change, and get a soda. You want anything?"

"Yeah, grab me some black coffee," he answered.

"Got it." I rummaged around on the floorboards until I found the bags I wanted, then climbed out of the car and shambled across the lot and through the glass doors marked with tape that showed feet and inches. I kept my mouth shut and made sure the holy items I wore were really, really obvious. There was no point in inviting trouble.

The bathroom was in the back of the store. I used the facilities, then changed into clean underwear, socks, and a new T-shirt before pulling my suit pants and jacket back on. That done, I took a minute or two to wash my face in the sink. I looked bad. My hair was a wreck, and the makeup I'd started the day with was long gone, leaving me looking vampire white.

Glancing down at my watch I saw that time was flying by, despite the fact that I was so not having fun. And I still needed a better plan than just walking into the cavern and letting Hasan take me over. I'd slept through a good chunk of research and planning time. But I hadn't been in any shape to think or plan, not with my bat attempting to take over.

Drying off, I took a minute to brush my teeth and comb my hair. I hadn't thought to buy makeup at PharMart, so I went without.

By the time I was finished, I looked better; not good, but better.

I went back into the main part of the store and grabbed coffee for Bubba and soda for myself before getting in line at the checkout. Attached to the ceiling above the Lotto machine was a pair of black-and-white monitors that displayed a patchwork of images from the various security cameras around the truck stop.

One display showed the perimeter of the parking lot. If I'd

blinked, I would have missed the blur of motion caused by a pair of dark figures moving at vampire speed. They hadn't crossed onto the property. Yet. And they might not, if the magical perimeter around the edge still had enough charge. If it didn't . . .

Bubba, keep an eye out. There are bats just outside the perimeter.

The man in front of me took his change from the clerk and shambled out to a waiting truck with his six-pack of Bud and pack of cigarettes.

I moved up to pay. "Is the charge on your perimeter still good?"

The clerk blinked at me a little stupidly. He was in his late fifties, gray hair, gray eyes, and gray skin. He looked tired, like he'd been on shift for a while. He also might not have been the brightest bulb in the display.

"Our perimeter is checked regularly. Why?"

Checked is not the same thing as charged, but most civilians don't realize the difference.

"I thought I saw vampires moving around outside."

"You must have been mistaken." He sounded bored or tired, maybe both. "We're only five minutes away from O'Hare. This close to the airport we're under regular patrol."

I damned well hadn't been mistaken, but I didn't want to argue. And if he was telling the truth about the patrol, the police would be here shortly to take care of it. So I paid for my drinks and headed for the car, first making a short detour to make sure that there was enough charge in the perimeter to last the night. Just in case.

"Did you see them?" I passed Bubba his coffee before taking my seat and fastening my safety belt.

"Nope. But I decided to stay in the car just in case." He glanced at the clock. "We made good time getting here. You've got time to make your calls." He passed me his cell phone, fully charged.

I pondered for a whole minute who to call first. The dream was still bothering me. My subconscious was trying to tell me something. But what?

When in doubt, call an expert. I dialed El Jefe's number from memory. He answered on the first ring.

"Hi. It's me."

"Hello, Celia. How can I help?"

"You know what's going on?"

"Dawna and Kevin both called and brought me up to speed."

Good. I didn't have to brief him from scratch. And he'd gotten the warning. Yay. Here's hoping everybody else had too.

"What do demons want?"

There was a long pause. Apparently my question wasn't one he'd been expecting.

"Angels and demons have been at war since the beginning of time, if not before."

"Right. And our planet is just one of God knows how many inhabitable planets in countless solar systems."

"Yes."

"So, why our planet? What do we matter? I mean, it matters to us. We live here. But what difference does it make to them?

There have been prophets, and a messiah, and angels and demons fight here all the time. Why?"

"I don't know. Why do you ask?"

"I'm pretty sure there's a major demon behind the theft of the ifrit. I need to know what he wants. I feel like we're missing something. I'm flailing around here and I need more information. What could an ifrit do that a demon can't?"

Demons are hideously powerful, plus they have the ability to influence and corrupt humans. Those powers combined gave them seemingly unlimited possibilities for mayhem. So why would they need an ifrit?

Warren was silent on the other end of the phone. I could sense that he was pondering my questions.

I continued, "It all fits together. All of it: the attack at the Needle, the one at the Zoo. And this."

Warren knew what I was referring to. The Zoo had been a prison for magical beings, werewolves mostly, although a few other things had been housed there. The place had become infested with demons. I'd had to rescue Kevin from there, and it was his time there, more than his work with the Company or any other trauma, that had caused his PTSD.

When Warren finally spoke, his voice sounded tentative, like he was still thinking his way through everything. "There were demons at the battles at the node. And there was a demon rift at the Zoo. And there's a demon here. It does seem like it should all tie together.

"But I don't know how."

Well, hell. I tried to stifle my disappointment. After all,

Warren is only human. And now that I'd brought it up, I knew he'd keep working at it. That was his nature. He *hated* unanswered questions . . . and he had access to some of the greatest minds in the world.

"Next question," I said.

"Shoot."

"How can a demon appear in a place if it hasn't been summoned?"

"A singularity would have to be formed."

I muttered under my breath, something to the effect of, "Why the hell don't they teach you these things when you're getting your degree?" I didn't expect him to answer, but he did.

"There's only so much time, Celia, and it's important to cover the basics. Rarities and more esoteric items are hardly likely to be encountered by your average student.

"If a demon has been summoned enough times, it is very nearly able to make a permanent manifestation; and *if* it is being summoned at the precise moment that a soul is being taken into hell, a soul that that particular demon has had personal interactions with, there is an infinitesimal chance that that individual demon can take advantage of the opening. *If* he is aware of it and moves quickly enough. Although, frankly, since they can alter time, I suppose the latter is relative. I take it you ran into one?"

"Started to. We sealed the opening with holy water before he could get through."

"That's my girl," he said with an audible smile in his voice. "I'm very proud of you, Celia."

."Thanks." Warren doesn't give praise often. It meant a lot to me to hear it.

"Any more questions?"

"Just two. First, why would an ifrit need the use of a physical body for more than the couple of minutes they get by possessing a corpse?"

"Is that what he wants? Your body?" Warren did his best to sound professional and not alarmed, and failed miserably. I mean, normally he is a baritone and his voice does not squeak like Mickey Mouse's.

"Appears to be."

"Oh, Celia."

"Any ideas?"

"No, but we'll look into it. What was your second question?"

"I thought you needed to be a really talented mage to handle node magic."

"You should. Yes."

"Matty isn't ranked that high."

"No," Warren admitted, "he isn't. Which was why the church gave him dispensation to marry Emma. They, and he, fully expected that he would die that night."

"Why didn't he?"

"I only have a theory."

"Give it to me."

"He's related by blood to Isabella and Bruno. They both have power to spare. I can't be sure, but I'm betting that his mother used her control of the magic to protect her sons, taking more of the burden onto herself. That would explain why she's suffered such severe ill effects, even though she'd worked node magic previously without any problem."

That pretty much confirmed my own suspicions. Isabella would do anything to protect her Bruno and Matty. I wondered if they knew, or guessed, what she'd done. She'd never tell them, but they're both smart men.

"Any other questions about the ifrit?"

"Gordon briefed my team earlier. Is there anything he didn't tell us?"

Warren chuckled. "Just that we figured out that the Guardians are the only ones capable of trapping and disarming an ifrit—because they have djinn ancestors in their bloodlines."

Ah, that explained a lot of things that I'd noticed about Rahim, and Abha's comment as well.

"Look, Hasan threatened to slaughter everyone I care about. You need to get to safety. I don't want anything to happen to you." My voice cracked a little when I said that last.

"Oh, Celia." Warren's voice softened. "Be careful. When you get back and this is all over, we'll go to dinner at La Cocina. My treat."

"I'd like that." My voice was a little raspy, the scenery outside the car window a blur. In the driver's seat, Bubba was shaking his head in wry amusement. Apparently big, tough, bodyguard types aren't supposed to get all mushy in the clutch. "I gotta go. Bye."

"Bye."

I tucked the phone into a little cubbyhole in the dashboard and sat back, closing my eyes.

"You are such a wuss," Bubba teased.

He was trying to cheer me up with humor. It worked. I found myself smiling in spite of myself. I mean, yeah, he was managing me, but he knew me well enough that he was doing a good job of it. "Oh, bite me."

He laughed and started the car.

The bad guys were trying to kill me. The Patels wanted me dead to the point of hiring assassins. The ifrit wanted to possess me. Oh, and there was a demon who wanted me dead, so another demon could torment me for eternity.

I've been in tough places more than once. But this was looking worse than anything I'd seen in a while. I was scared, and coming up blank as to how to stop the all-powerful and seriously evil genie from destroying everyone and everything I loved.

So I spent about a minute and a half (which was all the time I could afford) throwing myself a nice little pity party while Bubba took us back onto the highway and then off at the O'Hare exit. Then I took a deep, steadying breath and focused my mind on the image of Rahim Patel.

Hello, Rahim.

Celia. His mental voice was cautious and he didn't sound thrilled to be hearing from me. No big surprise there. Hell, if I had any choice, he'd be one of the last two people I contacted. But beggars, choosers, and all that happy crap.

Can Hasan hear this conversation? I'm wearing a sujay.

He didn't say anything for a few seconds, but his thoughts had a distinctly sour tone.

No. Bitterness there. Lots of it.

Good. Did you absorb enough energy from the vosta to get back on your feet?

How did you know—

I hadn't known, I'd guessed, though his reaction confirmed it. If he was the Guardian and had djinn blood, it would make sense that he might be able to absorb magic like a djinn—magic that would enhance his healing abilities, much like my vampire nature improved mine. A Mrs. Patel had bought a very powerful vosta from the DeLuca's for a life-or-death matter. It could have been someone else. But my bet had been Abha. She had, after all, said she planned to "revive" Rahim, although she hadn't mentioned how. No doubt she'd given the vosta to her husband, who could use its power to heal himself.

There was an angry pause in Rahim's thoughts; then, *My wife talks too much.*

Your wife is why you're not going to jail for the rest of your life at a place like the Needle. I'd cut her a little slack if I were you. Besides, I got my information about your bloodline from another source.

What source?

None of your business.

Mental silence. Finally, he spoke again. *I am fully recovered.*

Good. I am on my way to the caves in southern Colorado. I have a plan, but I need your cooperation. Actually, I didn't have a plan. It was more of a wild, Hail Mary sort of idea that was coming together in my mind even as we spoke. Rahim didn't need to know that. I needed him to think that I knew what I was doing so that he'd follow my lead. Maybe. I hoped.

Tell me.

I heard there's been a falling out between you and your grandfather?

Wow, that opened up a can of mental worms. Shame, rage, humiliation, and the memory of some really harsh insults Pradeep had heaped on his grandson washed over me in a mental tidal wave.

Yes. He thinks me incapable of recapturing Hasan. He has summoned Tarik to Florida. They will attempt a ceremony as soon as he arrives.

Good. We can use that.

We? He sounded incredulous.

Look, do you want to get the bad genie back in the bottle or what?

Okay, not a smart move on my part. You don't goad a man who has already tried to kill you. Black rage left him wordless for a long moment. I waited it out. When he finally had himself under control, his mental words were cold and clipped.

Tell me your plan.

21

I'm not a big fan of airports in general. I suppose as airports go, particularly the big international ones, O'Hare is as good as any. It's mostly metal and glass with brightly colored lights—and of course the ever-present banks of screens showing arrivals and departures. It's pretty, in a sterile, impersonal way, but it's clean, well organized, and remarkably well run for being such a huge enterprise.

We returned the car to the rental company and hopped on the shuttle, which dropped us directly in front of the doors marked for United. The lines for ticketing and check-in were long, but we had no choice but to join them. Directly in front of us was a group of college-age men wearing hockey gear proudly emblazoned with DU PIONEERS in bold gold lettering, along with the University of Denver seal and a cute cartoon character. They were boisterous in a way that made me think they were heading home from a win on the road.

Most of them were big guys, and a couple were large enough to make Bubba look positively petite. They carried luggage and skate bags, and more than one had a hockey stick poking out from a nylon duffel bag. Whenever our eyes met, they grinned, and one winked. But they were refreshingly polite.

Eventually it was my turn to go to the counter and check the bags. Bubba had bought us tickets online while I'd been in the rest stop, but we still had to declare our weapons, which can be a real bitch of a process. There are so damned many rules. The questionnaire alone runs six pages: List your name, address, and carry permit number; state how many of what weapon is in each bag; cite what ammunition you have for each weapon; guarantee that it is in a separate bag from the gun it fits; give the number of spell disks and/or spell balls you are carrying; describe what each does and what kind of containment packaging each spell is in.

Back in the office I keep a file full of photocopies of completed forms that I can take with me when I travel. I just cross out whatever I don't have with me at the time. I suppose I could've asked Dawna to send me a copy electronically—if I had gotten a chance to unpack them, or had a freaking clue as to which box they might be in, or a way to print them out on my end. I didn't.

So, I wrote as fast as I could, but it was taking precious time. I watched the hands of the clock above the counter racing forward as I heard the relentless ticking of the seconds counting off in my head.

Our regular weapons were bother enough. But my knives? As major magical artifacts, they got their own declaration pages—and had to be packed into special, airline-provided, locked-and-sealed packaging that could only be opened by my bio-readings and thumbprint. Setting that up took more time. The hockey players, who were halfway through the line to security just a few yards away, were staring openly. I suppose it was quite a show.

The people behind me in line were angry and growing angrier. Somebody like me slows the whole process down and puts other people at risk of missing their flights. Of course, that's why the airlines tell you to get to the airport at least two hours in advance—although almost nobody ever actually does.

"Do you have any actual luggage, Ms. Graves?" The uniformed attendant smiled at me when she spoke, but in addition to the note of real curiosity in her voice, there was more than a little hostility. A quick glance showed me that, nope, she wasn't wearing an anti-siren charm. Great. She might make my life more hellish just for grins because of that lack of protection. Women often felt anger in the presence of a siren, even if the siren wasn't using her powers.

"Just carry-on." I gestured to my brand-new bag. "It's a short business trip. I left in a hurry. I figure I'll do some shopping in Denver."

"Not in so much of a hurry that you couldn't pack an arsenal." Her tone was ever-so-polite spread thinly over downright bitchy.

"It's a *business* trip. My *business* is personal protection. Weapons are necessary. Extra clothing is a luxury." I smiled so hard it made my face hurt, making damned sure that not even the tiniest hint of fang showed. Because this woman—like anyone working an airline check-in desk—can refuse a ticket to any passenger they deem threatening and even have them detained by security in the interests of national security. So I would be nice, even if it made my blood boil and my face ache from smiling. I didn't have time for this. I really didn't. But there wasn't anything I could do about it other than be as pleasant and non-threatening as I knew how to be.

Bubba was standing a little behind me and to my left, keeping an eye out for trouble. Very quietly he said, "Chill, boss. You're starting to glow."

Oh, hell. Glowing was bad: very vampity; not at all non-threatening. Even without showing fangs, glowing could get us in trouble.

I closed my eyes, picturing sandy beaches, warm sun, the sounds of waves lapping the sand, the occasional call of a gull. My pulse slowed; I felt calm roll over me. Right up until Bubba grabbed my arm.

"Um, boss? You might want to lay off the ocean sounds."

I opened my eyes. "What the . . . ?" Sure enough, the exact sounds I'd been using to calm myself were now being projected through every speaker in the airport. *Every* speaker, including individuals' iPods and headphones. At least I assumed it was all of them. I could certainly overhear it from the headset of the guy in the next line over.

I'd only ever done anything like that once before—when I had first awakened my siren powers. Apparently I was more stressed than I'd admitted to myself. I might have regained control of the vamp side of my nature, but it was costing me on the siren side. Shit, shit, shit.

I turned to the attendant, whose male supervisor was now

standing right behind her, providing the same support for her that Bubba was for me. The senior attendant's expression was one of concern, but Halle-fricking-lujah, he was wearing an anti-siren charm around his neck.

Fleetingly I wondered if he'd taken the time to hunt one up or if supervisors at every airport were required to wear them, then said a silent prayer of thanks that he had arrived and was protected. Smiling again, I bobbed my head as a sign of apology and said, "Sorry about that. It's been a rough couple of days. Stressful job."

"No problem," he said firmly but without heat. "Identification, please."

I handed it over. At her boss's touch on her shoulder, the original attendant stepped aside. He reviewed my paperwork and licenses very carefully before finally stamping them approved and printing out our tickets.

"Have a safe flight." He handed the paperwork to Bubba. Not to me. I noticed that, but decided not to make a fuss. It so wasn't worth it.

"We'll do our best," I assured him.

"Do that," he said, then called for the next passenger, dismissing us.

Bubba handed me the papers as we joined the line for security, which was long, but moved pretty swiftly. I made it through the scanner without incident, but was treated to an extra bout with the wand. All the while I kept my breathing steady, reminding myself that this was just part of the process. No big deal. *Calm: I am calm.*

As they cleared me, I heard the boarding announcement

for our flight. Bubba and I looked at each other, grabbed our shoes and bags from the conveyor, and dashed barefoot through the concourse, shoes clutched in one hand and bags banging against our legs. We made it to the boarding area, breathless and annoyed, just as the gate attendants were making the last call.

We hustled down the gangway and onto the plane. The flight attendants had already closed most of the overhead bins and were rearranging items in the rest. I could hear the pilots running through their preflight routine behind the cabin door.

Because we'd gotten our tickets late, there were only two seats available on the flight. I wound up close to the back, in a center seat, between two of the biggest men I'd ever laid eyes on in my life.

Derek had dark hair and eyes, his handsome face made roguish by the fact that his nose had been broken at least once. Bobby was a freckled redhead with a merry grin and sparkling green eyes that made him look younger than the twenty-one he swore he was. They were defensemen for the hockey team, and while I was able to squeeze into my seat, I felt like a cork stuck in a bottle. It had to be worse for Bubba, who was in similar straits two rows behind me.

I managed to shove my carry-on under the seat in front of me and strapped in. Not that the seat belt would be necessary. I was sufficiently trapped in my seat by my seatmates that I wouldn't be going anywhere, even in the event of a crash.

The flight was awkward and uncomfortable, but could

have been much worse. Derek and Bobby were good company. They plied me with liquor, each buying me a screwdriver, then kept me laughing with stories about their road-trip adventures. I knew enough about hockey that I wasn't completely ignorant of the game that was their abiding passion, which pleased them to no end. When Derek went to the bathroom, Bobby confided in me that there was a good chance "D" would be joining the NHL next draft day. All in all, the flight passed quickly, and I only caught myself checking my watch twice.

Even so, I was glad when the plane taxied up to the gate. I checked my watch, calculating flight times and drive times. I was going to be cutting it close on my end. I hoped Rahim could deliver the way he'd said he could, but I had no control over that, so I forced thoughts of him out of my mind.

Since we were seated near the back, both Bubba and I were caught up in the usual bustle of disembarking as the rear passengers moved around, bumping into each other and pulling down their luggage while they waited for those seated in front to disembark.

The assassination attempt was so subtle I missed it, should've been dead where I stood despite Kevin's warning. Everybody was distracted. A loud dispute broke out in first class. A tall, gray-haired man in an expensive black suit was arguing viciously with another passenger. People close by were trying to get clear of them and make enough space for the flight attendants to intervene. Some passengers farther away stopped in their tracks to watch.

While that was happening, a petite blond woman in an

off-the-rack navy suit was struggling to pull her bag from the overhead bin after having refused offers of help from both Derek and one of his teammates. She stumbled backward and would've fallen right into me if Bobby, with the reflexes of a trained athlete, hadn't moved between us to catch her.

He caught the injection meant for me.

Bobby fell into the space between the seats, taking me down with him. I was pinned, immobilized by his dead weight and from being jammed into such a small area. The bat in me made me plenty strong, but I had no leverage. I shouted for help, trying to push Bobby off me.

He was gasping for air like a landed fish, and I could hear his heart stutter, then stop. The blond started screaming hysterically and an attendant rushed back, shoving his way through the crowded aisle, pushing the still-screaming woman out of the way—and closer to the door. I saw a man help her off the plane as she pretended to sob in his arms, but I was in no position to stop them and nobody seemed inclined to listen to me, though I was shouting for someone to stop her.

They pulled Bobby off me and into the aisle. The team trainer and a doctor who'd been a passenger began doing CPR. Emergency personnel arrived quickly, walking into a crowded plane that had fallen eerily silent except for the harsh breathing of the men struggling to revive Bobby. As the EMTs moved to set up a stretcher, I stared at the dead man who had just unwittingly saved my life.

22

Emergency personnel wheeled Bobby out on a stretcher, an oxygen mask on his face. His heart had been restarted, but its rhythm was unsteady, and I worried that he wouldn't make it. Derek, stunned and scared, sank back into the nearest seat; other players gathered in the rows around him, silent and solemn. Someone, maybe the coach, led them in a prayer, and I prayed right along with them. So did most of the other passengers who were still on board.

I was scared for Bobby. I was also just flat scared. I kept looking at my watch and shifting nervously in my seat as the minutes ticked relentlessly by.

The people who'd been seated in the front half of the plane were long gone—along with the blond who'd actually done the deed. But those of us who'd been in the back were considered witnesses and were being held for questioning by a group of four TSA agents.

If I kept my mouth shut, what had happened would be considered a medical emergency, not attempted murder. The

TSA cops would let us go more quickly—and time was of the essence. But they also wouldn't know to test Bobby for the poison curse, wouldn't have the chance to find the right antidote or counterspell in time to save his life.

He seemed like a good guy. I didn't want him to die.

I also didn't want my gran or anybody else to.

I wasn't the only one checking my watch. Nobody was actually complaining, and for the most part the passengers were as cooperative and helpful as could be. Oh, there were a few people making calls on their cell phones, letting others know they were delayed, and one or two were frantically trying to rearrange flights. Most people had been shaken by what they'd witnessed, and sat quietly and respectfully, waiting in relative patience to be questioned.

As I checked the countdown on my watch for probably the twenty or thirtieth time, a female officer came to question me.

She wasn't wearing an anti-siren charm. I forced myself not to sigh. Without the charm, she'd have an instant, irrational antipathy toward me. Women are jealous of sirens and react badly to them. Unless they're gay. That hope dimmed when I saw the very elaborate wedding band on the officer's left hand, and the "World's Best Mom" necklace around her neck. Oh, she could have been part of a same-sex couple, but the odds weren't in my favor. And when she looked down at me through narrowed eyes, I knew I was in trouble.

"So, *princess*," she practically spat out the word, "tell me what you *think* you saw."

Before I could answer, a stout brunette in the TSA's standard blue blazer and gray dress slacks rushed breathlessly through the gangway door and down the aisle, and everyone turned to watch her approach. I was glad of the interruption—I wasn't at my best and whatever I was about to say would have been completely misunderstood by the TSA agent. The newcomer was carrying five or so anti-siren charms. Their chains glittered in the artificial light, the bits of hair in the various colors of the sirens who'd donated them shining brightly. Even from this distance I could feel the magic coming off them.

Thank you, Jesus. I'm not normally religious, but I meant it. Tension was singing through me as I felt time passing and knew that I was going to have to drive like a lunatic to have any hope of making my meeting. I was terrified of what was going to happen once I got there, too, but that was a terror I was familiar with. I'd fought the big bad before, and knowing my luck, I'd probably do it again, if I survived Hasan. It was the thought that I might cause the deaths of innumerable people, including people I loved, through no fault of my own, because of obstacles placed in my way by others, or because I just wasn't fast enough—that was hideous and wrong and terrifying. I looked at my watch again. *Come on. Come on!*

"They were locked in the magical supplies closet. Good thing the folks from Chicago called to give us a heads-up." The TSA agent handed charms to her fellow officers as she moved through the plane. "Here you go, Lang." She offered a necklace to the woman interviewing me, who was visibly reluctant to take it. "You know the rules."

Lang almost growled, grabbing irritably at the inoffensive

bit of jewelry. The instant her skin touched the metal, the expression on her face changed dramatically: barely controlled anger simply melted away, revealing shock and surprise. She turned to me, eyes a little bit too wide. Swallowing hard, her face lightly flushed with embarrassment, she coughed and said, "Now, where were we?"

"You wanted to know what I know." I put on my best fake smile and put a lilt into my voice. Anything, anything to make this interview go faster.

"Right."

I didn't tell. I felt like absolute dog crap about it, but time was flying by and I was on the clock. I was hustling through the gate area with Bubba just ahead of me when an idea hit me. Concentrating, I contacted Dawna telepathically, asking her to get a prepaid phone and call in an anonymous tip. It wasn't much, and for all I knew, no one would follow up. But it was better than doing nothing.

Actually, it was worse. Because I didn't know the TSA somehow monitored telepathic communications in the airport.

I'd barely gone another twenty feet when I was surrounded by TSA types. Smart man that he was, Bubba ducked into the nearest waiting area, taking a seat as if he were waiting for flight.

"Ms. Graves, if you'll come with us, please." Lang said it nicely, she really did: probably because she was still a little embarrassed about her earlier antipathy. Even so, it wasn't a request and we both knew it. Not with the entire group of officers surrounding me, staying close, but not too close.

I've always envied people who get to ride on those little golf-carty things through busy airports. No, I don't want a disability, but man, those things can move when the driver's in a hurry. Today I got my chance. They drove me through the concourse, then, to my surprise, out onto the tarmac via a set of doors that had been hidden by illusion. Then we sped across the asphalt, dodging a couple of planes on the way, to a similar door in the main part of the terminal.

Between the wards and the illusion spells on both sets of doors I was in quite a bit of discomfort—and that was before I was escorted to an interrogation room. The TSA, NSA, and whoever else had had a hand in planning the building had spared no expense in making sure any prisoner would remain secure. Crossing the threshold into the interview room made my knees wobble and brought tears to my eyes. I had to steady myself on the table and almost fell into the chair.

The door shut firmly behind me, the lock sliding into place with an audible scrape of metal and a loud click.

God, I hated this case. This was the *third* time in as many days that I was being held for questioning—a new record, even for me. Not to mention that I didn't have the time for this, or the inclination.

My new accommodation was an interior room with no windows, plain white walls, an acoustical tile ceiling, and industrial-grade, gray carpeting. A simple metal table was bolted to the floor, and the chair I was sitting on was one of those black molded plastic things with metal legs that aren't really comfortable, but aren't uncomfortable enough for anyone to bitch about. The chair was bolted down, too, just far enough from the table to make it uncomfortable for a seated person—assuming they weren't in the NBA (or maybe on the Pioneer hockey team) to rest their arms or head on the table's surface. The only decoration on the wall, if you could call it that, was a clock. Black hands relentlessly circled the white face as precious time ticked away.

Even the air was empty, with that stale, canned quality that comes from having been recycled and purified until there's no trace of any scent or life in it.

In the course of the past few years, I've spent more time than I'd like to think about sitting in rooms not too different from this one, either waiting for, or enduring, an interrogation. It's enough to make you think. And weirdly, a room like this can actually make you start to feel guilty, even when you haven't done a damned thing wrong. Yes, that's a psychological trick used in questioning suspects. But the authorities use it because it works.

Right now I had no doubt in my mind that I looked guilty as hell. I was squirming in my seat, checking my watch and the damned clock repeatedly and wishing I hadn't had that second screwdriver.

Dammit, dammit, dammit. I do not *have time for this right now. If they heard the warning to Dawna they have to have heard her comment about the ifrit and the deadline. If they run a check on me—*

If they ran a check on me they'd get so damned much information at this point it might take them a week to wade through it. *Dammit, dammit, dammit.*

The one small plus I had going for me was that I wasn't feeling vampity. But I really needed to get to a bathroom sooner rather than later—another thing an interrogator would use to their advantage.

I checked my watch again. If I left this room right now, and got to a place where I could safely use my siren call, I could try to reach the ifrit that way. Maybe, if I talked fast enough, I could put a pin in what he had planned for humanity. Probably not. But, I had to try. I remembered watching the oil rig go up in flame, the people scurrying like ants, trying to escape a hideous death.

Sure, it could have been an illusion, something the ifrit conjured up to scare me. But it had felt real. And I'd felt Hasan's dark glee at causing pain and damage. That hadn't been my imagination. I'm not that creative.

Screw it. Trouble with the law was bad—but it was nothing compared to the kind of pure evil the ifrit was capable of. Rising to my feet, I was just about to stride over to the door when it opened. The man who entered was short, five five or five six at the most, with sandy blond hair cut very short, and watery blue eyes. He wasn't handsome, wasn't ugly, wasn't really much of anything at all—you'd never notice him in a crowd.

Instead of a TSA uniform, he wore a low-end, off-the-rack navy blue suit that was too big at the waist. The sleeves of the pants and the arms of the jacket needed to be hemmed. His shirt was white, with narrow red and navy stripes, and his tie was the same color as his suit. I didn't see any weapons on him, and didn't feel the kind of spells that would conceal them either. He was wearing an anti-siren charm and there was a radio attached to his belt.

The plain black-and-white plastic name tag read Ned Turner. It had no other identifying information or organization logo. Turner tossed the manila folder he was holding onto the table and pulled out a chair that had been hidden behind illusion until he touched it. Made me wonder who and what else might be hiding in plain sight.

"Were you planning on going somewhere?" He waved me back to the chair intended for me but I didn't move. He didn't sit either, just with his hand on the chair back, willing me to cooperate.

So not going to happen. "I need to find a bathroom. And I need to get out of here. I'm going to be late for a meeting." I tried to keep the panic from my voice and failed.

One look at the expression on his face told me that Turner had no intention of letting me go any time soon. "A meeting." He gave a snort of laughter. "Yeah, you'll be late all right."

"You can't hold me forever without charging me, and I've done nothing wrong." I crossed to the door and put my hand on the knob. "If you want to escort me to the john, feel free. But I am leaving this room."

"You don't think attempted murder is wrong?"

He'd said attempted. Bobby was alive. Thank God! I liked him. I would've felt horrible if he'd died in my place. I still felt guilty. Not that I'd show that to Turner—not a chance. I kept my voice neutral as I answered. "Not me. Didn't do it. I was the intended victim. The perp was a blond woman, maybe five two. She was wearing a cheap blue suit, glasses, and had her hair in a bun when she left the plane. But she probably lost the jacket and glasses and let down her hair by the time she was more than a few steps into the concourse. You probably can track her using your surveillance software."

I tried to turn the knob. It was locked, and probably spelled. But the lock itself was just an ordinary bolt and I couldn't feel the spells, so they probably weren't too intense. I took a deep breath and concentrated, the way you do before you try to break boards for the first time in martial arts class.

Behind me, Turner said, "You're not going anywhere. And I'm not interested in some other woman. I'm talking about how you saved yourself by pushing an innocent man in front of you."

Gathering every bit of strength I had, I slammed into the door with everything I had. The lock didn't give. The door did. I popped out into a narrow, anonymous hall with Turner at my heels.

He hit me in a tackle like a linebacker, smashing me into the far wall with an impact that gave me whiplash and rattled my teeth. I rolled, threw him off, and struggled to my feet as three other agents boiled into the hallway.

Time ran out.

Hasan's voice was everywhere, filling the air. Its power translated into actual pressure, pushing against every inch of exposed skin, and a hot wind that blew even indoors. It wasn't just in my mind, either—everyone could hear it.

"*You are not here. You are not dead, but I cannot see you. Where are you, Celia Graves?*"

Turner's eyes widened until the whites showed all around the irises. He swallowed hard. The other agents froze, looking around in almost comical panic.

I grasped the *sujay* at my neck. With a sharp yank, I pulled it off, then shoved it into my pocket.

"I'm here," I shouted. "I'm doing my best. I was on my way to you when somebody tried to kill me. I'm still trying to get to the temple." The air was so filled with magic, it felt like it was burning my lungs. Hell, maybe it was. The exposed skin of the agents in the hall with me was reddening as if from a sun- or windburn.

There was a nanosecond's pause. Then, "*DO BETTER.*"

Those words were followed by a roar of sound like nothing I'd ever heard before. Like a jet engine up close, but much worse and much louder. The walls of the terminal began to vibrate, then shudder, before peeling away with a scream of protesting metal. The air pressure changed and my ears popped. Thirty seconds, maybe less: that's how long it took Hasan to tear apart the entire building, leaving me looking out through twisted, exposed metal at the swirling vortex of a tornado that took up much of the horizon.

The tornado had to be more than a mile wide. It tossed jumbo jets like children's toys; ragged bits of metal, cars, semis, and anything else in its path were pulled up to circle in the green-tinted black clouds. The mass was backlit by flickering lightning and the crackling, popping flickers of man-made lightning that were the last gasps of destroyed electrical junctions.

Most disturbing of all, I could see Hasan's face in the clouds, beautiful and implacable in his rage.

23

The city of Denver and its suburbs were about to have a really bad day and there wasn't a damned thing I could do about it. My head was pounding like a drum. The noise, the rapid change in air pressure, and tension combined gave me an instant headache that brought tears to my eyes.

"What the hell was that?" Turner gasped. When I returned my attention to the hallway, I saw that he was the only one still standing. The other three were lying on the floor and none of them were moving. *Shit.*

"That was a pissed-off ifrit. He'd given me a deadline to meet with him and I missed it." I started taking stock. A huge section of the airport was completely flattened and most of the walls around me had been reduced to twisted metal spikes. But I stood in a six-foot-wide circle of perfection. Walls, floor, doorways—everything was intact.

Also intact was someone's cell phone. I could hear it ringing, somewhere in the rubble to my left. Could hear it over the wind, and the creaking and settling of the building, and shouts as people began looking for the injured.

There hadn't been a lot of warning before the tornado hit. I doubted that the authorities had been able to get more than a few people to the shelter of the tunnels. I guessed a lot of people were hurt. Or dead. Damn Hasan anyway.

The phone rang again. Usually, a call went to voice mail after four rings. It rang a third time, and then a fourth, and then the sound stopped.

"That was your meeting?" Turner asked.

"Yup. Now shush." I concentrated, picturing Dom Rizzoli's face in my mind. I didn't know if he could help me, but he was the highest-level law-enforcement type I knew. Maybe he knew somebody high enough up to get me some backup and serious transport. Maybe. I hoped.

What the hell is going on, Graves? his mental voice thundered.

I winced. The headache I'd had earlier was suddenly back with a vengeance.

Stop yelling. Please. My head is killing me.

I could actually hear him take a deep breath and start counting. He got to about eighty before he was calm enough to be civil.

Look, just tell me what's going on. Please. I know you had a case involving the ghost of Connor Finn and what happened at the Needle. But what I just heard was no ghost or sorcerer, not even a demon.

I told you I was dealing with an ifrit. I'm sure I did. Though now it occurred to me that maybe I hadn't. I couldn't really remember. It had been a rough couple of days.

No. You didn't. That's not the sort of thing I'd forget. His mental voice was not quite a snarl.

Oops.

Sorry, I apologized. *The ifrit's name is Hasan. Bad guys used Finn's ghost to let him loose. I got hired to protect the guy trying to put him back in the jar. Things went south . . .*

No kidding? With you *involved? I'm shocked.*

It was my turn to growl at him mentally. *Anyway, Hasan gave me an ultimatum: get to a specific location by a specific time or he'd start killing people.*

Is this why I have a message from your business partner?

Seriously, didn't *anyone* bother taking Dawna's calls?

Yes, probably. I was on my way when some bad guys made a run at me on the plane and injured a civilian instead. I tried to do the right thing by the victim and wound up stuck here, and the deadline came and went without me.

So what we heard was an angry ifrit?

You heard him? I was shocked. Dom had said he'd heard the ifrit before, too, but I hadn't really taken that in. I'd assumed that Hasan's voice had only appeared locally.

Celia, everybody on the freaking planet *heard him.* He gave a huge mental sigh. *It's not just Denver. An earthquake hit California, there was a tsunami in Thailand, at least two volcanoes have erupted, and several off-shore drilling rigs were hit by explosions. And there's more. There were simultaneous disasters all over the planet.*

Oh . . . dear . . . God.

So tell me. What do you need to fix this? I suspect I can get authorization to give you whatever you need.

I gave him a list.

It's good to have friends in high places. The military scrambled helicopters from Buckley Air Force Base—to get help to the folks at DIA *and* to ferry me down to the caves pronto. My sad little carry-on had been lost in the rubble. My weapons were God knows where—that part of the airport had been completely flattened. There was no telling how high the death toll was going to be. I didn't dare think about it.

While waiting for the cavalry, Turner and I checked on the other agents. One was dead. The other two had been knocked out, but it didn't look like they were seriously injured. They were groaning and starting to come to when I heard the roar of engines and *thwup thwup* of helicopters coming in fast.

I took a moment to mentally check on the people I cared most about in the world.

Bubba was stuck in the airport bar—pinned under some rubble with a badly broken leg. He was in a lot of pain, but he was alive, so I counted my blessings. Gran was fine. El Jefe and Emma were unharmed but stranded. They'd watched the Landingham family home get swallowed by a crevasse created by one of the California earthquakes—a crevasse that made a perfect circle six inches outside the jeweled casting circle they were standing in. Dawna was on her way to the hospital after a car wreck. She'd been heading back to the protective circle

Tim had put up. She had been badly injured but was expected to pull through. The rest of my staff—and Minnie the Mouser—were fine.

When my thoughts brushed Bruno's, I found him in the kind of complete concentration he gets when he's working a particularly dangerous and tricky bit of magic. I knew better than to interrupt him. Besides, he had to be alive to be working said magic.

That was as far as I got before the choppers landed.

The noise was tremendous as three big machines landed gently on a relatively clear section of tarmac some hundred yards or so away. The wind from their rotors sent up clouds of dust and sent little bits of debris swirling, but it wasn't too bad. I stared in awe as a group of military specialists dressed in tan desert camo emerged from the first chopper, carrying enough armament to take over a small developing nation. They ran toward me in a wedge formation, each bowed slightly at the waist, expressions intent. It was impressive as hell and more than a little scary. I wasn't the only one the spectacle affected, either. I heard Ned Turner swallow and he stammered a little as he spoke into his radio.

"Um, we have . . . military personnel here."

The radio crackled. Then a voice said, "They're here for the princess. Cut her loose, Turner."

"But . . ."

"*Now*, Turner. We have more important things to do, like saving lives."

"Right."

While they were talking, more troops were arriving, more

choppers landing in the fields of long grass beyond the runways and beginning to offload emergency gear. I saw teams of medics streaming across the landscape and breathed a sigh of relief when a couple targeted the injured TSA agents in my hallway.

By the time Ned finished stammering into the walkie-talkie, seven members of the military were waiting at parade rest in a perfectly straight line six feet in front of me. The eighth man stepped forward and held out a hand. I took it and shook hands.

"Ma'am. We've been sent to assist you with the mission. I am Command Specialist Cox, a level-seven mage specializing in defensive magic." Cox was a big man, standing about six two and broad boned, with a square jaw, penetrating brown eyes, and dark hair in the classic military cut. He filled out his uniform completely and thoroughly, without an ounce of fat to be seen, and he moved with the kind of confidence that comes from knowing what your body is capable of.

Cox began introducing the rest of the group, speaking so quickly that I was glad they all had their names sewn onto their uniforms. There were four other men and three women of various apparent ethnicities, and other than Cox, they all looked younger than me. Cox set a pack gently on the ground by my feet.

"Weapons, clothing, and protective gear," he informed me. At his nod another soldier set a four-pack of nutrition shakes next to the backpack.

"Which of you is the best shot?" I asked.

"Rifle or handgun?" Cox replied.

"Both."

"Finlay has had sniper training. Vargas has the best scores on the range with handguns."

I debated for a moment. Who should get the necklace? Not me. Hasan needed to see me coming. But I wanted at least one of our team to be invisible to his eyes; someone who could and would shoot me if they had to, to slow me down or, God forbid, kill me.

"Vargas." I pulled the *sujay* from my pocket and offered it to a beautiful Hispanic woman who might, possibly, have been old enough to drink. She looked from me to Cox, her expression questioning.

I continued, "You'll need to fix the chain, or tie a knot in it, but wearing that will make you invisible to the ifrit. If it looks like he's taking me over, shoot me. Please don't kill me unless you absolutely have to."

At Cox's nod, Vargas took the necklace from me and began fiddling with the chain. At another gesture from Cox, a man who appeared to be in his mid-twenties stepped forward, holding a large-ish wooden box. "We had to scramble a bit to get the artifacts you told Agent Rizzoli you needed," Cox commented. "Cooper."

The young man passed the box to me, his expression not quite neutral. I saw a hint of regret. Mostly he looked very tough and very determined. "Ma'am." His voice was a soft, melodic tenor. "I realize these are not your own weapons, but they were spelled by the same mage and are of excellent quality."

Cooper flipped open the lid of the box. I felt the magic

imbued in the knives wash over me in a burning wave that took my breath away. I knew that the military gave their corpsmen good gear, but not this good. Knives like these were rare and expensive.

"Those are not military issue." I met Cooper's eyes when I said it.

"No, ma'am, they are not."

I stared down at the matched pair of plain silver throwing knives where they lay on black crushed velvet, and knew without being told that they were Cooper's most prized possessions.

I opened my mouth, intending to say something, but he spoke first.

"Ma'am, the general made a personal request that I give you these knives. I'd be honored if you'd take them."

"The general?" I turned to Cox, my expression inquiring.

"Ma'am, everyone heard the ifrit. When we were notified by Washington that you were here and needed our help, General Abernathy took a personal interest."

Hell, what could I say to that? I'd asked Dom for artifact-grade knives if he could get them. There was a really good chance I'd need weapons like these if I was going to get through the day without becoming Hasan's sock puppet.

I sighed, running my hand over the spelled silversteel of the first blade, feeling the familiar power of Bruno's magic.

"All right. But when this is over, I'm giving them back." I winked at him. "I don't know you well enough to take a present this valuable from you."

Cooper grinned, which made him look years younger. I could like this man. The realization made me cringe inwardly. I was about to take him, and the others, up against Hasan. Yes, they were trained professionals. But this was going to get ugly. Who knew if any of us would make it out alive?

Cox had been surveying the damage around us. Now he nodded in the direction of a table that lay overturned atop a pile of rubble. "Vargas, Finlay, bring that table over here."

They snapped to it. The table, while battered and dented, still had all four legs. Screws and twisted metal plates dangled from those legs, showing where it had been ripped from the floor.

Finlay and Vargas set the table unsteadily upright in front of me, then stepped back. Cox stepped forward and spread a map onto the tabletop. Everyone, including me, moved in to get a good view. Out of the corner of my eye I saw Turner moving out of the way, toward the medics and the injured TSA agents.

"So, ma'am," Cox said, "What's the plan?"

"Do you have a privacy disk? I'd rather the enemy didn't hear this."

Cox reached into the pouch attached to his webbed belt and pulled out a spell disk. He muttered words that would set the perimeter of the magic and broke the disk. In an instant we were enclosed in an echoing bubble of silence.

It took a while to explain. Once we were all on the same page, and my team had made suggestions to make my plan better, it was time to go. Cox released the bubble and I followed him across the littered ground until we reached the helo, carrying the pack they'd given me earlier. Cooper carried the box with his knives. Once aboard, I changed into the nice, clean uniform and protective gear. The others were polite enough not to watch.

Clothes don't make the man, or woman in this case, but it felt really good to get into them just the same. It was also going to make it a lot easier for the illusion specialist to make me look like just another soldier if I dressed the part. Here's hoping that confused the enemy, even if only for an instant. And I absolutely adored having body armor and weapons. I'd felt so naked without them.

Now I not only had one of Cooper's throwing knives strapped onto my wrist, I had a 9mm handgun, a weapons belt filled with various spell disks, top-of-the-line body armor, and a nifty set of gloves that would not only protect my hands if we had to exit the chopper by sliding down ropes but would convert the friction into energy that would be released when I hit something. How cool was that?

Once changed, I sat down, strapped in, and began chugging nutrition shakes as I went over the plan again in my head. It was a good plan.

I felt almost confident as we lifted off the ground.

Then I made the mistake of looking out the window.

The devastation was much worse viewed from above. Most of the airport was completely flattened. Planes and rubble were scattered over literally miles of prairie, like toys thrown in a toddler's tantrum. A swath of destruction blazed a trail miles wide heading west, through the heart of the city and beyond. Glass skyscrapers that should have glistened in the sunlight didn't, and I realized they'd shattered, spraying deadly shrapnel all over downtown. We were far enough away that I couldn't see details. I was glad of that.

I swallowed hard. Hasan had done this, and more, and he hadn't even broken a sweat. *I* was going up against a creature capable of *this*.

Somebody had to, I knew. And while I felt hideously inadequate to the task, the clairvoyants all seemed to think I was our best hope.

Which was freaking terrifying.

On the other hand, I wasn't the only one opposing him. Rahim was supposed to be meeting me, helping me with my plan. Maybe Pradeep and the other Guardians were taking action, too; I didn't know.

The helicopter wasn't the smoothest or quietest ride I've taken, but it was definitely fast. In next to no time we were hovering over the crossroads where, according to my perfectly lovely plan, I was supposed to meet Rahim and his group of the Guardians.

Unpleasantly, the crossroads was empty. No sign of Rahim or his team, not even a stirring of dust in the distance.

I scanned the whole area. The ground was uneven, rocky, and scrubby desert with sparse, scraggly plant life. It would be easy to hide. Not so easy to move without kicking up dust.

I'm a planner. I do not like having to improvise. I particularly don't like being forced into it by people not doing what they've agreed to do, dammit.

Focusing my mind, I reached out. *Rahim? Where are you? You were supposed to wait at the crossroads.*

You were delayed—we knew not for how long. Every minute

costs lives. So we have gone ahead and are entering the caves now. You were right. My grandfather's ceremony has drawn off Hasan's attention and most of the—

A mental scream replaced his mental speech. In my mind and in the distance, I heard automatic weapons fire, saw spurts of dust rising from where bullets hit the ground.

Shit! I shouted mentally and physically to my people. "*Rahim and his Guardians are under fire! They're the only ones who can trap the ifrit! We've got to help them!*"

24

Pradeep and Tarik might have drawn off some of the
enemy, but the bad guys hadn't left their lair unde-
fended. Not that I'd really expected them to. That was
why I'd asked Dom for military help.

Rahim, however, had been overconfident. Again. If we
both survived the day I was *so* going to kick his ass.

Still, while I'd known we were liable to take fire, it's a very
different thing to experience it firsthand.

We used ropes to get from the helicopter to the ground. The
journey took only a few seconds, but they were long ones. I was
grateful that the gloves worked. So did the body armor. Without it I would have been cut into hamburger by weapons fire
before I hit the ground. The bullet impacts felt like someone
was whaling on me with a lightly padded baseball bat. Less
than two yards away, someone screamed. I looked and saw
Vargas fall thirty feet to the ground, the back half of her head
just gone.

Shit, Vargas had the *sujay.*

I hoped I wasn't the only one to remember that, because

there was too much going on for me to be able to concentrate and remind someone using siren telepathy, and too much noise for anyone to hear me say anything.

On the rope beside me, Cox reached onto his belt and pull off a grenade. Pulling the pin with his teeth, he flung it into the bit of cover from which most of the shots were coming. We were already on the ground and running when the grenade exploded, sending clods of earth, rocks, and things I didn't want to think too much about flying at me.

I could still hear Rahim in my head. There were no words—he was too far gone for that. But his sense of urgency was unmistakable. Magic and bullets were flying at us as I ran in a zigzag pattern toward where I'd last heard from Rahim. I stumbled more than once on the rocky and uneven ground, but kept moving, keeping low enough to use the scrub and rocky outcroppings for cover when I could.

I would've missed the body if it weren't for my inner bat, which smelled fresh blood and lots of it. I wasn't hungry—the nutrition shakes had taken care of that—but the smell hit me just the same, and I swallowed hard as my mouth started to water. I followed the scent and found Jones sprawled dead on the ground. Beside him, Rahim should have been. Bullets had chewed through so much of his torso that it looked like ground beef, but he wasn't dead. He also wasn't alone. One of the enemy had squatted down over him and was working to remove the dying man's gore-soaked pack.

Pulling my nine, I fired repeatedly as I charged forward. Unfortunately, the other guy's body armor was every bit as good as mine. My slugs hit hard, knocking him onto his ass, but he recovered instantly, pulling his gun and firing back.

He was a good shot, but not perfect. Plus, it's hard to hit a moving target, particularly one moving at vampire speed. I heard the buzz of the bullets flying past—felt a sharp, burning sensation, then wetness as one of them clipped my ear— but there wasn't time to think before I was on him. I kicked at his chest, but he moved aside, blocking my blow with the arm holding his gun.

That was a mistake. I've got more-than-human strength. I heard the bone of his arm break with an audible crack at the impact of my leg. His weapon dropped from his now-useless hand. Swearing, he rolled away from me as I regained my footing and drew a knife with his other hand.

I pulled the trigger, my gun aimed at the center of his face, only to hear it click, empty.

That made him smile. I snarled in response, pulling a spell ball from my belt. I could tell by feel that it was a full-body bind. When I flung it at him, he ducked, so it shattered on the rock behind his head. I felt the magic of the spell flow out, only to be countered by the wards on his gear.

He rose to his feet and faced me.

It was my turn to swear. I drew Cooper's knife and moved carefully forward.

My enemy was injured, which gave me some advantage. And I had vampire speed. But that hadn't seemed to impress him much so far, and he was bigger and taller than I was, more than six feet, and heavily muscled. That gave him better reach.

We circled each other warily.

I opened my mind, focusing my siren abilities, trying to influence him. Nada, despite the fact he wasn't wearing a charm.

"Your siren mind games won't work on me, chickie." His smile was a baring of teeth.

Chickie? "Then I guess I'll just have to waste your ass." I moved in with a blur of speed, my knife slicing side to side before I danced out of reach. I heard the ripping of cloth and his hiss of pain, and smelled fresh blood, but the blow hadn't been lethal.

When I went for him again, he was ready. He sliced at my knife arm, scoring a long, shallow gash that burned like hell itself and bled freely. I danced back, out of reach, and he moved forward on the attack. His third step took him out of the protective shadow of the rock face.

The sniper round hit him in the face a split second before I heard the crack of the rifle. The impact drove him backward, blood and worse spraying behind him as his legs crumpled. It was a lot more gruesome and hideous than movies and video games make it look. I swallowed a little convulsively and looked away—I had no time to be sick. I wiped my knife on my pants, slid it back into its sheath, and hurried over to Rahim.

Squatting down beside him, I was appalled. He still wasn't dead. Despite his terrible injuries, he lived. Blood bubbled from his chest with his every shuddering breath, yet somehow there was strength in his hand as he grabbed my arm, guiding my hand to the bloody strap of his pack.

He projected the image of Ujala's face into my mind. Then he was gone. At last.

Tell me you didn't bring your ten-year-old kid into this hell.

But he had.

I heard a child scream *"Papa!"* from a shadowy cleft in a rock formation some twenty yards away. Looking toward the sound, I saw the boy trying to break free from a man who held him fast. I recognized the captor's face from the odd little meeting Rahim had held back at the condo in Treasure Island . . . which seemed like an eternity ago now. So he was one of the Guardians, and on our side. Good.

I closed Rahim's eyes, then stripped the bag from his corpse as the gunfire died out, leaving behind an almost echoing silence broken by Ujala's heartbroken sobs. In the distance, I heard a wolf's howl. I sent my mind outward and found a familiar mental signature.

Kevin.

Don't shoot the werewolf. He's with me.

I could sense negative reactions to that particular order. The troops weren't happy. They didn't trust the monsters. I got that. If Kevin went too wolfy, he'd be dangerous to both sides. I didn't think that would happen; his control is excellent. But . . .

Don't shoot the wolf unless he attacks you.

In the back of my mind, I heard Kevin's dark chuckle, but when I reached out to him there was no answer. Then again, I didn't really expect one.

If Kevin were human right now, his PTSD would make what was happening here impossible for him to handle. The wolf wouldn't care. But I was pretty sure his wolf-self had enough self-preservation instinct to bury his human-self deep enough to protect his sanity. Which, unfortunately, might be deep enough to endanger us.

I was willing to take the gamble.

Three soldiers followed me across the stony ground to the cave entrance. All three were alert, continually scanning the area for danger. As I dropped Rahim's bloody pack gently at the feet of the middle-aged Indian man who held the weeping Ujala, I opened my mouth to offer my condolences.

I couldn't speak. The minute Rahim's bag left my hand, power washed over me in a tidal wave that stole both thought and breath and left burning agony in its wake. I dropped to my knees, the jolt of the impact on the hard stone buried beneath a deeper, stronger pain. Tears streamed from my eyes. I felt Hasan's satisfaction.

You have arrived.

He was coming.

I fought for enough strength and breath to gasp out a warning, both psychically and aloud. *"He's coming! Go,"* a bare fraction of an instant before Hasan slipped into my body and, with gloating satisfaction, said, "He's here."

25

Ujala made a gesture with his left hand. There was a sound like a thunderclap, so loud I felt it as pressure. It shook small stones loose from the ceiling of the cave and raised a cloud of choking dust that set me coughing. Burning power washed through me, bringing a gasp to my lips. When my tears finally stopped and I could see again, everyone was gone—except Hasan, who was riding me like I was his favorite pony.

He dragged me to my feet; I made him work for it, fighting him for every damned inch until my muscles ached from the strain.

You will stop fighting me! he snarled in my mind.

The hell you say.

He didn't answer. His thoughts had moved elsewhere. I felt him gathering his will to send magic flowing through the cave to heat the rock. He was shocked to stillness when the magic simply wouldn't come. He tried again . . . nothing.

I wanted to crow with surprised delight. I'm not much of a siren, even if there is royal blood in my veins. But one thing has bred true from my heritage. The siren gift cannot coexist with any other major talent. So long as Hasan was inhabiting my body, he had what I had, no more. This was great news for our side—if only I could tell them. With Hasan in the driver's seat, that wasn't likely to happen.

When he overheard my thought, he snarled in wordless fury. He picked through my memories to come up with a plan. Using my hand, he rifled through the spell balls in my belt pouch until he found what he wanted. A smoke bomb.

Our fingernail pierced the gel coating; then Hasan rolled the ball, underhanded, across the floor, into the caves where my allies had gone. Three seconds later acrid smoke, the equivalent of tear gas, began spewing from the little thing, blocking the light from the magical and more prosaic electric lanterns that hung at intervals along the walls, connected by thick, snaking cables.

A second or two later, a strong breeze born of magic blew it all right back into my face.

I bent double, coughing until I choked and gagged. The stuff tasted hideous, like some obscene combination of cayenne peppers, garlic, and fruit juice, and made my lungs burn like they were on fire. The effect only lasted a minute or two before the strong wind from inside the cave cleared it away— but they were really miserable minutes.

Hasan untucked my shirt and used the fabric to wipe our eyes and nose. Once he could see clearly again he led us cautiously forward, gun in hand, moving from one rock formation to another, using them for cover.

He'd been in these caves before, so he knew what to expect. I didn't.

The place was bigger than I expected. I'd caught a glimpse through the porthole during the ceremony in Indiana, but that hadn't really given me a true feel for it. Nor had the small cave opening give a clue. Just a few steps in, along a narrow path and around a bulge in the rock, the cave opened up into a passage at least twenty feet wide and fifty feet high. Magical light flared to life at our movement, revealing fangs of rock in every shade of brown and gold from pale tan through cinnamon and umber. Some of the stalactites and stalagmites were tipped in the palest cream. The cavern was stunningly beautiful.

Hasan listened hard, hoping to use sound to track his enemy. I heard the distant trickle of water but there was no sound of any human movement. Hasan growled, the sound coming from my lips. It was an eerie sensation, and God how I hated it. I wanted him out of me! I struggled with renewed vigor but he beat me down brutally.

He took one step, then another. At the third step I felt a spell snap into place. The ground beneath us melted into thick, viscous mud.

A mudder that worked on stone? I admired the spell even as I felt myself sinking rapidly to the hips in the equivalent of localized quicksand. At that point I stopped being admiring and started being scared—well, more scared. Drowning in mud was not how I wanted to go. My survival instincts started to rise in full-fledged panic, but I drove them back by sheer force of will. Better to die than let Hasan get whatever it was he wanted.

Hasan didn't agree. He started flailing around, which only made us sink faster. I was up to my armpits in goo when one wild arm wave found the solid rock at the edge of the pit.

The spell had a limit.

Relief flooded through me in spite of myself. Hasan gently tossed the gun onto the ground just past the edge, then grabbed the rock edge with our fingertips and pulled until we had a full-hand grip. Pulling harder, he got us close enough to get hold of the base of a nearby stalagmite. Using every ounce of vampire strength available in my body, and every ounce of energy that had been poured into my nifty special-duty gloves, he pulled against the sucking mud. I felt my muscles straining and tearing, but he forced our body forward, finally managing to drag us to the edge of the spell and then out.

I lay on the floor for long minutes, sodden and spent, my breath coming in grateful, heaving gasps, my muscles screaming in protest at the abuse they'd suffered. I heal well, but it would take days before the damaged muscles in my upper body stopped giving me hell.

I would have been content to stay there a while longer, but I felt the stirring of magic thrumming through the stones beneath me.

Hasan felt it too. It was his turn to panic. Rahim was dead. The Guardian child did not have enough mages with him to do the spell. How—

Mages! You brought mages with you, he accused me.

Yup. Good ones.

You'll pay for that, he hissed in my mind.

How exactly do you plan to do that? I'm your ride. Damage me much more and you're screwed.

You have loved ones.

Yeah, and your magic isn't working. Pull out of me now to do something and you won't get back in. I'll drown myself in the muck if I have to.

Wordless rage consumed him. He knew I'd do it. And even if he animated my corpse, there wasn't enough strength left in my damaged upper body to haul me out again.

Never having possessed a living human body before, he had no understanding of physical limits. He was startled—and disgusted—by the realization that he had damaged me, that I could not be manipulated without consequences. Startled, he pulled back. Not out, but back, and only for an instant.

Long enough for me to unsnap the sheath to my knife, but not long enough to draw it, and not nearly long enough to cut myself.

Oh, no you don't. Hasan scolded me as if I were a toddler. *You are a child. I have existed for eons here, and longer than that at home. What does your text say about the humans? Ah yes, a grass that grows one day and withers the next.*

Our "text"? The Bible?

Indeed.

I was weak, but he managed to drag me into a sitting position, then slowly, painfully, got us onto my feet, though most of my weight was supported by a column of rock.

The boy has power, Hasan said with grudging admiration. *More than either his father or the old man. But less skill.*

Give him time.

No, Hasan answered firmly, *I don't think I will.*

He bent down, intending to pick up my gun.

It wasn't there.

He stared, wide-eyed, at the spot where he'd tossed it. Someone had taken it—and he hadn't seen, or heard, a thing. Though I had.

You distracted me.

Maybe. Or maybe somebody in the cave had thought to grab the *sujay* from Vargas's body. Either way, score a point for our team. Hasan might be inside my head, but Great Aunt Lopaka had been training me about shielding my thoughts from other sirens—and apparently the same trick worked pretty damned well against evil ifrits. Yay.

You think you're clever. But every act of defiance will cost you dearly in the end. He showed me hideous images, things that would haunt my nightmares, silently promising that he'd do all that and more to the ones I loved.

Right, like you wouldn't have done all that anyway.

He couldn't deny that.

The power of Ujala's working was building, I could feel it. I wondered how many of the Guardians were helping, how many of the mages I'd brought along were still alive. One of them had to be: Someone had taken that gun.

Hope flared to life. I might be alone fighting for control of my body, but I wasn't fighting alone.

A wave of magic washed outward, stealing my breath and affirming that hope. I rejoiced as I felt it burn against my skin.

Hasan was much less happy. He forced our body forward, moving in virtual silence. All the lights within sight of us had been extinguished, but the cavern wasn't dark, not to my eyes. Faint but distinct lines and swirls appeared as if etched into the rock, glowing in faintly fluorescent green, in patterns that I knew had meaning but couldn't comprehend. It was hauntingly beautiful. As we moved deeper into the cave, they grew in number, brightness, and intensity.

Hasan was worried. If he didn't hurry, the boy might be able to bar the way before we reached the altar. That was unacceptable. He would not be thwarted. Not this close to his goal.

What altar? I asked. Of course, he didn't answer, but he was eager enough that I could finally tap into his mind and figure out what he wanted, why he was doing all this.

The ifrit wanted to go home.

Oh, not in the warm, fuzzy way. No, he wanted revenge. Hasan had been exiled because he was a serial killer. He'd slaughtered his fellow djinn in the double digits, after putting them through unspeakable horrors. I saw that he wanted to hunt down the ones who'd discovered his crimes, then prosecuted and punished him. He intended to extract the most hideous, painful revenge on them that he had been able to imagine. And he'd had eons to plan every bit of it. My stomach roiled at the images that played through his mind.

But, eager as he was, he still remained cautious. Now was not the time to make a mistake through haste. Humans, while puny and generally ineffectual, could show surprising resourcefulness when roused. There was also the demon to consider. He would be remiss indeed to think it hadn't taken steps to keep him on Earth until he'd done what he'd been released to do.

Hasan paused, looking for traps. Without success. He couldn't use magic to search while using the body, and the boy and his allies—and the demon and his—had cloaked their traps too thoroughly. Our head snapped to the left at the faint scrape of a boot echoing slightly in the open area he knew lay just a step or two ahead; there was a sharp intake of breath and the rustle of fabric to the right.

I could hear from his thoughts that he was tempted to slide out of my body and use his powers to destroy the foolish humans who were scattered throughout the cavern, lying in wait to oppose him. But he didn't dare. He knew he couldn't trust me. I heard him curse me mentally with frustrated fury.

The ifrit's frustration was intense enough that my I felt my fingers actually dig into the stone of the column where I stood. How dare she threaten him, *fight* him. When he no longer needed her body he would make her pay, and he'd take time and pleasure doing it.

But first, he had to deal with the boy. He considered the layout of the cave complex. He knew it well, having been sent from the djinn world to the place of his imprisonment through this very temple—and been jailed here by the demon and its servants until he'd stolen and consumed the vosta.

He was almost certain where we were—two steps from a crossroads—but in the confusion of the fight, he might have gotten turned around. Too, there was always the chance that the boy had thought to use illusion magic to change the appearance of the tunnels.

Hasan moved us cautiously forward. As he did, the lights and swirls rose up to dizzying heights, to the ceiling of an enormous cavern. The pattern there was dominated by a feature that was recognizable to anyone who'd ever read a map: a compass rose, and at its center, a glittering diamond the size of my head. Even the dim light provided by the magic made it glitter. In the faint illumination I saw tunnels branching in each direction. Hasan paused, debating which path to take to the main cavern with the altar of ceremony.

PAIN.

I dropped to the ground, my body slamming onto the uneven stone with teeth-jarring force as my left leg gave out beneath me in a spasm of pure agony. A knife, glowing eye-searingly blue-white with magic, was embedded in the muscle of my left thigh. Dark blood flowed from the wound, soaking the leg of my pants and wetting the cavern floor beneath me. The blade hadn't hit an artery—the blood wasn't spurting—but this was no minor injury. I instinctively grabbed for the knife with both hands, swearing.

Then snatched my hands back at the realization that I wanted that knife in me. It was my only hope of keeping Hasan at bay.

The moment I knew that, so did he, and he redoubled his efforts to regain control of our shared body. The struggle probably only lasted a few seconds, but it felt like an eternity. I watched my arm start to lift from the floor, the muscles visibly trembling from the strain of conflicting messages.

You will do this.

I will not.

I heard someone take a step but saw no one.

In the distance, indistinctly, I heard the sound of male voices chanting, felt the flow and eddy of power moving more strongly than ever through the stones beneath me, seeming to thicken the very air I drew into my lungs.

The cavern played tricks with sound, but there was no mistaking the direction from which the power was coming. It poured from the mouth of the eastern tunnel in a blistering wind that brightened the runes and sigils on the wall.

No! Hasan's fury gave him strength enough to overpower me. With a hiss of pain, he ripped the knife from the wound, flinging it away to clang against a rock somewhere out of sight.

He rolled us over, my blood splattering and smearing on the ground as he tried to drag us to our feet. He almost couldn't do it. My body was reaching the end of its resources; exhaustion and injury compounded by blood loss made it increasingly hard for him to move.

When my body lurched to its feet, a stifled scream broke from between my gritted teeth. My right leg bore the bulk of my weight. My left dragged, almost useless, blood pouring steadily from the knife wound. Each time Hasan put any weight on it, every time it bumped against anything, the deep, throbbing pain became a piercing lance of pure agony.

Cursing under his breath, Hasan used my hands against

the stone walls to steady himself and we shambled drunkenly forward. He staggered from one rock formation to the next. Even as he did I could feel the spells being wrought to the east draining him.

But nothing they did could drain his will. I knew that even if I bled to death, he could keep my body animated for several minutes, moving toward his goal. For a moment he rested, leaning against a column, digging through the pouch of spells, looking for something, anything he could use to kill the boy. Without Ujala, the other mages in the working would lack the knowledge to complete it. Nothing then could stand in his way.

I fought for control, tried to use my fear and pain to my advantage. I stopped him in his tracks for a moment, but only a moment. Then we moved inexorably forward again.

The mouth of another cavern was only a yard in front of me, the golden light of magic illuminating the way. Each word of the chant, clearly audible, struck Hasan like a small hailstone. I felt them hammering hard against my skin. When each struck, a wisp of smoke and the scent of myrrh rose from my body, covering the increasingly strong smell of spilled blood.

The trail of blood marked my passage like slime behind a snail. Something . . . some*one* was behind me, following that trail. I was pretty sure I knew who. I tried not to think too much about it, lest Hasan overhear the thought. Instead, I focused on the pain and my continuing battle for control.

I might be losing, but by damn I wasn't giving up. It was costing him, too. I knew that because I could feel both his frustration and eagerness building. Success and freedom were mere heartbeats away.

We stepped into the doorway and I had to blink several times to adjust to the brilliant scene in the next space. Before me was a casting circle, with a mage holding a gemstone at each compass point and a djinn jar set at the exact center. It stood, a barrier, between Hasan and the elaborate altar at the opposite side of the cave, which was set between huge stalagmite columns that had been carved in the shapes of towering nude figures. One male and one female, they must have been a hundred feet tall.

The chanting grew, building toward a crescendo, and each mage raised the vosta he held over his head: To the north, Ujala, with a diamond; the south, one of his uncles, holding the sapphire; on the east, Cox, with a topaz; and in the west, another soldier, whose name I didn't remember, grasping an emerald.

Hasan pulled a spell disk and cracked it as he stepped away from the wall, intending to throw it directly at Ujala. I pulled back, not fighting until the crucial instant, when I used my concentrated will to foul his aim, so that the full-body bind hit a column three feet to the boy's left, far enough away to do no harm at all.

Something about one of the shadows caught my attention, tugging at the edge of my consciousness as Hasan grabbed another spell ball. A blur of motion from behind ended with a huge, fur-covered body slamming into my injured leg and bowling me over sideways. The magical flame ignited by the spell ball streamed off course, a good eighteen inches to Ujala's right.

I fell, my newly empty hands grabbing deep into the fur of a huge golden wolf who dug his claws into my belly and chest. I wouldn't have thought I had enough strength left in me to do it, but adrenaline can let you do amazing things. Hasan flung Kevin aside, hard. The wolf hit the cavern wall with a bone-cracking impact that left him crumpled on the ground at the foot of the altar, neck twisted at an impossible angle.

Hasan tried to make me stand, but couldn't. My body had taken too much punishment. I had lost too much blood. He looked around the cave, trying to figure out his next move, while I tried to see if anyone else had been hurt. The magical blow Hasan had loosed had missed Ujala, but found another target. On the far side of the room, perhaps a half-inch away from the circle, was a body so badly burned that it no longer looked human. I thought it a corpse . . . until it moved.

I shuddered. She wasn't dead. She, because the body was too small to be any of the men. Morales then, it had to be, but her uniform and flesh were charred beyond recognition. The pain I felt had to be nothing compared to what she was going through. Yet she still fought, trying to move an arm that was so badly damaged it shouldn't be able to move at all. Why?

My own memories supplied the answer. If she touched the circle, she'd become part of the magic, and her death by magic would activate the node. The spell Ujala and the others were working was powerful, but it wasn't powerful enough. Hasan was still free, still strong enough to inhabit my body. But weakened as he was, with my body failing beneath him, he would not be able to resist the power of the node.

Hasan either heard my thought or came to the same conclusion. Whichever, it didn't matter. He knew, and with a hiss of fury he tried to dig in my pouch for another spell.

I didn't let him. Ujala and the others might not have freed me yet, but their spell was working. The ifrit was weakening.

I called on my vampire strength, but more than that, I embraced my siren heritage.

I should have done it sooner. Reaching out with my mind, I sought help from my aunt, my cousin, from everyone I knew, everyone I loved, from the men and women fighting with me in the cavern.

And they were there: Three soldiers besides those in the circle; Kevin his neck broken, but alive, human essence determined, his wolf furious; Emma and Dawna, steadfast and loyal; Gran; my aunt; Isaac and Gilda Levy; John Creede; El Jefe; all there, all willingly giving me their strength of mind and will. I reached for Bruno and found . . . nothing. Just a vast, echoing void where his presence would normally be. I sought and found Matty, felt his pain, his sorrow, and his determination to exact revenge—revenge for the loss of his brother.

Bruno was dead.

The knowledge hit me like a sledgehammer to the gut. "No!" I howled as pain ripped through my heart and soul. The agony of my loss, combined with the strength given by my loved ones, became a weapon. I struck Hasan with all its power.

The blow staggered him and in that instant my body and mind belonged only to me. Grabbing Cooper's knife from its sheath, I slammed it into my injured thigh.

Hasan screamed in agony, but not through my lips. He was out of me.

He was out of me.

He was out of me and he looked like *hell*. If I'd had the energy, I'd have cheered. Hasan was mostly incorporeal by nature, but while he'd been beautiful, all smoky and glimmering, on the beach in Florida, now he looked a lot more like smog, yellow, dull, shot through with darker streaks, like cuts and bruises. It made him seem more substantial, almost solid.

The burned, bloody hand of the dying mage touched the edge of the circle. As she breathed her last, power, light, and sound exploded through the circle with an intensity that beggared the imagination. I was blinded and deafened, lifted off my feet and sent airborne for several yards. When I hit the floor, I rolled, from pure instinct, coming to an abrupt, jarring stop against a stone wall. The knife in my thigh slammed into the floor, causing me an indescribable amount of pain, and I screamed in agony.

When I was able to move, and to see, I pulled the knife from my leg; blood poured from the wound. Thanks to my vampire abilities, the place where I'd been stabbed earlier was already healing—slower than usual—but I'd lost so much blood that I was growing weaker with each moment.

Cleaning the knife on my tattered shirttail, I slid it into the sheath. I needed both hands to steady myself.

The floor of the cavern began to shake. I hadn't thought I could be any more afraid than I had been in the last few hours. I was wrong. Adrenaline coursed through my body at the realization that we were underground—in the midst of an earthquake.

I'm from California. I know about earthquakes. If we stayed where we were, chances were good we'd be buried alive. Heading for the cave entrance right now might save my life . . . but Kevin and the others were still down here, and I could hear Hasan's bellows of rage. An earthquake might not be enough to stop him.

When I glanced over my shoulder, in the dim light of the cave entrance I could see stones bouncing across the ever-narrowing gap. Saying a prayer for strength, I turned toward the burning brightness of the spell circle.

I couldn't stand, so I didn't even try. Stripping off my belt, I tightened it around my wounded leg, just tight enough to slow the bleeding. Using my good leg, I pushed myself across the stony floor. Pebbles and larger stones rained down on me. Sharp, jagged bits of golden brown rock dug into my hands as I dragged myself forward, the already-damaged muscles in my arms and back screaming in pained protest.

It was slow going, and I was treated the whole time to human screams and inhuman bellows. Beneath me, the stone floor was growing uncomfortably warm from the heat of magic—the battle was still going strong. Reaching the altar room, I found that Hasan had his back to me. Semi-corporeal, he was gathering power to his fingertips and trying to make his way to the corpse of the downed mage. At the same time, the magic from the node, concentrated through the stone in Ujala's hands, pulled him inexorably toward the mouth of the djinn jar.

When all you have is a hammer, everything looks like a nail. When all you have is a throwing knife, everything becomes a target. Hasan's broad, muscular back was directly in front of me. I had no idea if the knife could harm him in his current state, but since it was a magical artifact, it might. I didn't take time to think it out—there was no time. If he loosed a blow at Ujala from that distance he wouldn't miss and the child, the Guardian, would die. I struggled until I was in a sitting position, drew the knife, said a quick prayer, and threw.

I put everything I had into that throw: All my remaining strength, all the years spent honing my skills, all the rage and grief I felt at Bruno's loss. The blade flew through the air with a slight hiss, then sank with a meaty thunk into the ifrit's spine. I collapsed onto my side, incapable of anything more.

Hasan's scream could have shattered glass. His arms flew wide, the blow he'd prepared for Ujala flying into the statue to the right of the altar. As I watched, his body melted to a fine mist the dark red of heart's blood. The vapor was sucked slowly into the mouth of the jar. When the last of it was inside, the power of the circle died. Most of the light died with it: Most, but not all.

Ujala set the still-glowing vosta he was holding onto the

ground and stepped forward. Pulling another stone from his pocket, he slammed it into the mouth of the djinn jar. Using a black candle, lit by magic, he created a new seal, muttering a spell I couldn't make out, scratching sigils into the molten wax.

I heard the sound of stone scraping on stone, coming from the column next to the altar, the one shaped like a woman. The one Hasan's blow had damaged.

It was . . . moving . . . and not from the earthquake.

"Holy shit." Cooper's awed comment came from a corner of the room where I'd noticed something wrong with the shadows. He stood in opened-mouthed wonder, the camo spell that had hidden him expended.

Holy shit was right. The brown stone resolved itself into a living being of incredible beauty, her skin shining like polished brass, her eyes and hair black and gleaming, like obsidian.

She was a hundred feet tall if she was an inch, but before our eyes she shrank. As she did, a thin, iridescent dress materialized around her, sheer as a cobweb and held at the shoulder by a brooch in the shape of a *sujay*. When she was down to nine or ten feet tall, she stepped forward and down onto the floor of the cave. There was no rock-on-rock sound when she moved.

Inclining her head slightly, she addressed Ujala, who held Hasan's jar with both hands, offering it to her. In the background, Cox gestured to his people to hold fire, because battered as they were, when she first manifested, they had prepared themselves to fight.

The djinn's voice rang through the cavern like an enormous gong. "You have done well, Guardian. We are proud of you, and of your father before you. Take Hasan away for safe-keeping."

Ujala bowed at the waist, but not before I saw tears gleaming in his eyes, which were now the clear gray and white of the sparkling diamond vosta he'd used during the ceremony. His hair was still dark brown, and he otherwise seemed to show no ill effects from the enormous power he had wielded.

He is the Guardian, the giant djinn said in my mind, answering the question I hadn't voiced.

She glided forward another few steps until she stood directly over me. I looked up, and up, into unreadable, inhuman eyes of total black. Her expression was totally alien as she regarded me for a seemingly endless moment. When she finally spoke, her voice was soft and intimate, pitched so that I, and only I, would hear.

"You, too, have done well. They would not have succeeded without you." She regarded me for another long moment, those unsettling eyes seeming to bore into my very soul. "I will give you three things you wish." A small smile played at the corner of her lovely mouth. "Without strings."

She gestured at Kevin. The golden light of magic surrounded him and his body straightened into its normal, human form. He lay on the stone, naked, beautiful, and whole.

"Give me your hand," she said.

I struggled to sit up. It wasn't happening. My body simply would not move. Exhaustion, my injuries, and blood loss combined to leave me helpless at the djinn's feet. I was too tired to even be frightened. Intellectually, I knew that I really didn't want to piss her off. I'd had enough of angry djinn for one day . . . hell, for a lifetime. But I simply could not comply.

She squatted gracefully and set her hand on my forehead. Her hand was warm but hard, like the brass it resembled. I felt strength flow into me, strength and comfort. My breath caught in a sharp sob as I remembered. Bruno was gone. I'd never see him again. Never hold him. Never tell him how much I loved him. Never get to say good-bye.

Time stopped. Everything around me froze in place. Falling stones hovered in midair; Cox stood balanced in midstep. Then, in less time than it took me to blink, I was standing, in my dirty, bloody uniform, in a hospital emergency room.

The scene was one of controlled chaos. Doctors and nurses in bloodied scrubs were working full out. EMTs came running through the automatic doors, pushing a gurney with a still and mangled form on it, the face covered by an oxygen mask. Another EMT was perched atop the body, doing heart compressions. With every push, blood pumped out of the bullet wounds that riddled the victim.

We have gone back in time, the djinn said in my mind. *You wished to save your lover. It is too late for that, nor am I willing to cross his deity. But I have brought you to a time and place where you can bid him farewell.*

Without hesitation I turned and raced after the gurney. Too late, I tried to shift around a man who was pushing a crash cart toward the curtained cubicle where they'd taken

Bruno, but instead of colliding with him, I passed right through him. Apparently I was here, but my body wasn't.

There was no time to think about that. I stepped through the curtain and came face to face with Bruno's spirit, which was staring down at the body on the gurney in shock. A doctor shouted for people to clear before zapping him with a defibrillator's electrified paddles. The body bowed, its chest rising off of the gurney, but the heart machine continued its relentless, monotonous beep.

Bruno . . .

Celia? He looked at me. *What? How?*

I threw my arms around him and they didn't pass through. He was there, real, warm to the touch, his soul whole even if his body wasn't.

I'm so sorry. I'm so sorry. My non-body was wracked with sobs as tears poured unheeded down my cheeks. *I love you. I've always loved you.*

The body was electrified again and I felt Bruno shudder in my arms.

So I'm dead? His voice was shocked. *Are you . . .*

No. The djinn brought me here.

A djinn? Celia! He squeezed me tight. *You shouldn't have. You really shouldn't.*

I couldn't save you. I wanted to, but I couldn't. But I had to say good-bye.

Oh, honey. He gently cupped my cheek in his hand. Leaning down, he kissed me, his warm, gentle lips pressing against mine.

I felt a surge of power that I'd felt only once before—not magic, something different, purer, and more powerful. It was exactly the same feeling I'd encountered when my sister's ghost had finally been called home.

We were out of time.

As if from I distance I heard the doctor announcing the time of death for the official record. A slit of light appeared by the head of the gurney, swiftly becoming a doorway that hovered six inches off the floor. The rectangle was filled with light so bright I couldn't look at it directly.

A tall, male shape dressed in blinding white stepped out.

What is this? Power sang through each word and I found myself falling back a step. Bruno stepped protectively between me and the figure, using his soul to guard mine.

The angel, for that was what he was, stood at alert, his expression stern and forbidding.

The djinn, who'd appeared behind me when the slit first appeared, raised her hands in a placating gesture. *She is here to tell him good-bye. That is all. We have no quarrel, you and I.*

The angel gave her a long, wary stare, then stepped aside. He gestured for Bruno to precede him.

Bruno turned to me. With a sad smile, he pulled me into his arms one last time, trying to put everything he had, everything we were to each other, into that last embrace.

I love you, Celie. I always have, and always will.

I couldn't answer. Tears had choked words and breath from me. So I held him tight, willing him to know, to understand.

His arms tightened around me one last time. Then he let me go. Squaring his shoulders, he stepped forward, into that doorway of brilliant white light. The angel followed, closing the door behind him and leaving me in a room that seemed very dark without it.

26

I stood staring after them for a long, long time. The djinn waited patiently. In the background, medical personnel covered the body and left, moving on to new patients, new emergencies. I heard someone talking about a burn patient, Connie DeGarmo.

That registered dimly: Connie DeGarmo was Bruno's aunt Connie, Sal's wife. But I couldn't rouse much interest.

Bruno was gone. Dead. Yes, he'd gone to heaven—but that didn't make the loss of him any less hard.

When I was as ready as I was going to be, the djinn took my hand. Magic washed over me and we were back in the cavern, back in the present. We reappeared maybe a second after we'd left. The scene in the cavern was just the same. No one had moved—in fact, most of them probably had no idea I'd been gone. Cox knew; I could see it in his eyes. The look he gave me was filled with a lot of caution and a little distrust.

I couldn't blame him. In his place, I'd feel exactly the same.

He was still giving me a hard stare as the djinn withdrew

the stickpin that held her brooch in place, keeping the bit of
jewelry in her hand as the fabric of her dress fell to pool on
the floor. At a twitch of her fingers, the left sleeve of my uniform shirt dissolved to mist. I held perfectly still as, with great
care, she used the sharp pin to etch a perfect circle, a few
inches wide, in the flesh of my upper arm. Blood welled up,
but only a little. The scratch wasn't deep. She pressed the
brooch, which was now the size of my palm, against the
wound. Magic filled the air, but instead of the heat I normally
felt, this was cold, so cold I shivered, my teeth chattering. The
skin beneath the brooch turned red, then nearly gray, before
the metal simply melted away before my eyes, leaving behind
a mark that was both scar and tattoo. It had the shape of the
sujay and tiny gems were embedded at each of the compass
points.

*Your third wish, granted. Never again will any creature be
able to possess your body against your will.*

Three wishes: Healing Kevin, saying good-bye to Bruno,
and this. No strings attached. I knew I should be grateful, and
eventually I probably would be. But now, it was all too much.
I was spent, physically, mentally, and emotionally.

Turning her back on me, the great djinn strode over to the
altar. She pivoted and backed into her place, her body growing and changing until it was, again, a colossal figure carved
of brown stone, reaching up to the cavern ceiling.

27

The army medics patched me together enough to go home. Once there, I slept for two full days, only climbing out of bed to use the facilities and eat. I didn't watch the news. I really didn't want to know how much damage Hasan had caused the world. He'd done more than enough damage to me.

On the fourth day, Dawna sent Kevin to drag me out of bed. She was healing, but it would be a while before she was completely herself again. She sent Kevin because I had a flight to catch. I had appointments to keep. The military types who'd assisted me were to be given special commendations at the White House. I was invited to attend and I wanted to show my support. Cox and his people had been amazing; they completely deserved the high honors they were getting.

The president had offered me civilian honors, but I'd decided to pass. I'd done my best, but it hadn't been enough. I didn't know how many had died, but even one was too many.

I dressed conservatively and made sure I ate before and after the flight. The trip itself was uneventful, as was the limo ride to the White House. Security was tight enough that my skin reddened and blistered as I passed through the building's perimeter, but everything had healed up by the time I'd swathed myself in sunblock and taken my assigned seat in the Rose Garden.

The autumn day was chilly, but the garden was still beautiful. Classical music played softly in the background. My seat was in the second row, behind the family members of the honorees. Everyone was dressed in their absolute best. Some faces shone with pride. Others, probably relatives of the fallen, bore signs of grief. A few children shifted uncomfortably in their seats. One, a bright-eyed blond in pigtails and pink ruffles who couldn't have been more than two, stared at me with wide eyes over her mother's shoulder.

Cox and his surviving crew, in full dress uniform, were lined up in front, beside the lectern with the presidential seal. They looked good. Some of them would have fairly spectacular new scars, but they all stood tall and proud, at parade rest. Cox's hair had gone completely white and his eyes, which now glowed, had taken on the color of the topaz he'd been holding during the ceremony. Tucker, who had stood at the west point of the compass, had white hair too, his eyes as vivid green as the emerald he'd used. Awaiting their commander in chief, the whole team nonetheless acknowledged me subtly. Every one. It made me proud.

The music changed to "Hail to the Chief." We stood. Cox and his people came to full attention.

The president of the United States had arrived.

I found myself blinking away tears as emotions threatened

to overwhelm me. The ceremony wasn't long. Medals were awarded. Each soldier got a personal thank you and a handshake from the president. Cooper was presented with another set of knives. Maybe I shouldn't have been so impressed; after all, my great-aunt Lopaka rules the sirens. But I'm an American, and I choked up. I almost regretted declining my honor.

Cox, his team, most of the families, and many of the other spectators, including me, went directly from the Rose Garden to Arlington National Cemetery, where Specialist Morales was buried with full military honors. She'd been posthumously awarded the highest honor the military could grant a mage. Her father accepted it and the folded flag from her coffin, his face solemn, as her mother sobbed in the arms of her son.

Vargas's funeral was just as sad. Her big, apparently close family was obviously devastated. Full military honors were given, and when they fired off the honor volley it was as if they'd fired straight into her mother's heart.

While I was in DC, I met with Dom Rizzoli, who debriefed me. Then he did something totally unexpected. He gave me a hug. At first, I held back, but it felt good having his arms around me. When he said, "You did good, Celia," I even believed him. But the cost had been so damned high. Too high. Living without Bruno . . . I wasn't sure I could bear it, even though I knew I had to. It wasn't like I had a choice.

I went to a lot of funerals in the next couple of weeks. The service for Jones was small and simple, and attended predominantly by very scary people who looked remarkably ordinary. Dawna, Chris, Kevin, and I all went.

Jones had been there when I was turned into an abomination. He'd been beside me when we rescued Kevin from the Zoo. I hadn't liked him. He had plenty of power, a brilliant mind, and, as far as I could tell, absolutely no conscience. It was a frightening combination. No, I hadn't liked Jones much—but I'd respected the hell out of him.

I sent flowers to Rahim's funeral. It didn't seem right to attend. I didn't think Abha would hold anything against me, nor Ujala. They'd paid our bill—which was quite large, in the end—without complaint. Still, I stayed away.

For Pradeep I sent nothing. I still had hard feelings about the guy. I'd learned from contacts at the Company that the contract he had taken out on me died with him when he was killed on the beach in Florida, with Tarik and the others, trying to work their own version of the magic needed to trap Hasan. He was felled by the bad guys, who'd used one of those heart attack guns on him.

I hadn't liked Pradeep, and the fact that Tarik had betrayed his family and calling was only partly mitigated by his eventual change of heart. Still, I had nothing but sympathy for both Divya and Abha. I felt even worse for Ujala. He'd been forced to go through something no kid that young should face, and he was taking on duties grown men would blanch at. He had power and intelligence, but he was going to have a hard life. Still, I was glad the djinn in the cavern had said what she had to him. It's important to a kid that his father be remembered with respect.

Bruno was given a huge Catholic funeral mass at the Cathedral. Since he'd never been part of the Mafia, he wasn't an excommunicate. Matty didn't officiate; he sat with his family. Part of me wanted to sit in the general audience, with El Jefe, Ram Sloan, and other professors who'd worked closely with Bruno, or with Dawna, Chris, and Kevin.

Instead, I was in the third row with the dignitaries, sitting between my great-aunt, Queen Lopaka, and King Dahlmar of Rusland, who was married to my cousin, Adriana. As often happened on state occasions, my aunt insisted Baker and Griffiths act as my security team. I didn't argue. We'd worked together before; they were good at their jobs without being annoying about it and I liked them quite a bit. Griffiths was an imposing redheaded male; Baker a blond woman with a beautiful smile and the gift of clairvoyance. Both were businesslike, alert, and armed to the teeth in their somber black suits.

Because of the solemn occasion, they, and all the other security types, were trying to be discreet. It wasn't easy. There were so many of them present. But nobody objected. Bruno had been murdered: murdered by a traitor to his uncle, who had also planted the detonation charges that took out Sal and Connie's mansion. Every time I thought about it, I was overwhelmed with grief and rage.

I was just a wreck. Even when Bruno and I hadn't been together, he'd always been a presence in my life. Now he wasn't—except in memory. Knowing he was in heaven and at peace didn't fill the void of his absence. My friends tried to help, but they were grieving too. John Creede called, and sent flowers to the funeral. He couldn't come. Because of the trouble he'd gotten into by helping out at the Needle, he still couldn't return to the United States.

Just a few short weeks after Bruno's funeral, his mother, Isabella Rose, died. Matty was devastated all over again. I was so glad he had Emma to lean on.

Isabella had wanted her funeral to be a small family affair, and it was. But they insisted that I was one of them, so I attended, sitting beside Emma. Isabella and I hadn't really liked each other, but we'd both loved Bruno, and eventually we'd reached a point of mutual respect.

When the ceremony was over, I excused myself to find the restroom. On my way, I passed an alcove filled with votive candles. Two people stood inside, and though I did not stop, I couldn't help but overhear what Sal was saying to Connie.

"Sweetheart, you've got nothing to worry about. Pretty faces are a dime a dozen." His arm slid around her waist. "But beauty? That's in here." He poked a stubby finger onto a spot just above her left breast. "And baby, you're fucking *gorgeous*."

He meant every word, too. Connie's hair might never grow in again because of the burns to her scalp, and no amount of magic would ever fix the mass of scars that covered her back from having gone into a burning building to save Joey's children. But she was beautiful, and courageous, and absolutely amazing. Sal was lucky to have her and was smart enough to know it.

Joey himself was waiting for me when I exited the bathroom. Pulling me into the same alcove, he shoved a recording device identical to the one Rahim had brought to my office into my hands.

"This is the security footage from Sal's house, from that day. I know you've been blaming yourself for what happened to Bruno—because of the ifrit. You shouldn't. None of it was your fault. Bruno chose to come back to Jersey, even though he knew what was going on, knew how dangerous it was. And he chose to be a hero, to sacrifice himself to save Connie and the kids." Tough as he was, Joey choked up then, his voice failing. He rubbed impatiently at his eyes with the back of his hand.

Rather than risk showing more emotion, he squared his shoulders and walked away. I stared down at the recorder wondering if I'd ever have the courage to watch what was on it. Because Joey was right about one thing: I did blame myself. Bruno had made his choices, but Hasan had rigged the game—and because of me.

The ifrit was back in the jar. I suspected that his jar, and the others, had been moved to a different, safer location. We'd dealt the bad guys another setback, but they weren't dead, and I knew their master wouldn't give up. So I was very cooperative when, two weeks after Isabella's funeral, Matty and a representative from the Vatican showed up on my doorstep to question me. I hope they succeed in finding out what the demon's plan is, and stopping it. And I *really* hope that plan doesn't involve me.

EPILOGUE

It was almost a year before I could bring myself to look at the security footage: a year and some heavy therapy with Gwen to get past the worst of the anger, guilt, and loss, to put my grief into some sort of perspective. I loved Bruno and part of me always will.

Whether we would have worked, in the long run, as a couple is anyone's guess. We didn't get the chance. I blame Hasan for that. And while it's not particularly Christian of me, in my heart of hearts I hope that the knife I stuck in his back—the knife Bruno crafted—hurts him every second of all the eons of his imprisonment in that damned jar.

Almost a year to the day later, early on a Friday afternoon, I opened my center desk drawer and pulled out the recorder. It was time. Taking a deep breath, I hit the play button.

I was looking down at an angle, the view of one of the security cameras posted at regular intervals around Sal and Connie's estate. It was mounted on a corner of the building that served as both multicar garage and pool house, giving me a great view of an expanse of the manicured back lawn, the kidney bean–shaped in-ground swimming pool, and the flag-stone patio with its inset silver casting circle. The very back of the image showed the bottom six inches of the back of the house.

Bruno was walking the casting circle. My heart ached as I watched his familiar figure, dressed in his usual black jeans, Converse sneakers, and a worn Bayview T-shirt. His hair was mostly hidden by his favorite Mets cap. He moved with calm assurance, doing something he'd done a million times, but still taking care, making sure he did it right.

Power blurred the image behind him as he walked, placing a jewel at each compass point.

Connie floated on an inflatable in the middle of the pool, her body brown and glistening in the bright sunlight. She wore a red string bikini, a big floppy straw hat, and sunglasses. She sipped a drink from a tall glass, watching Bruno at work with unabashed interest.

Toys were scattered around the yard and I could hear children's laughter coming from the direction of the house. Deeper, male voices came from the garage.

There was no warning. The whump, whump of demolition charges came out of nowhere. The house shuddered, smoke and dust filling the frame as childish laughter changed to screams. Orange flames flared from the house toward the patio.

I could smell oily smoke and the taste of concrete dust coated my tongue.

Connie didn't scream and she didn't hesitate. Dropping her drink, she rolled off the inflatable and swam with strong, sure strokes to the side of the pool.

Bruno stood in the center of the circle, arms extended, his

expression one of total concentration, his entire body glowing with the power of the magic he was wielding. His voice was a strained rasp as he called out, "I can't hold it long."

He was using magic to hold the house together, I realized. The strain had to be stupendous. His body quivered with it, and the jewels he'd set into the circle glowed neon bright.

"I'll get the kids," Connie said, and ran off screen, directly into the inferno.

She was still inside when the gunfire started.

The first shot came from the front—off screen. It took Bruno in the shoulder, spinning him around and dropping him to his knees. More bullets tore into him, each impact making his body jerk. Blood and tissue flew everywhere. He could have shielded himself—if he'd dropped the spell on the house. I knew that wouldn't even have occurred to him. His first choice would always be to protect Connie and the kids over himself.

A limo drove into the frame, Sal at the wheel. He drove like a lunatic over the grass, crushing toys, slamming lawn furniture aside, engine roaring as the limo bounced over uneven ground and onto the flagstones, putting the spell-protected vehicle between Bruno and the gunfire.

It wasn't enough. It only protected Bruno from one side. I recognized the man coming up from the rear as Louie Santello, one of Sal's own men. He was carrying a Glock 9mm and took the time to aim carefully. One shot, two, then three, tore into Bruno, who continued pouring everything he had into holding his spell stable as four terrified children raced out the French doors with Connie at their heels. She was hunched over a blanket-wrapped bundle, her hair aflame and her back already *a mass of charred flesh. She leaped into the pool and ducked herself and the baby underwater just long enough to put out the fire on her head.*

The boys scattered and ran as fast as their legs could carry them.

Rolling down the limo window, Sal smoothly drew a gun that was just short of a cannon from beneath the seat. His first shot took Louie, the traitor, between the eyes, blowing out the entire back of his skull.

In the distance I could hear sirens, but they would be too late. Bruno lay crumpled on the ground in a spreading pool of blood, his body utterly still, eyes staring blankly up at the smoke-filled sky.

Keeping low, Sal rushed to the pool. He took the baby and set him on the floor of the limo before helping Connie out of the water.

My vision blurred and I hit the pause button, unable to continue. *Oh, Bruno.*

"He was a hero."

I brushed the tears from my eyes with the back of my hand, turning to see who'd spoken. It was Cox, in civilian clothes, faded blue jeans, a tight black T-shirt, and a leather biker jacket. He'd been handsome in camo. In civilian clothes he was devastating. Everything was just tight enough to show off a totally ripped body. His white hair and honey gold, topaz eyes made for an interesting combination. If there were any other side effects of working the node magic, I sure couldn't see them.

Men like Cox don't use the word "hero" lightly. Looking into his eyes I could see sympathy, not pity. I appreciated that. A lot.

"I was in town, and figured I'd look you up. I got the address from your Web site. But if this is a bad time . . . ?"

"No. It's okay. I . . ." I stammered awkwardly. Grabbing a tissue from the box on my desk, I scrubbed my eyes dry. "It's been a year." My voice was raw.

"You still miss him."

There was no point in lying about it. "Yeah."

He gave a short nod. "I get that. There are people I miss, too." A shadow passed over his face and he gave me a crooked smile that was more than a little wistful.

It made sense. In his line of work, even more than mine, death was a fact of life. Hell, it's a fact of life for everyone, come to that. Sooner or later.

I took a deep breath to steady myself and shut off the recorder. Tossing the damp tissue into the trash, I met his gaze.

"I'm surprised to see you here." I said, then added hastily, "Glad, but surprised." I blushed a little at how lame I sounded.

He smiled again, more broadly this time, and I felt my heart flutter a little. "I'm on leave. Thought I'd stop by, see if you wanted to have lunch."

"I could use some lunch," I said as lightly as I could manage. I hadn't realized I was hungry until he suggested food. But I was. And company might be the best thing for me right now. "What did you have in mind?"

"It's your town. What do you suggest?"

"I know this terrific little Mexican restaurant near campus."

He smiled. It was a good smile, sincere and a little bit nervous. "Do they serve alcohol?"

"Oh, yeah. Barbara makes a killer margarita."

"Good. We can raise a glass to fallen friends."

"Sounds like a plan to me."